Strange Malady

Alison Anthony

STRANGE
MALADY

HEINEMANN : LONDON

William Heinemann Ltd
Michelin House, 81 Fulham Road, London SW3 6RB
LONDON   MELBOURNE   AUCKLAND

First published 1992
Copyright © Alison Anthony 1992
The author has asserted her moral rights

A CIP catalogue record for this book
is available from the British Library

ISBN 0 434 02324 8

Phototypeset by Falcon Graphic Art Ltd
Wallington, Surrey
Printed in Great Britain
by Clays Ltd, St Ives plc

Contents

This book is dedicated:
to Bob, my husband, for his love,
support and strength;

to my family, for being there;

to Grace, for my life.

And to the people of my past and present,
in the hope that they might have a future.

With special thanks to
William Heinemann Ltd, East Midlands Arts,
The Oppenheim/John Downes Trust and
The Society of Authors/Authors' Foundation,
for all the moral and financial help they have given.
Thanks also to
Nottingham Polytechnic Computer Services
for the use of their facilities, and to
the Nottingham Victoria Street Branch
of HFC Bank PLC, for helping us survive
a time of crisis!

'When morning comes, and your soul struggles to rise again, does it ever trouble you – this endless searching, this hoping, this dreaming?

'I'm afflicted with some strange malady, to recover from which would be another kind of death. I cannot make sense of disorder – cannot balance, define or explain. The moon howls, but I can't hear her. The earth spins, but my eyes remain level. It's going on without – and inside me. But beneath it all, at the centre of it all, beneath the slough, confusion and despair, this certainty remains. And will remain.

'The sense of one universal, beating heart.'

The Sign

'YOU WILL LOSE' the sign said.

In letters six feet high, ten feet from the top of a cavernous railway cutting, close to the city centre. The cutting was sixty feet deep: its sides dropped almost vertically to a weed-stricken base at least two hundred feet across. At one time trains would have emerged from the tunnel that was now concealed by a giant advertisement hoarding, and passed through the cutting to a station that no longer existed. Now the only things likely to emerge from the tunnel were rats; their heavy bodies shuffling silently through the dense vegetation where once the tracks were laid. 'YOU WILL LOSE' it said.

This had once been the location of the city workhouse. Seemed it would always be the site of despair. Someone had risked the fall, the rats, the strong possibility of arrest to pass this message on. But was it challenge or statement? Battle-cry, or protest in defeat? 'YOU WILL LOSE'

A strange battle, when no one knows the enemy. The police could have written it. Or the miners, willing to enter this pit to protest their right to keep others open. Or the Government, telling miners that the right to work was as outdated as compassion. Or football supporters, chiding their rivals. Or one of millions unemployed, in defiant optimism, given to abseiling down cutting-walls with a paintbrush in their hands, celebrating democracy with one eye out for the Law; making their statement to the ghosts of the workhouse poor.

There was a chasm, slicing through the heart of a green and pleasant land. Those who lived above worshipped the sun, and were blind. Down in the chasm it was cold. The slopes declined steeply. Few footholds existed. Those who lived above were called 'Winners'. 'Losers' were pushed to the edge, and fell.

But there were those who would neither win nor lose. Some were born above, but chose to worship something other than the sun. Some were born in the chasm, but taught themselves to fly. These remained on the edge, wishing that the chasm did not exist and, when another Loser fell, they'd reach out to take their hand. But the decline was inevitable and irreversible. The weight became difficult to bear. The Winners refused to help, even taunted: 'Let them go. If they deserve to be with us, they should fly. If not – let them fall!'

And so it was that, one by one, those who would neither win nor lose, burdened, strained and unable to move, crying out in pain, released their grasp.

The Losers fell. The Winners cheered. And those who'd tried to hold on felt lighter for the release but refused to move from the chasm's edge and lived, therefore, in perpetual torment. They prayed that the chasm would cease to exist, that there would be neither Winners nor Losers, that there could be a different kind of sun. But the sun grew brighter and the Winners more blind. And the chasm grew deeper, gouged out like a vast bloody scar on the landscape.

There were no angels here. No devils. No beating wings. No infernal horns. Only people. Bad, sad, good, mad people. Outside transmissions unacceptable. The world was grey with a man-made sickness. The pit and the sun were illusions crafted into reality. Life was as useful and expendable as a pocket of loose change. And when the sign appeared no one cared.

'YOU WILL LOSE' the sickness said.

All Roads Lead To This

Summer, and everything seemed grown out of all proportion. While the grounds were kept bright for the new owners, the small footpath that began halfway up the hospital lane and cut through the fields to what had once been the church, was left untended. Nature took over, submerging the rickety wooden gate beneath bramble and bryony, while nettles rose defensively through the wild grass to prevent intrusion.

She left the bus at the foot of the hill. Just beyond the derelict hospital houses, where the lane began to rise upwards, a wide, red metal mouth with white lips and white teeth announced menacingly: 'ROAD AHEAD CLOSED.'

She skirted the sign and walked on to the place in the hedge where the gate used to be.

It was difficult to find. The path was almost completely overgrown. The only clue to its existence was a small copse – much larger than she remembered – of silver birch. She pushed through the nettles but found the gate padlocked, so she held her breath, looked round once, and climbed over.

Her dark chestnut hair is pulled back in a ponytail. Her eyes are darker, but it's hard to tell what colour. Look into them and you notice only their darkness. Look at her directly and you have the strangest feeling that sends shivers up your spine. She returns your gaze but seems to go further – beyond you somehow – as though she actually sees something else.

Her face is no longer pallid, but the bones of her hips show through her jeans, as do her ribs through her t-shirt. She eats when she remembers, but often forgets. Other things matter more to her now.

She sat on what remained of the path and looked down the hill, her back to Anydale. The hospital no longer exists. She had no desire to explore new buildings and old memories. Sticking out of the back pocket of her jeans was a faded yellow booklet: 'A Service of Remembrance for Anydale Hospital, 1902–1987.'

She had not been available for prayer that day. Her mind had been fragmented, dislocated . . . she could not be gathered in. So while the priest, standing before the assemblage of staff and patients, tried to inject a little soul – perhaps a little meaning – into the hospital's closure, Gail was pinned to another hospital's bed while the Ward Sister aimed to inject her with something entirely different.

The booklet was a gift from a friend – an old colleague – who had sensed when the time was right for Gail's private Service to begin. That time was now. For Gail, at least. For us, it must be later.

First we must find her. We must find her with Rose, because Gail by herself could not show us the way. And remember that there are no angels. Only people.

The pendulum has cracked. It swings back and forth, between 'now' and 'then', and only Rose can steady it. When Gail walks into the room Rose shuts the door, and then the two of them are alone. It's a small room in a large building. Gail sits in one chair, Rose takes the other. The wind's up. It looks set to rain.

'Have you seen it?' Gail asks the older woman.

'Seen what?'

'That sign on the cutting-wall.'

'I don't go that way.'

'You should.'

'I don't need to. You see it often enough for both of us.'

'I dream about it too. Only when I dream it's more like a chasm. Half the nation's at the bottom, up to their knees in mud. They can't get out. The other half's at the top, jeering.'

'Where are you?'

Gail rises and walks to the window, resting her forehead on the cool glass. Outside, the trees are shedding leaves in showers. Winter isn't far away.

'Do you think it will rain?'

'I think it must, soon,' the therapist replies.

'Mum once said that the rain meant God was crying.'

'Only God?'

'God cries too much.'

'What about you?'

'I can't cry.'

'I know.'

'I wish it would rain.'

'Do you think it needs to?'

'You can feel the pressure rising.'

'Tell me what you're thinking, Gail.'

'It'll be fierce when it comes.'

'But no worse than the wind.'

Gail closes her eyes. 'I wish I could cry.'

'Come and sit down. Tell me.'

Instead Gail moves to the far side of the room and crouches by the wall.

'I'm afraid of you,' she whispers.

'Of me?' Rose smiles gently.

'You seem very powerful.'

'Why?'

'Because you make me afraid.'

Gail is in pieces. Her marriage failed, she gave up her career and finally, through a series of extraordinary circumstances, she slid off the plate. In moments of elation she can convince herself – and others – that these are temporary setbacks. But then she sits alone in her bedsit, counts the stripes on her orange sink curtain or the cracks in the ceiling and considers, quietly, how her world will end. When the sun comes out – even for a moment – she turns to the wall and hopes it will soon go away. She needs a different kind of sun. One on the inside.

She isn't beyond hope. She tells herself that she's

hanging on for something. Working something out. Putting a jigsaw together. Repairing and fitting the broken pieces.

But first she must find those pieces.

She's afraid of what she might find.

She puts her arms across her chest and looks cautiously up at Rose: 'I'm afraid of myself,' she says.

Bricks And Mortar

(Or 'A Nice Little Development')

In one corner of the grounds of Otherville Psychiatric Hospital (obsolete) stands an isolated building,
surrounded by walls, that once belonged to the
Hospital Superintendent. Its correct title is 'Otherville
Rehabilitation and Therapy Centre', but all the locals call
it 'Otherville Road', as it's the only building on Otherville
Road still standing.
Correction: there are plenty of houses on the opposite
side of Otherville Road, but their residents long since for-
mulated new addresses. People tend to think of a 'stigma'
as something wrong with the eye: these residents know
better. It's the way people look at you when you say you
live on 'Otherville Road'.
Stoney Street runs down the back of these houses,
parallel to Otherville Road ... how far back doesn't
really matter. All that matters is that Stoney Street is
there. So that even those houses whose front doors open
directly on to Otherville Road, provided they're close to
a side street that runs towards Stoney Street, manage to
address themselves as somehow 'off' Stoney Street, or
'near' Stoney Street. It's a postman's nightmare.
Gail once drove past a hospital patient walking down
the middle of a city road. People were pointing but he
didn't notice. He kept to the right-hand side, facing the
oncoming traffic, and near to the kerb. Gail recognised
him as a patient by the involuntary twitching of his limbs,
caused by medication, by his hospital-shrunk trousers

9

and his half-shaved head. But he looked purposeful as well. He carried a shopping bag.

Gail pulled up at the kerb to go across to him, then noticed a knot of pedestrians struggling along the path. It had been snowing heavily and the paths were treacherously icy. Two middle-aged women clung to each other as they slipped and slithered their way to the shops. One man walked slowly, sprinkling sand from a satchel hung over his shoulder. A young man slipped and fell over, jumped up instantly, brushed down his trousers and looked around nervously, to see whether anyone had witnessed his humiliation.

Meanwhile the patient forged ahead, having sensibly elected a clear and gritted road as the least dangerous route to the shops.

People will go to any lengths to prove they're not mad.

The Therapy Centre gardens are a triumph of conceal-ment. Oak, ash and beech trees rise conspiratorially into the air and hide the old hospital site from view. Which is probably a good thing for Gail, as should she be forced to watch the demolition during her therapy sessions, she would probably not recover.

Of all the odd terms used to describe mental ill-ness, and Gail's breakdown in particular, suggesting that she 'slid off the plate' is perhaps the most bizarre. What plate? How do you slide off a plate? What has a plate to do with anything? Better to say 'she dropped the plate' – at least that suggests something shattered. And assuming that one dropped plate is roughly equiva-lent to one breakdown, then for Gail to witness what they're doing to Otherville would arouse a reaction similar to a nuclear explosion in the Staffordshire Pot-teries.

Otherville belongs to the Developers, who are doing what Developers always do. They've flattened the hos-pital. Now they're building charming little houses in 'a most unusual location' (they're keeping the perimeter wall) for young London couples who, with electrified rail, can afford to commute. And a bloody good job that they want these houses too, as no one else in the city can afford them.

For this was the decade in which Things Were Happening.

Something unpleasant had occurred.

Something dark and monstrous had sucked the nation in and spat compassion out like an indigestible pip.

Otherville's 'development' was one of the consequences. The same had happened to Anydale Hospital, a few miles out of the city. Were you to stand at the foot of Anydale's hill you would see ... nothing. No boiler chimney peeping over the horizon, no hospital church, no nurses' home by the orchard: no orchard. Nothing.

All that's left is in the city now.

Somewhere between the Salvation Army and the Night Shelter. Somewhere in the Arboretum. Somewhere near the Market Square, or the railway embankment, or by the river. Subject to all the elements.

Spot a man shouting at pigeons, or a confused woman in summer dress and carpet slippers wandering the streets in the rain ... Or a man without dentures muttering obscenities as he rifles through the municipal bins – or an old boy sleeping on the bench beside the winos, or the woman with lipstick smeared across her cheeks, collecting nubb-ends from the gutters ... Pick them out, there's plenty to choose from – or better still, slap a roof over the whole city and you'd have the latest community-conscious, well-integrated asylum – with one important difference. There's nowhere warm for them to go.

Is there only one black and one white – one right, one left, one fence to sit on, one good, one bad, one mad, one sane?

Then take a look at Gail as well. For she'd dispute these assertions. She's tall, old and wise enough to look over the fence and see the truth on the other side.

Are you wondering how tall the fence is?

How tall do you want it to be?

She was once a psychiatric nurse. To look at her, you wouldn't think she's mad at all.

Time

One hour. Sixty minutes. Sixty seconds to a minute.
When Rose arrives and they enter the room, Gail has
three thousand six hundred seconds in which to speak.

Gail bought a calculator. Time worries her. Eighty-six
thousand four hundred seconds to a day. She could
count them. She could just sit and count them.

Martha's clients average thirty minutes a go. She works
strictly by appointment. She calls herself a Sex Therapist.
She doesn't hang about on street corners. She doesn't
need to. No frills, no fancy equipment, just Martha in
the flesh. Men flock to her for thirty minutes of warm
liberation. From six p.m. to two a.m. with, on average, a
thirty minute break between each. That's eight on a busy
night. She charges around £45 a trick. £45 for half an
hour. One thousand eight hundred seconds. Twopence
ha'penny a second.

Seven times 86,400 seconds. Six hundred and four
thousand eight hundred seconds to a week. Minus 3,600
seconds, that's 601,200 seconds between walking out of
the therapy room and walking back in again. But with
sleep at eight hours a night it's 201,600 seconds less.
Four hundred and three thousand two hundred seconds
of consciousness between each session.

Martha's door opens as she walks her last client downstairs. It's two a.m. Gail switches off the light and yawns,
wishing that she'd taken her sleeping tablet half an hour
ago. Now she must wait another one thousand eight

hundred seconds before sleep.

She climbs into bed, lights a cigarette and stares at the ceiling. Four cracks in the plaster. The largest runs from wall to wall, directly over her head. It has twenty-three capillaries. She stood on the bed to count them. She's less concerned with the others. She's scared the big one grows while she's asleep. She's afraid the ceiling might collapse on top of her.

Her face is pale but expressionless. It has developed a translucency peculiar to the ill. All the blood, it seems, has retreated defensively to her vital organs. Her body thinks she's in danger. How does it know?

Rose suggested yoga, but Gail's mind is too busy to relax. Every second counts. She doesn't have the time.

On her desk is a piece of A4 paper, with a list of figures and calculations. Beneath it, a straight horizontal line, and beneath that a message to herself:

1) DONT WAKE UP TILL 10.30 A.M.!
2) CHECK THE CEILING!
3)

. . . She left the third blank. It was meant to be something constructive. She couldn't think of anything. Underneath, one final calculation for the following morning: '10.30 a.m. 259,200 seconds to go!'

'A busy brain!' concluded Rose at their next meeting.

Gail had just taken the clock off the wall and placed it behind Rose's chair, out of her line of vision. She sat down and immediately found herself counting the bars on the radiator.

'I can't stop myself!' Eight panels of glass in each of the two overlapping window panes. 'I had so much to say to you last week, and so long to wait . . . '

'You don't have to wait.'

'What else can I do?'

'Why not write down the things that you want to say?'

Gail caught the bus home. Her car was now a memory. The bus journey was three miles. Thirty pence. Ten pence a mile. Conveniently simple. She bought a pack of writing paper from the newsagent's for ninety-five pence. When she found herself calculating the cost per sheet she threw the calculator out of the window.

She wrote a page, studied it, shuddered and resolved to find a job. A mindless job. A physical job. Not Martha's sort of physical, but a job without people. The less people the better.

E.G. Pluckett, Proprietor of Pluckett's Egg Packaging, manoeuvred his cigarette to one corner of his mouth, let the ash drop down his shirt front before, unknowingly, rubbing it in as he loosened his tie. He puckered his lips, hummed tunelessly and referred again to her application.

'But you're a nurse!'

'I was. I'm not now.'

'Why?'

Gail looked out of the office window at the girls on the factory floor, picking eggs from an endless array that passed before them and deftly filling the soft cardboard trays.

'If eating eggs made you ill,' she asked, nodding her head in that direction, 'would you go back on the production line?'

Pluckett was balding. He scraped the little that remained across the top of his pate – as if that fooled anyone! It irritated her profoundly. She wanted to cut it off – and then have a go at the hairs coming out of his ears. She crossed her legs, wondered if he might interpret it as a defensive gesture and uncrossed them again. Then she wondered if uncrossed legs looked forward. She didn't want to appear forward. The man had forest sprouting from every visible orifice. Forward was the last thing she wanted to appear. So she inclined towards him slightly and looked him straight in the eye. Unfortunately he only had one good eye. The other – his right eye, had wandered recklessly and was currently watching the factory floor. I bet that eye keeps the staff on their toes, she thought.

His left eye, meanwhile, returned her insistent gaze.

'And you say you've packed eggs before?'

'Before I started nursing, yes. I picked, packed, denested, candled, worked on the casing machine and I know what to do with melange.'

That'll floor him! she thought.

It did.

'We'll need references.'

'You'll have to write to the School of Nursing. The hospital's closed.'

'How did you get here?'

'There's a bus that runs to Shellingham. I walked the rest of the way.'

'Did you? Hmm.' His wandering eye caught sight of his secretary outside the window. 'Sandra? Two teas please . . . '

His good eye can't be looking at me, then, Gail thought. She let her gaze wander and found herself counting a stack of egg trays in one corner of the office. It *was* his good eye. It followed her.

'One of the perks!' he said. Dizzy with disorientation, she didn't dare look straight at him.

'Well!' he announced decisively, pushing back his chair and correcting both eyes at once: 'I think you'll do!'

'Does that mean I've got it?' She squinted at him.

'You can't work Wednesdays. That's all?'

'Every other day is fine, but I take 'A' Levels part time,' she lied, thinking of Rose and Otherville Road. 'I want to widen my horizons,' she added, thinking also of his wandering eye.

'We can arrange transport for you, so that's one problem less. Now, I'll show you around, find you a uniform and that cup of tea, eh?'

He was actually quite nice. Better a nice balding man with one good eye and sprouting ears, than a smart-suited bastard, she thought.

That night, she started a new page and wrote: 'Society will always need eggs!'

'And eggs don't die,' she added quietly, as she stood on the bed to check the ceiling.

The Road To The Hill

'I've been thinking about Celie.'

'Have you?'

'I might go round and see her soon.'

Rose waited.

'We were in hospital together . . . I told you, didn't I? There's a stream in the grounds. We decided to paddle. We used to paddle together as kids, in a stream near the farmer's house. I suppose it just took us back.

'Celie wanted to stay on at school, but as it turned out, she was pregnant before her sixteenth birthday. She married Jack and moved into a flat in the city – twenty miles away. Jack worked in one of the big city factories – it's closed down now. She met him through a cousin, I think. He was such a nice lad: he sounded tough, he had a real accent, but he was lovely.

'I thought at first that she was making a big mistake – but when you're pregnant the mistake's already made, if you can call it that. But I went to visit once they'd settled in and Jack treated me like a sister. He did everything for the two of us. I never knew a man more comfortable in company.

'They had a few days in London as a honeymoon and they were full of it . . . The Tower, Oxford Street, Buckingham Palace. They were so excited, and so happy together . . . They loved each other very much. I stayed overnight and, when I left the next day, Jack came down with me in the lift and walked me to the bus stop. It was a

rough area – they lived on the fifth floor of a tower block –
but with Jack, you felt protected. He didn't make a fuss
about his size – he was taller than me and quite stocky –
but he didn't play it down either. He simply carried himself well. He had an aura of quiet, gentle confidence that
just radiated from him. And he loved to talk! He waited
for the bus with me, then waved me off. I could see why
Celie had fallen in love with him. I think I loved him too.'

'You say you met Albert at their flat . . . ?'

'I did. Years later. I think I saw another Jack in Albert.
I expect I was just looking too hard.

'About a year after they married, Jack's parents separated and Frank, his younger brother, went to live with
them. Frank always was a difficult boy. I suppose he must
have been ten or eleven then . . . Very sullen. He seemed
to scowl at everything. But Celie took him in and cared
for him as well as she could, with Joe only six months
old. Jack kept a firm eye on Frank, but you could tell
that Frank was destined for trouble, even then.

'I visited as often as I could but circumstances at
home seemed to bleed most of my enthusiasm for going
anywhere. I left school at sixteen with a few 'O' Levels.
My headmistress said that I should be a vet. I wanted to
be a social worker. At sixteen the Social Services wouldn't
have me. I should learn a little about life first, they said.
Now I know all that I care to know about life, and I don't
want to be a social worker.

'I hated school too much to stay on after the exams. I
went to work as an egg-packer for a few months and then
I started at the Wimpy full time as a cook. The manageress
was a large jovial woman who mothered me and all the
other girls. On my seventeenth birthday she paid for me
to have my ears pierced. She said I could clean the tiles
at the back of the grill like nobody else. But I hated making
doughnuts. You had to mix the stuff by hand and get the
egg-fat so hot it smoked. We never had doughnuts while
I was there. I cooked a mean beefburger, though!

'Cafés are like day centres for the lonely. Working
in them, you learn how to listen. You learn patience.
You learn a lot about people caught at the fag-end of
life. Displaced people, society's outcasts; the victims of

abuse and the butts of malicious humour who just want
to be accepted, for whom a smile means the world. We
took them in.

'One day I saw an advert in the paper. It was a
huge photograph of a young woman sitting on a park
bench talking to a distressed young man. The caption
said: "Could you do this?"

'Something clicked inside me. Determination maybe –
or compassion. Or perhaps just the feeling that it could
be Mum sitting on that bench. It could be one of the
lonely people in the café. It could be me. So I applied,
sat an exam, was accepted and continued to work at the
Wimpy until the following October when, aged eighteen
at last, I could begin nurse training.

'Like most town girls, I found my society in pubs, drinking under-age. And parties, where we drank so much it
nearly put us off alcohol for life. And boys. Unlike most
of the others, however, I didn't really have a home to go
to. Dad went to work and I went to school: Dad watched
the telly and I did my homework. Then I left school and
we both worked. I paid board, cleaned and cooked, but
most of the time we hardly saw each other. Dad went to
the pub and I went out with friends. We didn't go on
holiday because that would have meant being together.
Other people go on holidays to get away from it all. We
didn't – for exactly the same reason. Growing up after
Mum's death was like climbing a ladder, because the
only way out was up. I took the pill, met a few lads,
learned something about sex, grew up a bit, had a good
time on Friday nights and waited. That's how it was.

'When I was sixteen Dad met Deirdre and got married
again. A very quiet Register Office do: some of Dad's
mates from work and Deirdre's family. I developed a
migraine three days before the event and was so sick
that I had to stay home in bed. I know how that sounds
and it's true, I hated her, but she hated me as well. I was
glad to start nurse training, to get away from it all.'

Early Departures

'Sometimes Mum would just go away. Somewhere inside herself. For hours, sitting motionless on the settee, staring at the wall. Coming home from school, I'd find her like that. I don't know where she went. The light was never on. So I'd switch on the gas-fire and sit with her in the darkness. Somehow, even when she seemed so far away, just being beside her felt comforting. I'd cuddle up to her and watch the fire. I often fell asleep like that. She'd come back gently, while I was still sleeping. She'd put her arms around me, stroke my forehead and whisper, very gently, "My baby."

'"How's your Mum?" people would ask. I can never forget the look in their eyes. Part pity, part curiosity, part fear. I was still at infant school. What did they expect me to say? Mum was Mum after all. She was my mum, that's who she was and how she was, so I'd say "She's alright, thank you," because Mum had taught me to be polite, even to the rudest people – even to the "little" people who were Mum's age, Mum's size, had grown up with Mum, but whose concern never stretched as far as a visit now and then.

'There were times, of course, when she went the other way. To Skegness once. She sent me a postcard of a donkey called Dobbin and a message in huge letters:

"I'm going to buy a hotel. We shall live by the sea!!!!!!!"

'I stayed with Gran and Gramps while Dad went to fetch her home. Once she got as far as the Lake District.

It cost Dad a fortune in train fares. I accepted it as a part
of my childhood. It wasn't that strange. Either Mum went
away inside, or she went off for days at a time. She always
came back: that's all that mattered. I shut myself off to
everything else: the police coming when Dad reported
her missing, Gran crying, the strange looks from neighbours, the comforting hugs from the teachers at school
– sometimes comfort hurts more than anything.

'I learned patience at a very early age. After the Lake
District episode I dreamt of mountains, post-Skegness I
dreamt of owning a donkey called Dobbin like some
girls at school owned ponies. I looked at other children's mums and loved mine even more, because she
was special. My Mum didn't just make beds and cook,
my Mum went away and then came back with a hug, or
Kendal Mint Cake, or Skegness rock.

'First Grampy died, then Gran, then Mum.'

Gail stopped.

'That's a very blunt statement, Gail. You should try
to talk more about it . . . '

'I just remember how it was without them. I remember
Grampy being taken to an old folks' home, but I don't
remember seeing him there. He died soon afterwards. I
remember sitting with Granny while she showed me his
medals in a Woodbine tin. I hated to see her cry. I just
held her hand. Not long after she fell and broke her leg,
developed pneumonia and died in hospital.'

'And your Mother?' Rose prompted.

'Nothing.'

'What does "nothing" mean?'

'It means no.' She closed her eyes and tried to breathe
deeply.

She was in a stream. She frowned.

'Where are you, Gail?'

Celie was with her.

*'There's water still getting through, Gail,' Celie said, wading
up to the dam.*

'That's because we haven't finished yet.'

Gail said it aloud, surprised herself, opened her eyes
and saw Rose.

'Who were you talking to?' Sometimes Rose assumed

a stillness, a hypnotic stillness, that seemed to reach
out . . .

'It must be time now, Rose. Is it time? It must be.
I've got to go.'

When Gail left Rose checked her watch. They had
fifteen minutes left to run. She frowned, reached for her
notes, clicked her pen and began to write.

As Gail grew, she followed in her mother's footsteps.
Often she would simply go away – somewhere inside
herself. She had no idea where it was or that she was
in any sense unwell, but she pulled sleep towards her
as her best companion during those times.

If flight was a spiritual, rather than physical process,
then on occasion she felt almost able to fly. She was
filled with an irrational optimism – a sense of incredible
power and faith in the future. But these moments usually
preceded a downward descent. Unlike her mother, she
had no time to 'take off' to Skegness, or wherever. She
had very little chance to view life from the top of her
condition. For her, it was like a glimpse of a brilliant
sunset before night fell, and when night fell, it consumed
her.

To understand depression, you must understand the
complexity of descent. It is not straightforward. You
don't hit the bottom and wonder how to get back out
again: you can't distinguish the pit from the sky. You
forget what the sky looks like. The pit is your world. It's
dark and clouded. You can see nothing clearly. There is
no before and no after: there's nothing to look towards and
nothing of comfort to remember. You're raw and naked
and darkness surrounds you. You stand absolutely alone.
It isn't life, it's existence and existence hurts. You don't
want life's responsibility. It all seems very pointless when
you have nothing to offer and the very act of living hurts
so much.

During adolescence it touched her merely as waves
of numbing tiredness and she succumbed because sleep
was the only way out. When her mother died the tiredness
became almost overwhelming, but then she began pushing it away because work – and leaving home – seemed

the only way out. But it matured with her. It followed her.

When she began nursing she felt instinctively that she had come home. She learned about illness but never once considered that she, too, might be ill. Gail could not objectively consider the fluctuations in her own mental state – they were a part of life. But it gave her an edge. Often she felt able to understand people better because she saw her mother in them, but it was not true. What she saw in them was herself. On several inexplicable occasions she found herself contemplating suicide. She had no idea why. And when the moment passed it seemed as violent as a storm that had simply moved away.

The old mental hospitals had two types of inmate. One was trained, the other was treated. One wore a clinical uniform, the other did not. So the young man who took fifteen baths a night in the nurses' quarters was indeed a nurse, as the next day he'd put on his white coat and resume his duties. Should a young man attempt this feat in the ward baths he would be medically prevented from doing so again because he was a patient. If you are a nurse, you cannot be ill. The two are not compatible. That many patients would make better nurses was not disputed, nor was the fact that nurses make lousy patients. But the conclusion that this might logically lead towards was studiously avoided by the nursing profession. Nurses are not ill. It's impossible.

Gail was not ill. Whatever took hold of her during those dark times had no name: she felt incapable of expressing what it was. Sometimes, startled at the destructiveness of her thoughts – standing at the sink with a razor in her hand, or sitting against a wall that rimmed a multi-storey car park – she tried to look into the darkness, but it was almost like a dream – something insubstantial. Even as she turned her eyes towards it she felt herself turning away again . . . it was like a paralysis of conscious thought, blanking out an incomprehensible truth.

She tried hard to be a good nurse. She became angry when her colleagues discussed 'objectivity' as the most

essential nursing requirement. How can you help someone, she wanted to say, if you don't try to reach them?
How can you reach from behind a wall of 'objectivity'?
It isn't possible! Their reply was always precise. Without
that 'wall', you'll go mad yourself. Then you won't be
a nurse at all. And when Gail, many years later, went
officially mad and was admitted into Otherville, many of
her former colleagues said, well, it was always bound to
happen, wasn't it? Do you remember the time she asked
one of the consultants to give her ECT – electric shock
treatment – so that she'd know how it felt for the people
she nursed? She was always doing things like that! Bound
to go crazy, sooner or later.

Had there been someone in whom she could confide
– a nurse counsellor perhaps, Gail might have been able
to communicate those moments of darkness. But this
was her career, and it was generally assumed that nurses
do not need counselling. So while her colleagues spoke
excitedly about the future, Gail avoided the future whenever possible. She stood without shelter as the clouds
passed over her, she knew, when left with only the sound
of receding thunder, that they were growing ominously
large . . . then she donned her uniform. And while she
seemed on the outside to be as enthusiastic and sociable
and strong and capable as any of her peers, there were
times when she shut herself in her room in the nurses'
home and watched helplessly as the clouds swept the
sky with increasing ferocity, threatening to shroud her
in a final darkness that would lose her completely and
lead her to an absolute conclusion.

Rose did not deal in absolutes. Rose guided people
towards a greater understanding. Gail had gone from
sleep to work to nursing to marriage and ultimately to
the cutting-wall in her search for a way out. And then
came Rose.

Rose lifted her head at the sound of the storm, frowned,
then made one final note. Finally she returned everything
to her bag, slipped on her coat and left the room. Outside,
the wind *was* wild, but she set herself against it and walked
briskly to her car.

Shades

'I grew up in grey. Concrete seemed the foundation to everything. It still does, sometimes. It's like walking through a spoiled canvas.

'Grey concrete houses that browned in patches as they soaked up the rain, grey roads, grey pavements – even the primary school at the end of our road was made of corrugated iron. And the street sign – a low municipal block of concrete.

'We had indoor toilets, nice bathrooms, big gardens, an outhouse, a cat, a rockery in the front garden, gooseberries and raspberries in the back. The town finished and countryside began just beyond our back garden. So as children, we never really belonged anywhere, apart from our street. In the countryside we were unwelcome visitors. We played in perpetual fear of being shot. It was like playing in a big open library. We whispered all the time, and made dens in the barley fields that would shield us from the farmer's eyes. The fact that the farmer was myopic, geriatric and had never owned a gun was irrelevant. We grew up in grey. We made our own colours.'

'Do you still make them?' asked Rose.

'It's an attitude of mind, Rose. I can't find colour these days.

'Mandy Potter's dad owned the chip shop. His wife worked behind the counter. She couldn't sell you chips without swearing.

'"Fred!" she'd shout, "Fred, get your arse out of that chair and make up some bloody batter you bloody lazy sod!"

'"Common as muck!" my dad would say.

'Mr Potter hid in the back room for most of the time. Mandy acted as though she didn't care about anything. She told some tales, though.

'Mr Potter bought a car. No one on our street had a car. Cars belonged to Other People. But the Potters lived above the chip shop. They could afford one. Mandy said so.

'Mandy painted it for us at school.

'Bright blue, with orange wheels and a rocket at the back. We wanted to go and see, but Mandy said her dad had hidden it, on account of there being a lot of jealous people about. We weren't jealous, just curious. We had nothing to be jealous of. People said you suffocated in cars if you didn't wind the windows down. Ron Pagett's uncle's dog died in a car. And anyway they stopped us playing rounders in the street when they appeared. But Mandy was adamant. She said her dad was hiding it for a special occasion. I couldn't imagine the Potters having any special occasions. Perhaps that's why Mandy told so many lies.

'She painted her television as well that day. It looked as big as her front-room wall. She said that was because it *was* as big as her front-room wall. We spent ages trying to figure out where the knobs were. She said the knob on the gas-fire had a dual purpose.

'She didn't live on our street.

'Patrick Fulham's family were tinkers. His uncle used to come round every other Wednesday and hang bargain bags on all the front doors. The bags were full of crayoning and tracing books.

'"They're only a bargain if you've got the money!" Mum would say.

'He'd come back the next day and take them all away again.

'We weren't poor. None of us were poor. We were all the same. We weren't rich, we knew, because we hadn't a car. But no one else had a car, either. The adverts on television were for things like washing powder, and *everyone* bought washing powder.

'Mandy Potter said her mum didn't need washing powder because she had a maid. She said the maid's name was "Chrysalis" and that she only had one tooth. Celie laughed and said she'd probably lost the other teeth trying to bite into Mr Potter's battered fish.

'Patrick Fulham's dad was always in trouble with the Law. Mandy Potter said he was a child murderer. We were glad she lived on the other side of the estate.

'Billy Foster was the only boy ever in the history of the entire world to sit in Devil's Wood for half an hour. Devil's Wood was a line of densely overgrown hedgerow that skirted the barley fields. We'd seen smoke rising from gipsy fires in Devil's Wood. We hid from gipsies. It was a magical place, but sinister. Dogs would wander into it and, to our utter amazement, emerge unscathed. So it was unanimously agreed that, because Billy was showing exceptional courage, we'd sit in the barley field to wait for him. Patrick took his shoes and socks off and fell asleep. Celie rolled around like an unravelling ball of wool to make the den larger and I was left to watch for Billy. Then Mandy found us and said she'd seen him hanging by his neck from a tree, with blood coming out of his eyes. We ran home and told Billy's dad, we were so scared. Poor Billy emerged triumphant through the gap in the bramble that day, with no one to witness his moment of glory. Instead he went home and had his backside tanned.

'Celie's dad had been in the RAF during the Second World War. My dad had been in the Navy. So my dad took the helm of a bright red ship while her dad provided air cover in a purple plane. Those were glorious painting days, when the sky started six inches above the sea, the gap in between was the "bit before the sky starts", the sun always smiled and you could paint flowers in the sea if you felt like it.

'Mandy Potter said her dad had been a spy in Russia and had worn a black cloak and dark glasses.

'"He kilt three thousand Jerries!"

'"He never did!"

'"And he made an atom bomb!"

'"Ooh Mandy!" We were disgusted.

'We were sitting on the concrete street sign. Celie was picking berries from the bush behind us.

'"Mum says not to eat them berries. They kill you. Dead. But you thrash first, Mum says, because Ron Pagett thrashed a lot but they saved 'im in the nick of time she says."

'Celie dropped one berry and crushed another between her fingers.

'"If I died I wouldn't thrash because I'd be a witch and cast a spell and be saved and everyone else would die. Thrashing. I'd be a witch and I could eat *anything!*" Then she added, a little ruefully, "Except my mum and dad and . . . and . . . nobody in *my* family'd die. They'd just thrash *a little bit* and then get better!"

'Mandy was pulling up a sock. She said: "But I'd be Queen and I'd make you drop your wand so all the magic spells would go. *Then* you'd die!"

'"No I wouldn't!"

'"Yes you *would*, Celie!"

'Celie licked her fingers defiantly. "There, I've licked the juice off me fingers!"

'We all turned to face her, gasping.

'Billy lay flat down on the pavement and poked ants with a bit of stick.

'"Hee! Look at 'em gettin' cross!"

'"You shouldn't do that, Billy. Mum says if you're cruel to insects and animals God won't 'ave you in 'eaven!"

'"I'm not goin' to 'eaven!" Billy said wickedly. He poked another ant.

'Next day there was just Mandy, Patrick and me. Mandy stood up to play with her whip and top. It wouldn't go.

'"It won't go!" Mandy cried, whipping the pavement.

'"It won't if you treat it like that, Mandy!"

'"It will! I'll *make* it go! I'll whip and whip and whip until it's so dizzy it *has* to go!"

'Then there was only Patrick and me. Patrick stood on the pavement, scuffing his plimsolls against the kerb.

'"Where's your mum gone then, Patrick?"

'"Don't know. But she's going somewhere really ace and then she'll come and get us!"

'"Did she say?"

'"She don't 'ave to. She'll come."

'"What's your Dad say, then?"

'"Not much. 'E's drinking."'

Gail tucked her knees beneath her chin and looked across at Rose.

'It's funny how you remember things. It's like that song about the green bottles, falling one by one, but it wasn't like that, not really.'

'What happened to the last bottle?'

Gail looked out of the window.

'I suppose I'm counting again. Five four three two one. There's such order in numbers. When I came here on the bus today everyone looked like sticks. I don't know why. Then I started counting limbs. Why limbs?'

'The last bottle, Gail?'

'There was a bus stop near the street sign. I stood there one day with a threepenny bit. When the bus came I asked to go to Anydale Hospital, to see my mum. But the bus conductor wouldn't let me on.

'"Wait 'til you're older," he said, "wait 'til you're older."'

The House On The Hill

The main road sliced through the cold countryside, busy constantly with cars, vans, articulated lorries; a hurried, impersonal artery of life. At sharp right-angles to the road ran a small, largely disregarded lane that led uphill to a cluster of buildings. Little could be seen from the foot of the hill: the nurses' home, the church, a chimney or two – and a row of grey hospital houses lined the left side of the lane, before it began the steep ascent. To the right, lush greenery swept down the full length of the hill; occasionally populated by grazing cattle.

Gail stood at the foot of the hill: the bus indicated and pulled away. She had a case in her hand. She felt bright and enthusiastic – albeit a little anxious. She coughed and looked up. She began the ascent.

As she climbed, it seemed as though the large Victorian buildings rose to greet her, silhouetted against a clear sky by the setting sun. Gail believed that she had never seen anything quite as moving as the dark mass of the institution etched upon such a brilliant sky. So she walked on, up, up towards the light, oblivious to the shadows cast by these buildings that grew steadily longer; that crept down the hill to greet her.

'At first the hospital seemed like a warren of corridors, and everyone spoke in a foreign language: "Go past Two's, turn left by the kitchen and you'll be outside the door to Eight's. Go through that door and take the first door on your right. That's Nine's."

'Nine's was my first ward. Elizabeth Ward: Nine's to staff and patients alike. The Sister would send me on errands to get me used to the geography. It felt more like orienteering. One day she sent me to Two's for a fallopian tube. The Sister on Two's had just put down the phone when I found her. Something struck her as very funny. She went to check in the stock cupboard but came back without one. "Try Fifteen's," she said.

'I walked round the hospital twice, burning with embarrassment when I realised that I'd passed the same notice-board five minutes before. The corridor was on a slight incline: a young porter who looked as though he'd just got out of bed was freewheeling down the corridor on the bumpers of a large meal trolley. He winked as he passed. I shouted after him: "Where's Fifteen's?"

'He continued to roll, but fell across the trolley in a short explosion of laughter.

'"Thanks!" I muttered. I tried Gunby Ward. The door was in front of me. I padded across the dayroom to Sister's office in a state of some desperation. Sister wasn't there, but a student nurse I recognised from the nurses' home looked up as I entered.

'"Gail, isn't it?"

'"Christine . . . Sister sent me to get a fallopian tube but they haven't got any on Two's so they suggested I try Fifteen's but I've looked everywhere and I can't find Fifteen's!"

'I sat on a chair by the desk and lit a cigarette.

'Christine grinned. "Fifteen's is the Mortuary, Gail. And fallopian tubes . . . "

'"Oh hell!" I suddenly realised.

'"They've been having you on!"

'"But Two's! Sister went . . . "

'"They do it to all of us, the buggers, then they ring round to warn each other we're coming!"

'Halfway back along the corridor I was stopped by a short, stooped little man in rather large spectacles, who looked up at me with frightened eyes as he tugged at the sleeve of my jumper.

'"I'm dead!" he said. "I'm dead! Where do I go?" Before

I could answer, a young man in dungarees appeared at the top of the corridor and called him.

'"George?! C'mon George, that lady doesn't want to know about your problems!" George turned at the sound of the voice, then turned back to me, whispering conspiratorially: "They said I was mad because I talked to my budgie. I don't tell them, but he's inside me, my budgie. They think I killed him but I didn't. I just ate him. Now he's inside me. He says he's much happier, being all warm and cosy inside . . . "

'"George!" The male nurse walked up the corridor towards us.

'George's whisper trailed away, leaving a sad, glazed expression behind the large round spectacles. He turned and shuffled miserably towards the youth.

'"I'm dead," he said, "where do I go?"

'The male nurse took his arm, then addressed me: "Are you Gail?" he asked.

'"Yes! How did you know?"

'"Everyone knows everyone here." He grinned. "Fancy coming to the pub tonight?"

'"I'd like that." I smiled. "What time?"

'"Nine o'clock. I'll meet you by the staff canteen!"

'I watched them walk away. George was holding the nurse's hand. Every now and then his elbows twitched in unison. The nurse didn't seem to notice – perhaps he'd grown used to it – but to me the little man looked for all the world as though he was testing his wings.

'After a couple of years' experience, we were fit enough to play our own practical jokes on newcomers to the hospital staff. The best I remember was when we had a new batch of general nurses, who'd arrived for their three-month psychiatric experience. One of them – Pamela – was greener than the rest. You develop a funny sense of humour in hospital, and the general nurses were easy prey. And we were in the third year by then – we could get away with things. Pamela believed everything we told her. She wore plastic gloves for two days because Sister White told her that mental illness was infectious! We were both working on the same ward, and one day we took a group of patients for a walk in the grounds. There was an airfield close by, where they used to train civilian pilots, and on this particular day a private plane flew low over the hospital and circled it three or four times. I could see her watching the plane. I couldn't help myself.

'"That's the Anydale Spotter," I told her casually.

'"The what?"

'"It's the hospital plane. We must have lost a patient . . . "

'Her eyes opened wide and she stared at me.

'"D'you see how it keeps circling? John Fells – you know the charge nurse on Midfield Ward? He's the pilot. And Harold Sharp – the SEN on Five's – will be with him, with the dart gun . . . "

'"What?"

'"There's always a trained pilot and marksman on duty at all times, in case – like now – someone runs off. Once they spot him they'll shoot him with the dart gun . . . don't worry, it's only a short-acting tranquilliser – and radio his position back to base. Then the staff just go and collect him . . . "

'She looked horrified, then her face broke into a smile.

'"You're having me on!"

'"You don't believe me? When we get back you can go down to Midfield Ward and have a chat with Fells – if you're lucky, he might take you up next time."

'When we returned to the ward I had a word with Sister, who phoned John to warn him of the story. We sent her off and managed to stretch the hoax out for two hours, with help from the other wards.

'John showed her a scar on his face that happened when he crash-landed the plane in a field by the hospital farm. He sent her to Five's where Harold showed her the tall metal cabinet where the gun was kept, but said that she'd have to get authorisation from the hospital administrator before she could see it. The administrator played along, giving her a note, signed by him, "To witness Anydale Hospital In-flight Emergency Restraining Equipment."

'When Harold had checked the note he tucked it in her uniform pocket and sent her to the Central Nursing Office for "New darts – we used the last one today. If

you're going to see the gun you might as well make yourself useful!" And of course the Central Nursing Office
knew nothing about it! The whole hospital fed on that
story for weeks, and she proved to be one of the most
popular general nurses we ever had, for taking it all so
well!

'When you start nursing, you shovel shit. If you
can't shovel shit you'll never be a nurse. Within a week
you grow accustomed to the smells, the sights and the
duties. Then you learn to love the people.

'Stan would rub the palm of one hand with two
fingers of the other, lick his fingers feverishly, hardly touching them, then begin again: "Bugger fuck off
bugger!" he'd shout. He was tiny – almost a caricature.
Sometimes you could get him to smile – but you never
stopped his hand-grooming. I once saw him lifted over
another patient's shoulder and swung round and round
the dayroom. He was still grooming even as the ward
carpet flashed beneath him.

'Every morning Samuel would give the same greeting as
the sheets were pulled back to reveal yet another night's
fun with the play-doh he found around his bottom. "I'm
starved to deeth!" he'd say. "Starved to deeth!"

'If Bobby started to wander we'd fix him a sandwich
and sit him on the edge of a pouffe. "Eat your snap,
Bobby," we'd say, and the old collier's face would break
into a smile.

'So you start with the muck, but never take it with you.
Instead you transcend the shovelling and find something
to love in everyone. The way they take your hand. The
way that a usually impassive face suddenly winks at
you, the way they gratefully pucker their faces as you
give them a wet-shave: little things that make you smile.
You might be washing someone down and they pee on
you – you start again and they suddenly stroke the hair
back from your face.

'After three months I moved to a middle–long stay
ward, where I met all the characters I had passed two
or three times a day since I started training. I discovered
why they shouted; I learnt their names and made friends
with many of them.

'After a further three months I was allowed to work
on an admission ward, where I met people I recognised,
not from the corridors or the patients' canteen or the
cinema or the grounds, but from the streets of my home
town. After those three wards I knew enough to realise
that mental illness isn't the frightening condition people
imagine it to be. Every shout that echoed down the
corridors had a human being behind it, and once you
knew the person you ceased to be afraid. I learnt that
the greatest danger is always the imagination: confront
the truth and fear generally goes away. Take Lester: a tall,
stooped man with severe Parkinson's disease. He'd come
shuffling down the corridor like a skier in flight: pushed
forward by an inner momentum he was unable to stop.
If you tried to help him he'd strike out: despite years in
hospital he was a very independent man. His dentures
never stayed in and he couldn't speak clearly because of
his condition, so the only way he could communicate his
independence was by lashing out with his hand. He had a
wicked sense of humour: I can still see him smiling now,
with his teeth in his hand, leaning forward to try to tell
me a joke. In the bath he tried to keep his independence
by washing himself, which always involved standing up.
Unsupervised he'd stand, lean forward, take a dive and
somersault in the bath. I called him a "Daft old bugger!"
which cheered him up considerably. Sadly he was left
alone once too often, took his dive and drowned in the
bath.

'I still miss him. And all the others. Johnny especially,
and George . . . '

'Who do you miss the most?' asked Rose. 'Staff or
patients?'

Gail glanced angrily across at her. 'There's always that
distinction, isn't there?' Then she studied the arm of her
chair, and sighed: 'I suppose we create that distinction
ourselves, as nurses. I say it myself, without thinking.
Always "patients" and never "people". You don't think
about it at the time, but it's dehumanising. I suppose,
as nurses, we never knew – never wanted to know –
what really went on inside the people we nursed. We'd
read their notes – especially the long-stay patients – and

think, "Well, that's it, then. I know all I need to know about this person." And if you treat someone like that, on a daily basis, for long enough, perhaps they begin to believe it themselves. Perhaps they lose their lives – their real lives – and become the people we perceive them to be.

'We say psychiatry has advanced so much that we no longer need locked doors, strait-jackets or padded cells and it's true, but we've replaced them with medication so strong that it wrecks the personality. We give them tablets and call it "treatment", but really it's a kind of legitimate theft. We dose them up until they're so stupefied that they can hardly walk in a straight line; we steal – I don't know – their very "essence" – the thing that makes them individual. And when they're "manageable" they're somehow "better" – consigned to a line or two of nursing notes and a lifetime of hospital routine on some miserable back ward. Take George, for example – the little man who used to say, "I'm dead, where do I go?" . . . He ran out of places in the end.'

Her eyes smarted. She stood to leave the room.

'Aren't you going to tell me?' asked Rose.

'It's a long story, Rose, and there isn't time. I'd rather leave before you announce that the hour is up. I feel more in control. By the way – do you want any eggs? I can get you two dozen from Pluckett's, slightly imperfect, for fifty pence . . . '

Gail never worked on George's ward, but George was a hospital 'character'. Subsequently everyone knew his 'history'. At least they knew the pertinent facts. Everyone was fond of him.

The slim volume of hospital notes did no justice to the little man. A few details on the first page of the slim green folder, followed by a couple of pages of nursing notes covering fifteen years of his life. On 16th December, 1978 he had 'a difficult night'. The next entry, dated 23rd March, 1979, pronounced him 'co-operative' without elaboration. On 8th July, 1980 he 'enjoyed day-trip to Blackpool' and in November 1981 he 'saw chiropodist, feet OK'. George was abbreviated.

On the cover of his notes it said:

NAME: GEORGE BEAGLE
DOB: 25–3–1944
DOA: 18–2–1975

An administrative requirement, these three essential facts
provided a quick reference as well. Date of Birth – he's
that old, Date of Admission – that long in hospital. In
some quarters, DOA meant 'Dead on Arrival'. George
would have seen the irony in that, had he been given
the chance to see his notes. In '78 the 'difficult night'
was caused by the death of the ward canary. In '79
the 'co-operative' little man washed the Sister's car. On
his day-trip to Blackpool he won a coconut which he
subsequently lost on the coach journey home. He ate
candy floss. He drank a pint of shandy. He bought a
'KISS ME QUICK' hat then blushed from the top of his
head right down to his toes when Queenie from One's
merrily complied. He even had lipstick on his collar!
And a little bit of something had happened on every
one of the thousands of other days left unrecorded.
Perhaps he found a nice book in the hospital library.
Or he tripped over someone on the hospital corridor. Or
they had fish three days in a row so Sister let him make a
jam sandwich instead! Or he found a five pound note and
bought everyone a cup of tea in the patients' canteen! Or
a film in the cinema made him cry. Or he lost a pair of
socks in the hospital laundry. Or another patient hit him
by accident. Or the geyser in the kitchen broke down,
and they couldn't scald the cups. Or someone soiled his
bed. Or he had a nice walk. Or the chiropodist tickled
his feet!

George lived every day of his life. Not just before
his admission and occasionally afterwards, when people
remembered to write a line on him before the consultant's
infrequent visits to the 'back wards'. He lived every
single day, but it didn't matter. People only mattered
who had thick volumes of notes. George was abbreviated and George disappeared. George was 'a character'
and George disappeared. George didn't matter. He only
mattered when they closed the hospital down. Meanwhile

he joined the ranks of patients who were known by their obvious characteristics. George was not the old woman who tapped every drainpipe around the old School of Nursing. George was not 'the man from Six's who runs errands for the staff', George 'comes up to you and says I'm dead!' Oh, *that* George! The budgie man! Yes!

Abbreviated, forgotten, tucked-away-like-his-notes George. Dead on arrival George. On the hospital mantelpiece and dusty.

George.

George: The Tale Of The Suicidal Budgie

George used to live in a basement. He had lived very quietly in the basement. It was a very tidy basement. George tidied it every day. He had his own entrance. He had his own key. He paid his rent regularly, punctually, diligently. He was quite terribly orderly.

George worked in a library. It was a very efficient library. George was a very efficient little man.

George wore spectacles that seemed disproportionately large for the rest of him. And a clean tweed suit that had lasted him for twenty years. He carried a briefcase that contained a packed lunch, two plastic rulers, a pen, pencil and a copy of *The Librarian's Friend*.

'Normal!' said his neighbour.

'I wouldn't be too sure!' said another.

George subscribed to neatness in all things because it gave him a sense of security. If he paid his rent on time the landlord wouldn't evict him. If he kept his filing system meticulously up-to-date the senior librarian wouldn't sack him. And if he kept his flat spick-and-span his modest little niche in the thundering mass of life would be assured.

George was a man of quiet intelligence and great generosity of spirit. Many people were fond of him, but George could not see what these people saw. He looked in the mirror and saw only himself: frankly, he thought, that wasn't very much.

George had a friend; a steadfast friend, loyal, loving and true, who kept him company in his little basement flat through every lonely winter's night: who called goodnight and roused him every morning.

George was a gentle man with gentle dreams. But gentle dreams are fragile things and shouldn't be disturbed.

Then one day the library had a fire. George thought he would burst with excitement as he smashed the fire alarm with his elbow and the big red engines came. Two fire engines and twenty firemen: a disproportionate number for what was in fact a very little fire. Nonetheless, George was so busy cataloguing the charred remains of twenty books that he forgot his pork chop that night, and faced with the prospect of a poached egg for two nights running he let slip a moment's irritation as he changed the seed in his budgie's cage.

'Not a very interesting life,' he said.

'What more do you require?' asked Herbert quizzically.

'Ah, Herbert, you know how to get to the root of the matter! The answer, of course, is nothing. I require nothing more. My cup is full.'

But Herbert could tell that George was lying to save his feelings, and the knowledge hurt him to the end of his tail feathers. He bowed his head in dismay.

George's parents lived in a small council house on the other side of town. They had grapefruit for breakfast and they also had a budgie – Herbert Senior. The hen, Hermione, had died giving birth to Herbert, and so Herbert Senior was, being widowed, somewhat disinclined towards small talk.

'Come along, Herbert!' said George's father, as he and George stared through the bars of the old bird's cage.

'Look who's here! Aren't you going to say hello?'

Herbert Senior turned his face away and hopped to the back of the perch.

'Never mind,' said George.

'Never mind,' said his father.

'Would you like sugar?' asked George's mother of George.

'Have I ever said no to sugar?' asked George, smiling.

His mother smiled back. His father also smiled, then clapped his hands together briskly.

'Let's sit down, shall we? Tea's getting cold!'

They laughed at his father's little joke, for tea was always cold. Every Tuesday evening at five o'clock precisely George arrived for tea with his parents, and left, after pink salmon sandwiches and fruit cake, at seven.

'Herbert will want his seed changing,' said George as he rose.

'Of course!' said his father.

'Goodbye, then, Mother.' George kissed his mother on the cheek. And 'Goodbye Father,' as the two men shook hands.

'How was it?' asked Herbert, when George returned home.

'The usual, you know.'

'Oh good!'

'Mm.'

'George?' asked Herbert, who'd been brooding thoughtfully for some time.

'Yes, Herbert?'

'Are you bored?'

George sighed, and resolved to be honest. 'I think I am rather, yes.'

'Then you must do something!' Herbert hopped to the other perch to face George more squarely.

'What can I possibly do?'

'Eat me.'

George stopped blowing the husks from the top of the seed bowl, and stared at Herbert.

'I beg your pardon?'

'I said, you must eat me!' replied Herbert, puffing out and shaking his blue-and-white feathers.

'What a ridiculous thing to say! Are you mad?'

'I'm trying to be interesting.'

'Is that all it is? Then Herbert, I'd much rather you were dull.'

'So you think I'm dull?' For this merely confirmed what Herbert had been thinking for some time.

'No! What I mean is . . . '

'That you think I'm dull!' cried little Herbert.

'Don't be ridiculous!'
'Dull and ridiculous now.'
'For heaven's sake . . . !'
'You should eat me.'
George was becoming exasperated.
'Herbert, I don't want to eat you!'
'Then I'm inedible as well?'
'I didn't say that!'
'But you inferred it.'
'I didn't!'
'Did.'
'Didn't!'
'George?' said Herbert.
'Yes, Herbert?' said George.
'I think I'm becoming depressed.'

Dear Mr Snidgrove,
I am afraid I am not able to fulfil my duties as librarian
at the moment, as a problem of a highly personal nature
has occurred and I must remain at home. I'm most terribly
sorry for the inconvenience. I hope you understand.
    Yours sincerely,
    George Beagle

Dear George,
Is it your parents? I hope very much that the problem is
resolved soon, but would nevertheless like to assure you
that your job is safe with us. Do take care.
    Yours sincerely,
    Ronald Snidgrove

That much was a relief to learn. Now George turned his
full attention to Herbert, who had taken to lying on the
floor of his cage, claws in the air, pretending to be dead.
    George sat patiently reading beside the cage. He had
taken it from its stand and rested it instead on the coffee table, in the hope that the change of scenery might
help Herbert. The hours ticked by, interrupted only by
the sound of George turning a page and muffled noises
from the flats above.

'George?'

George stopped reading and looked anxiously down at Herbert.

'Yes Herbert?'

Herbert was lying still, in the same position, his little eyes closed.

'I'm dead now. You could eat me if you wanted.'

'You're not dead, Herbert.'

'I am! Look at me!' His eyes were tightly closed, his face a grimace of concentration.

'You're pretending.'

'But if I was, would you eat me?'

'No.'

'Why?'

'Because you're very special to me. I couldn't possibly eat you.'

'Humans eat each other. I heard it on the radio.'

'Only when they're starving.'

'And cannibals . . . ?'

'Well, yes, but they're not British.'

'But I'm a bird! Humans eat birds!'

'Not budgies.'

'Why not? What's wrong with us?'

'It just isn't done. And you're no ordinary budgie. You're my friend.'

'You don't mean that.'

'I do.'

'You're just saying it to cheer me up!'

'I'm not!'

'But it wouldn't do any good, you know. I'm beyond being cheered.'

'Maybe it's the weather.'

'Must you always look for excuses! Can't you see I'm not happy? I should much rather be eaten!'

And so it continued. George's leave of absence extended to a week. At the end of the week, however, he decided it was time to do something. So he wrote again to Mr Snidgrove, requesting to be allowed to bring his budgie to work. The senior librarian, a little perplexed, nevertheless agreed. On the first day, delighted at his colleague's return, Mr Snidgrove visited the library with sherry to welcome him back. 'Here's to you, George! Not having you here makes me realise how much we would miss you! All the best, my boy!'

George smiled and sipped a little of his sherry, then placed it on the library counter. Herbert pulled himself out of George's pocket by his beak and hopped quietly on to the counter, as George and Mr Snidgrove left to discuss the possibility of employing extra help on a part-time basis. He dipped his beak gingerly into the sherry glass, supped a little, raised his head and looked around, then supped a little more.

By the time George noticed Herbert's absence from his pocket, a quarter of the sherry had gone. Herbert was lying on his back on the counter, his wings spread wide and claws curled.

'Oh my God!' whispered George. Herbert opened one very clouded little eye and mumbled: 'Hullo George. I'm pissed.'

George left the library with rushed apologies to an even more perplexed Mr Snidgrove and walked briskly home. As he walked, the little warm bundle in his pocket hiccoughed, whistled feebly, then muttered, 'I think I'm going to be sick. Didn't know I could drink, did you George? Nor did I.'

The following day, George accidentally left the cage door open as he changed Herbert's water. Both were beginning to show signs of the strain by now: Herbert's feathers were dry and untidy, his eyes still clouded and he refused to stand upright. George was unable to sleep for worry, and hadn't washed or shaved. A large, sleek tabby whispered down the steps to the basement and nipped in just as George collected the milk from outside. George didn't notice, but heard within seconds a delighted purring coming from the living-room. He rushed in to find the cat crouched over Herbert's little blue-and-white body, on its back, the small voice chirruping: 'Eat me! Go on! Eat me!'

George was becoming desperate. The flat was a mess, he was relying on his savings to survive, and Herbert couldn't be left. Even safely in the cage, he had attempted to drown himself in his water bowl. So George deposited him in his pocket once again – this time keeping a cautious hand over the aperture, and took him to the vet.

'He's depressed,' said George.

'Mm,' said the vet.

'I'm very depressed!' cried Herbert.

The vet seemed not to notice.

'There!' said George.

'What?' said the vet, looking up.

'He said it himself: you heard him!'

The vet lifted an eyebrow.

'Heard who, Mr Beagle?'

'Herbert, of course! It's all he ever says now: "Eat me!" or "I'm depressed."'

The vet looked worried.

'He tells you this, does he?'

George nodded distractedly.

'I see . . . ' He looked down at Herbert, lying on his back on the examination table. 'Well – he's certainly out of condition, and behaving oddly for a budgie. I'll give you some tonic for him . . . and, er, if I may suggest – perhaps you ought to visit your GP?'

'Why?'

The vet adopted his most reassuring approach.

'You seem out of sorts yourself. It might be wise . . . I'll write to your GP – do you have his address?'

A couple of days later, George found himself in the doctor's surgery; Herbert nestled in his pocket.

'And you say your budgie talks to you?'

'Of course! I have him here – listen!'

George recovered Herbert and deposited him on the doctor's desk. Herbert staggered sideways, rolled on to his back and cried, 'Eat me! Go on!'

'There!' said George.

The doctor looked worried. The bird had whistled vaguely – nothing more.

'Does he talk to you often?'

'He talks all the time. We have excellent conversations . . . or at least, we used to . . . ' George bowed his head.

'And it's just – um – Herbert's voice you hear?'

'Who else is it likely to be?'

'The television doesn't mention you?'

'We don't have a television.'

'The radio?'

'No.'

'There's nothing unusual about your electricity supply?'

'Pardon?'

'No – well, there probably isn't.'

The doctor assumed a practical voice, reaching for his prescription pad.

'I'd like you to take these three times a day for a couple of weeks, then come back and see me.'

'What are they?'

'Just something to calm you down. I think you'll find they'll help . . . '

George, feeling in truth slightly overwrought, complied. Took the tablets. Three times a day. For a while Herbert seemed no better, but then a remarkable thing happened. He rolled over from the prone position on the floor of his cage, shook his feathers, chirruped and jumped on to his perch. Then chirruped again. George was astonished. He rushed to the cage.

'Herbert! Herbert – you're feeling better! That tonic must be helping. Do you feel less depressed?'

Herbert put his head to one side, watched him silently through one healthier-looking eye, then chirruped again, shuffled to the end of the perch and shook his little yellow bell. George smiled through clouded eyes and spoke again.

'How are you, Herbert?'

Herbert shook the bell once more, then jumped off his perch and attacked the food bowl, vigorously throwing the empty husks to one side. Then he stopped, looked at George, and whistled.

'Herbert!' cried George happily. 'Speak properly! I can't understand you!' Herbert whistled again.

This was intolerable. Better to ask to be eaten, than to say nothing at all.

George's life stood in ruins, his one true companion lost to him. He didn't return to work, nor did he visit his parents, but continued mutely to observe the other routines of his shattered life. Meanwhile Herbert grew better and better, whistling happily through the day.

One by one the routines subsided until only Herbert was attended to, somewhat vaguely. Herbert whistled on, seemingly oblivious now to his owner's dejection. And one by one the tablets disappeared, until the final one rattled into George's hand as he lay on the sofa, unwashed, half-starved, mute. He returned to the doctor.

'He isn't speaking at all now, Doctor. I don't know what to do.'

'I think it's probably for the best. Here's another prescription for the tablets you've been taking, and also something extra to take at night.'

'What are the new ones?'

'Just something to lift your mood.'

But George's mood didn't lift. The better Herbert became, the more George declined.

George's father visited.

'You're letting life get on top of you, son. You should always have the upper hand.'

'But he doesn't talk to me any more!'

'Just because your budgie's lost the words you trained him to say . . . '

'I didn't train him! And it isn't the words that I miss. It's the conversations we used to have . . . '

'You've been on your own for too long, my lad. Budgie's don't "make conversation"!'

'Father,' said George, as he ushered him out of the flat, 'you never understood me.'

Silence stole upon George like an unwelcome guest. Silence filled his ears, and Herbert's whistles were an agony of silence. Silence crept down the steps to the basement, and eased itself beneath the basement door. Silence filled the kitchen, the bathroom, the bedroom, the lounge. The day ended in silence and silence rose with the dawn, until night and day became barely distinguishable stretches of emptiness. George gobbled the tablets in desperation. Mr Snidgrove wrote several letters, received no reply; his final, curt little note together with George's P45 and holiday pay lay on the doormat, together with a steadily mounting pile of bills and circulars.

It was dark. Even the clock had stopped. George lay

on the sofa, arms and legs akimbo, staring at the grimy ceiling.

'Herbert?'

Herbert stopped preening, shook his feathers and looked at George.

'I'm dead, Herbert.'

Herbert cocked his head, shuffled to the end of the perch and shook his little bell. The final round had come.

Next morning the neighbours stood in huddles on the street outside, greedily swapping information on the previous night's events. Some, they said, had seen it coming.

'He got the sack from work, I heard.'

'I told you all along he wasn't right.'

'What a to-do!'

'It's a shame, I think.'

'Oh yes, it's a shame. But they ought to lock him up.'

George had been arrested at two o'clock in the morning, by several enormous policemen who held him down in a manner totally disproportionate to his size, as he'd been running up and down the street, upending dustbins and hurling their contents across the paths. The police thought him dumb, for not a word did he utter on the way to the hospital, but once there the reason quickly became apparent. As he sat on a chair in the interview room, George's mouth slowly opened to reveal, little by little, a beak, an eye, a mass of feathers.

Man And Boy

'That nurse you mentioned last week ... ?' Rose prompted. 'The one taking George for a walk ... ?'

Gail grinned. 'His name was Terry. And after Terry there was Tony, who indulged in late-night black magic – mercifully he didn't involve me. We had parties, did some things you wouldn't believe ... Went camping *en masse*, took to the pub most evenings after shift, and had a great time. But there never seemed enough to the men. They seemed very irresponsible – I suppose we all were – it was what we wanted at the time. But we were "living in" – living together as a community. None of us wanted a serious relationship then. We just wanted fun.

'The mornings would begin with the distant trundle of trolleys being pushed to the wards by whistling porters and, in the background, the "thuk thuk thuk" of the boiler room. I'd climb out of bed and open the window to retrieve the pint of milk from the outside ledge. Yawning and stretching, I'd watch the birds fighting for food on the grass below.

'Terry slept with his face to the wall, slipping gradually into the space I had left without waking. I'd fill the kettle – we all bought our own kettles – put it on to boil, shut the door quietly behind me and walk down the long warm corridor to the toilet. When I came back I'd pull the covers from the bottom of the bed and tickle Terry's feet. I love to see men in the morning, when they're just waking. For all their size they seem so innocent ... ' She smiled at the memory.

'Didn't you get into trouble, with a man in your room?'

'No. We were never caught. We'd let them out of the fire exit by the orchard ... We were still locked into the nurses' home at night, but we all had keys!'

'Was Albert like that, first thing?'

'Albert was different.'

'In what way?'

'I was married to him.'

Rose lifted an eyebrow.

'Have I told you that Pluckett's pack eggs for a large Newcastle-based egg retailer called "HAWAY − LAY!"? Every box we handle has the name stamped on the lid with a bright cartoon-style chicken and a logo underneath that reads: "They're the best, Henny!"'

Rose laughed. 'What has that to do with Albert?'

Gail grimaced. 'He'd know them. He probably ate them every morning as a kid. He came from up there.'

When Albert's father departed, after twelve pints, a fish-and-chip supper and a cigarette that luckily expired between the expired man's fingers; when Stan Marsden gave up the earthly effort of his twice-daily visit to the pub and took off to the great Tap-room in the Sky. When he went without so much as a 'Thank you' to his wife for all her years of effort on his behalf (his last words to her had been: 'Here, tak me shoes off for us, pet. I canna see me bloody feet!') ... When he passed, pissed, into our Father's forgiving arms, Albert had been fifteen years of age, and already as close a replica of his father as an under-age boy could be. He bought his first packet of condoms, and after trying them out with the woman across the road, who'd been initiating young boys into adulthood for the last twenty years (her husband worked regular nights and she had a helpful disposition), he'd discovered Ale. His dad introduced it by example. And 'Her Across' had bought him a couple of bottles of stout as a thankyou.

Albert knew what a Wife should be, from his mother, who never, never complained. They lived 'up North' until his father died, when his mother's brother (Uncle

Alf, who could smoke cigarettes the wrong way round without burning his tongue), took Aunty Enid away to Bournemouth (a nice little bungalow he'd bought with his redundancy money), and gave the manless, penniless 'Northern' Marsdens his former Coal Board house for a nominal rent that paid the nominal mortgage for him.

So Albert arrived in a small, friendly oasis between coal seam and sky, where the only fights occurred on a Saturday night and everyone spoke 'Geordie' so much you could be forgiven for thinking it was Tyneside, with foxgloves replacing the coal-scarred beaches.

Albert came from a long line of colliers who suffered a deep-seated aversion to the pit and consequently managed to produce sick-notes with unerring regularity, covering a wide range of illnesses. Good old Uncle Alf had lasted thirty years in this manner until the colliery management finally lost patience and offered him redundancy terms which, being a sound man of unsound scruples, he accepted with such speed that the personnel manager would have nobbled him if he hadn't already buggered off to Bournemouth.

And whereas a common syndrome amongst the sons of mining families was a gut-wrenching struggle to break from the tradition of following Dad down the pit, Albert had no such qualms about following in his dad's footsteps to the Philistine Arms and a lifetime with a good woman who never complained while he propped up the bar. Albert's training had begun early, with school absenteeism almost as prolific as Uncle Alf's lack of attendance at work. He knew a) how to avoid the school inspector; b) how to get legless on two pounds' pocket money – his mum's purse being for ever on the hall table; c) how to charm the girls and d) how to talk as though you know everything about everything without knowing anything. At eighteen, he was untrained, unemployed, unemployable and extremely satisfied with life.

Life, as many will tell you, is a hazardous expedition, filled with pits, peaks, troughs, pain, pleasure and work.

Albert avoided this expedition by never putting on his boots.

Bugged

Gail wasn't keen to talk to Rose about Albert. Sometimes she found herself missing him. The girls at Pluckett's were always talking about their boyfriends. They often asked her out for a drink, but she generally declined. Occasionally she'd join them just to be civil, but they were too loud for her. After one drink the pub's atmosphere seemed to bear down on her. She'd notice the men looking her way and suddenly feel very alone. A few years ago – before Albert – before everything – she'd have met their eyes quite happily, and followed that first contact through to a pleasantly warm conclusion. But, in truth, that was over a decade ago. Now she simply felt uncomfortably out of place in company.

Martha had what she felt to be the answer. Martha simplified life. 'What you need, Gail, is a man,' she told her. Often. Although she didn't actually say 'man'. And Gail realised that she probably was right. Martha knew her as well as anyone. When Gail first came out of hospital Martha had been there for her, knocking on her door two or three times a day to check that she was all right. Most days she'd invite Gail to her room for dinner: 'You must eat,' she'd say. And on Sundays – before Gail started at Pluckett's – they'd take a picnic together at the local park, where Gail fed the ducks while Martha sat with her feet in the lake, chattering about politics, the price of things, men (generally and specifically) and sexually transmitted diseases. She knew an extraordinary amount about everything, and swore that most of her clients came for counselling. Moreover, Gail trusted her implicitly – Martha inspired trust – so that when Martha said, 'You need a . . . man!' Gail believed her.

The problem was – men always expected more than she felt able to offer. She was still a young woman – in her late twenties – but, for the time being at least, she felt unable to relate to the opposite sex. She thought about death too much, and felt too vulnerable to be able to approach any relationship with the opposite sex on a purely frivolous basis. And it would have to be frivolous, to be what she wanted it to be, to get what she needed . . .

She remembered frivolous.

She wrote it down.

It had different connotations now. It wasn't the right word.

She stared at it.

'FRIVOLOUS!' it said.

It climbed off the page and skipped across the desk. All buttercups and butterflies and lace.

She put a line through it.

'Be honest!' she told herself. '"Frivolous" is not the right word: "Fuck" is the right word! Spit it out! Say what you mean!'

She ached.

'No!' she whispered to the ceiling. 'Albert is the right word!'

She cried herself to sleep.

So the following week she returned the conversation to her nurse training. She really didn't want to discuss her ex-husband. She didn't want to think about him. But Rose had a way of getting to the truth. Not that she ever did anything specific. She just seemed to manoeuvre Gail in that direction. Sometimes she made Gail feel as though she was in a room with advancing walls that were gradually closing in on her: that sooner or later they would leave her with nowhere to run and then squash all the feelings out of her. Gail knew that running wasn't the answer. She knew she was running from herself. But until it finally happened she would examine every square inch of her metaphorical squashing-room, to see if there was another way out. She didn't want the truth. She could see it coming and she didn't want to face it. Sometimes she felt so full of conflict she imagined that this . . . this . . . *thing* inside her was like a high-pressure cylinder just waiting to explode in a moment of pure devastation. What she didn't realise was that Rose not only understood her fear, but that she also released the pressure little by little, every week that they sat together.

Rose knew therapy to be a box of surprises. While Gail struggled to contain what she imagined to be a cauldron of raw emotion, Rose helped her to open the box and take out the wrapping paper. Sheet by sheet. Layer by careful layer. Until they reached the final layer, confronted Gail's 'moment of pure devastation' and discovered it to be something, when held to the light, very small.

The trick's in the unwrapping, Rose knew. As every imagined sheet was removed, Rose stayed behind with her notes to tuck it back in again, so that when Gail finally reached the centre she'd discover that nothing had been lost in the process, and that *everything* actually mattered.

Gail was talking about cockroaches.

'If I was due to start at seven in the morning I'd make a point of being first in the hospital. We had frequent plagues of them and the only entertainment they provided was first thing in the morning, to the first person who switched on the lights. Imagine a corridor the length of a playing field, with fluorescent strip lights that flickered on in a chain, starting at the door. Looking down the corridor the dark floor would part straight down the centre, following the lights, and disappear into the walls. The cockroaches, some big as mice, disappeared through the heating vents into the tunnels below. They never made a sound.

'They weren't as much fun on the wards. Have you ever stepped on a cockroach? They laid poison, and in the mornings the ward kitchens would be littered with dead and dying beetles.

'If I had the morning off I'd take a leisurely stroll across the grounds to the patients' canteen for a pint of milk, maybe stop for a cup of tea if there was room.

Later, from my window, I'd watch Basil – one of the patients from Eight's – being escorted to the orchard to dig. Digging the orchard was deemed as therapy. Dragging Basil by his shirt sleeves was deemed a necessary evil. The therapy was good for him. It was the hospital's answer to "rehabilitation".

'Basil became incarnate and given to diabolic mutterings on Thursdays: on Monday, Tuesday and Wednesday he was The King of England and Grand Ruler of the Great British Empire: disposed to offering and retrieving knighthoods depending on whether his dinner was hot or cold, or if there were lumps in his semolina. On Friday he was blind for a day. At the weekends he became himself and sat in a corner, weeping.

'Or at least he said he was the devil. I never heard him curse a soul, and frankly don't believe he had an ounce of cruelty in him. I think that his Friday-blindness was a form of self-punishment for his quietly diabolic Thursdays. If he could only have changed his routine and kept his kingdom for a full seven days, I'm sure he would have been happier.

'Instead they made him dig the orchard. I never saw an apple: they dug too much for the trees to grow. Ray, who dug for a fag. Oswald, whose nervous energy seemed unstoppable, would, if left to himself, have dug a pit and disappeared in it. Norman, who complained of perpetual tiredness, was given the job of "monitoring the spades". He watched them out: he watched them return. He just didn't count them.

'By mid-morning the hospital corridors were littered instead with bodies: people who didn't want to go where they should have gone; who didn't fancy packing cottonwool in Industrial Therapy; or who couldn't contemplate another group crossword in Occupational Therapy. They sprawled against the walls or curled up on the floor and slept. They'd hunt for cigarette ends – nubb-ends: the essential requirement for hospital living. Cigarettes could get you anything – even sex behind the cricket pavilion or in the bus shelter. I once managed to persuade an old man to let me clean his jacket. We sat down at the table and emptied his pockets. As the nubb-ends piled up on the table his chest expanded with pride. He must have been carrying at least two hundred: he was a very rich man.'

Several years later, Gail had the first of many rows with Albert in the kitchen of their (her) house.

She came off duty tired one afternoon and drove home in a temper. Albert was dozing on the sofa. Three empty beer bottles littered the carpet. His socks smelt. He hadn't cleaned or stoked the fire. The sink was full of dishes. The front-room door was hanging off its hinges. The television was on. Albert had been watching *Trumpton*.

But it wasn't that. It was the full ashtray. Full of the remains of a new packet of twenty she'd bought herself the day before.

She stood by the sofa and contemplated hitting him over the head with one of the empty bottles.

'You bastard!' she said.

'Humph?' muttered Albert, trying to wake.

'You utter bastard!'

'What?'

'You total, total, total . . . ' She stormed into the kitchen, turned on the taps and furiously targeted the dishes with washing-up liquid.

He staggered after her and stopped at the door.

'Hmm. This needs fixin'.'

'It wasn't broken this morning!'

Albert swayed slightly from side to side as he contemplated the problem.

'Needs a new hinge.'

Gail smashed a plate over a grease-stricken saucepan and turned on him.

'You smoked my fags!'

Albert was still bleary eyed, but he lifted his eyebrows: 'Ooh! Lock me up, Mother, your son's a criminal!'

'I told you yesterday they were all I had left 'til the end of the week!'

He pouted. If only he knew how stupid he looked, she thought, but she was too angry to tell him.

'You haven't done . . . ' she looked around with her hands in the air, dripping water: '. . . anything!'

Albert stuck his chin out. 'It's not my place . . . '

'BUT YOU MAKE THE MESS! AND YOU SMOKED MY FAGS! HOW *COULD* YOU?!'

Albert buttoned up his shirt and tucked it into his trousers. 'Know when I'm not wanted,' he muttered, heading for the back door: 'I'm going to Mam's!'

'Good riddance. YOU BASTARD!' This, as he closed the door between them.

That afternoon she raided the decimal jar, hunted out an old cigarette rolling machine an ex-boyfriend had given her, and scraped together enough change to buy half an ounce of tobacco from the beer-off round the corner.

The next morning, while on duty, she took Mrs Brown for a walk. Down the corridor, out of the door, down two flights of cold metallic stairs, along another corridor, through a fire door, through another fire door and out into the grounds.

In those days she looked every inch the nurse, black moccasins, subtle tights, chestnut hair scraped back from her face and secured in a taut bun; shrouded in a black cape that covered her meticulous blue uniform. Mrs Brown wore a thick wool coat buttoned irregularly, so that her collar was lop-sided and unbuttoned bulges of wool protruded all the way down her front. She wore a pair of boots – brown leather, fleece lining, one with a bit of egg stubbornly sticking to the heel; zipped at the front like pensioner's slippers ... thick mauve tights, two stained jumpers, one green round-neck, the other red v-neck (inside out), and a tartan skirt with a short zip at the front when it should have been at the back, topped off with a small navy-blue beret with a dead beetle motif. Her eyes were half-closed, she didn't speak, but shuffled forward with expressionless effort. Gail chatted to Mrs Brown – the way nurses should to someone not speaking, but Mrs Brown had been given another of those big white pills just after breakfast and was too busy concentrating on shifting her legs regularly to hear what Gail was saying.

Mrs Brown squinted from the sunlight's glare and shuffled through a pile of dead leaves that the assistant gardener had spent an hour sweeping. Luckily the assistant gardener from Ward 14 had forgotten all about the leaves and was currently having a tea and a smoke in the patients' canteen.

They walked on, then stopped at a small Victorian rotunda surrounded by trees and sat on one of the benches, sheltered from the wind. Mrs Brown's tongue felt too large for her mouth. She wasn't at all sure what was in there – it didn't feel like her tongue. She hoped it would go away, but meanwhile concentrated on breathing through her nose.

Gail reached inside her cape and extracted a small silver tin, some hand-rolling tobacco and a slim packet of cigarette papers. Mrs Brown stopped breathing through her nose and watched with sleepy interest. Gail opened the lid of the small silver tin. Attached to both the inside of the lid and the base of the tin was a wide strip of thick pink canvas. She placed it carefully on her knee, where it balanced precariously, the lid being heavier than the base. She opened up the foil top of the tobacco and sniffed the inside of the packet. Mrs Brown continued to stare.

Gail poked her thumb and forefinger into the packet and pulled out the tangled shreds of tobacco. Some shreds scattered immediately over her cape, but the rest seemed determined to stay attached to the packet. She clamped the fingers of her other hand round the base of the tobacco she wanted and tried to tear it free. The small silver tin fell backwards and slid off her knee on to the grass. She put the tobacco on her knee and reached down for the tin. The tobacco rolled on to the grass and the bit that Gail had been pulling at was swept away by a mischievous gust of wind. She tugged at a flimsy sheet protruding from the slim packet of liquorice papers. It emerged, followed by all the other sheets stuck together.

In frustration Gail pulled the lot out and stuck one corner of the first paper on her bottom lip. Its companions unravelled and streamed down the front of her cape in a banner of brown fury.

'It happens,' she muttered, stiff lipped, desperately trying to recapture the stream of Rizlas as they wafted manically in the breeze.

This was good therapy. Mrs Brown was entranced.

All of Gail's composure disappeared as she fought with the cigarette papers and her anger towards Albert. Her bun unravelled and her hair flopped forward in sympathy. With a sudden burst of efficiency she caught one end, tugged the other end from her lip, pulled one liquorice paper free, retrieved the tobacco from the grass, tore a small clump from the packet, positioned the cigarette paper correctly within the strip of canvas, sprinkled some tobacco into the pink trough inside the lid and licked the paper's adhesive strip. She turned to smile at Mrs Brown. 'This is the clever bit!' she announced, shutting the lid on the tin. From out of a slot on the top came a thin stalk of rolled liquorice paper, festooned with strands of tobacco.

Gail picked up the stalk and squinted down the middle. Undeterred, she gathered tin, tobacco and papers and shoved them back inside her cape, half stood to brush the tobacco from her lap, then sat back down again. She found her matches, struck one and lit the cigarette. One third was immediately eaten by flames and strands of ignited tobacco dropped on to her cape, but she inhaled on what was left and sat back with a smile of immense satisfaction.

Mrs Brown was transfixed by a long strand of tobacco that hung miserably from the side of the cigarette, as though preparing to fall. But Gail was happy. She took another drag and turned to Mrs Brown as the cigarette started to disintegrate between her fingers.

'I'm trying to give up,' she said.

The dead beetle motif on Mrs Brown's hat *was* actually a dead beetle, but Gail was so cross at Albert that she failed to notice. Later, they discovered that Mrs Brown collected beetles as a reaction to her treatment. She came in suffering from depression, the doctors prescribed electro-convulsive therapy and she collected beetles.

Blame the system.

Blame the beetles.

Don't blame Mrs Brown.

Mrs Brown was married to the local Member of Parliament.

Blame wedlock.

Blame politics.

Daisy (And Disillusion)

For three years Gail was taught the skills and knowledge required of a psychiatric nurse. After three years she passed her final exam and acquired a belt, a dark blue stripe on her nurse's cap and a modest raise in salary.

'Nothing's ever perfect,' she said to Rose after some consideration.

'Does it have to be?'

'Sometimes, yes. At least, you have to aim for perfection. . .'

'But you're human. We're none of us ever perfect.'

'We should try . . . '

'Provided we accept failure.'

'Rose!' Gail laughed. 'You're very cynical for a therapist!'

'Proof of my own imperfection!'

She smiled in reply. 'We were taught shop window nursing. The best. The absolute best. Fit-for-presentation nursing. The model of nursing perfection that you want displayed for all the world to see because it's so damn good. It's like being taught window-dressing with the finest equipment, the finest costumes and in the most creative environment you could possibly wish for; and then coming back, fired with enthusiasm, to a shop filled with second-hand clothes in a dark back street, where the only equipment available is a couple of wire coat hangers, a piece of wood and some safety pins.

'I could see the difference between what we were

taught and what actually went on. Everybody said you learnt "real" psychiatric nursing by experience, and of course it's true. You learned things that you would never dare admit to your tutor, even though the tutor probably knew them anyway. You learned what was acceptable, rather than what was best. You learned how to cut corners. You learned to reassess your ideals, according to each situation. You learned how to make do with wire coat hangers, if that's all you've got.

'But I suppose I always hoped that I could change things for the better when I qualified and had a ward of my own. I thought I could work within the system for change. But the system's bigger than all of us. Somehow you seem to inherit it. Despite what you think, Rose, I wasn't looking for perfection. But if things are bad and you aim for the best you might find a compromise that's at least *better*.'

'What did you want to change so much?'

'Attitudes, I suppose. Entrenched attitudes.'

'Could you have done it?'

'I wanted to try.'

'Did you try?'

'You learn very quickly that it's better left alone.'

'So did you leave it?'

'I tried, but I couldn't accept it.'

'Not sure of what else I should do, I remained. Better the devil you know, I thought. At least for the time being, until an answer came along. One thing was certain, I now realised. There were no answers here.

'Daisy had no flesh left; what remained sagged around her buttocks. The urine seeped through the pad, down the sides of the chair and into the carpet. The seat of the chair had a hole big enough to take a fist – but it was the only one we had that tilted back to stop her falling out.

'She'd fall because she was always on the move but never getting anywhere. Her hands, feet, limbs, face – flickering, chattering neurones. Unintelligible conversations; endless, endless – even as we fed her. Sometimes they began sensibly: she'd call, "Harry, Harry, did you put the supper on . . . ?" and then, just as surely as a gust of wind might bring a dying fire alive, the storm that

followed would quickly extinguish it. The sense had gone
– maybe a word, maybe two could be gathered from the
verbal torrent – nothing more.

'She developed pressure sores that would never heal
because there was nothing to encourage granulation,
no way to secure a dressing, and no way to keep the
dressing clean. Only skin between bone and the seat,
constantly chafing, constantly wet. She may have been
unaware of the pain: we assumed that it hurt and tried
our best to bring relief. Incontinence pads were little use,
she was soaking all the time and the linings bunched up
and caused more friction. Had we had enough staff to
concentrate on individuals we could have encouraged
her to walk . . . she *could* walk, with help, but she needed
constant support and when there were just two or three
nurses to twenty-six patients . . .

'In bed, we could have turned her – but she would
probably have developed pneumonia! No use adding pillows to prop her up, she was too far gone . . . she'd either
try to climb out, or shuffle herself into the horizontal . . .

'I saw her, at times, reach out to someone with a shout
of recognition and the eyes became clear, insistent – for
a moment. Then she tried to speak and the words would
jumble and her eyes grew dim, and misted, and filled
with tears. You tried to comfort her but she couldn't
stop talking. Nor could you hold her because the damn
chair was tilted back for her own sake and the little table
had to be secured to the arms to stop her from lunging
forward suddenly if no one was with her. Her fingers
occasionally rattled listlessly against the table-top – that,
too, could spark a memory: one sharp knock, a shout,
"Elsie, you in . . . ?" Then it was all gone again . . . all
gone.

'Daisy had once been a large, jolly woman, who used
to serve in a factory canteen. You could tell she was a
loving sort – it showed in her eyes, in the laughter lines,
the aged dimples.

'They rarely found stockings to match, nor could they
be bothered to look, for the stockings would be wet in an
hour or less. Sometimes they even forgot knickers – was
there any point? It only meant extra work, after all . . .

Bras were out – only one patient had one. So the patients were usually clothed in a vest and a nylon hospital-issue dress with Velcro up the back for easy changing.

'At mealtimes they wheeled Daisy to the dining-area and fed her standing with the plate just below her chin to catch the spillage. It was a race, of course – so many to feed, so few staff. Most of the patients were automatised eaters: like baby birds, they opened their mouths when the spoon touched their chins. They rarely chewed – they rarely had the teeth to chew with – so everything had to be finely minced.

'A couple of the less demented patients were given the job of rolling up the stockings in the afternoons. In the afternoons the ward stank, and there was a gap between lunch and the arrival of the afternoon domestic, so the dining-area was filthy. Violet tended to wander at this time of day, so she had to be jammed between the table and the wall. More often than not a puddle formed beneath her on the yellow linoleum. The two old ladies looked almost normal until you noticed the flies gathering on their balding heads.

'The patients slept in their chairs; after lunch you tended to wander round with wet tissues, trying to get the crusted gravy from around their mouths.

'When Daisy died, she died alone. You could only call for extra staff to deal with difficult or violent patients. Daisy was dying, and "reliefs" weren't available for purely compassionate reasons. So she died alone, as they all did, surrounded by screens in the ward dormitory. We were so short-staffed it was a struggle just to keep the ward running and the patients cared for.

'She died silently, her eyes wide and wildly staring. She had a look of astonishment on her face. I suppose it was mainly that her mouth sagged open. But perhaps it came back to her, then. Perhaps she'd knocked on Elsie's front door again and Elsie had actually opened it! Perhaps Harry had been waiting for her, with the kettle already boiled. Perhaps it was a kind place that she'd just entered – after so much pain, it would have surprised her. I hoped so. We jammed a pillow carefully beneath her chin to hold her mouth shut. I'd laid people out before, but this was different, because I was pleased for her, pleased that she'd left all the torment behind. And if they wouldn't allow us an extra nurse to sit with her, at least they gave us a relief so that we could really make her tidy before the trolley came. So we washed and sprinkled some talcum powder on her, brushed her hair, clipped her nails, packed her as gently as we could with gauze, dressed her in the shroud, labelled her. We pinned a rose to the shroud before wrapping her, finally, in the clean white sheet . . . Then the porters came with the beaten metal trolley and took her away, while we finished up the paperwork, cleaned and disinfected the bed for the next patient and tried to pretend that we were inured to it all.

'That evening, I went over to Celie's flat in Beckwood. Beck's – the factory – was still in business then. Sometimes I stayed there overnight – falling asleep on the settee with little Joe snuggled up beside me. Jack always said I had too many late nights. I slept better on their settee than I ever slept at Anydale – or at home, for that matter. I'd drift off during the Nine o'clock News and wake the next morning snug beneath a couple of blankets, with Celie standing over me bearing coffee and a smile. When Dad died . . . I stayed with them for a few weeks. I think they put me back together. I don't think I could have gone back to nursing without them. They were my family.

'Jack was still at Beck's then. Frank was a handful. Joe had just started primary school. Cindy wasn't even born. I loved them all.

'Albert Marsden had just started work at Beck's – the unemployment office had found him a job and you can't refuse work when you're on the dole. Jack was supposed to teach Albert how to check and test the bike frames – that was his department, but Albert didn't want to learn – he simply wanted to be sacked, so it was safer to get him to make the drinks. Jack said Albert made him laugh so much he couldn't think straight, much less make him toe the line. The factory wasn't making a profit – everyone knew that: they knew their jobs were insecure, so when Albert came along and kept asking to be sacked – it cheered them up. Albert wasn't choosy – he asked everyone. The only people he didn't ask were the managers, but he asked the fitters, the painters, the welders, the testers, the cleaners, the young and the old. He asked them all. "Sack me!" he said. "I don't want a job!"

'Jack and Albert became firm friends, and arriving at Celie's I was introduced to him: a slim, dark youth in jeans and sweatshirt, with a jacket slung over his arm, and cap hanging out of the jacket pocket. He had slicked-back hair and a disarming grin.

'That night we all went to the pub together, leaving Frank to babysit. We walked through the streets hand-in-hand, as though it was the most natural thing in the world. We got drunk. Everybody seemed to be friends with Albert, but then he made everyone he talked to feel special – he had a way with strangers. At one point he dragged me across the tap-room to introduce me to an old man he'd just met at the bar who raced pigeons. I don't remember what the old man said, but Albert put his arm round him and the old man's eyes shone with pleasure at being noticed, for once.

'Later, as I told him about the hospital and how tired I'd become of it he listened gently, brushing the hair back from my face.

'"You're very beautiful," he whispered. Jack leaned over Celie and tapped my arm: "You've just got to stand your corner, Gail, and not let them knock you down. It's like Beck's. If you thought about it too much it'd drive you round the bend. Roll with the punches, Gail, but never let them bury you!"

'"But what happens," I shouted back, "if you haven't got a corner to fight from? What if they *have* knocked you down, and you can't get back up again?"

'Jack extricated himself from Celie and stood up. "Who's havin' another?" But then, as he picked up the glasses, he leaned over to me. "Don't let them get you down, Gail. Nothing's worth that!"

'We walked to the bus stop with Jack and Celie, but Albert and I fancied a curry, so we said good night and walked off alone. I remember Albert phoning for a taxi to Anydale. I fell asleep on his shoulder all the way there. He crept round the back of the nurses' home while I let myself in at the front with a key, then I let him in through the fire door by the orchard. We crept upstairs in darkness. To my room. To bed.

'He was the most beautiful lover I'd ever known. I wanted him all the time. And within a month we were married. Just like that.'

She clicked her fingers.

'Do you really regret meeting him?'

'I don't regret anything about our relationship, except that it ended so quickly in marriage. I thought I'd found a good man – a man like Jack, who'd protect me just as Jack seemed to protect Celie by his presence. He put work into perspective. I was in love with him. I just didn't know him well enough.'

Beached

The night had sharp fingers that scored the inside of Gail's
skull. A million mites bit their teeth into the ends of every
nerve in her body. The bed unmade itself in knots around
her feet. The claws drew blood, and then the shadows
came. They came whenever they chose: unannounced,
unwelcome. They clutched at her; her belly became a
clenched fist. She imagined her soul as dark and heavy
as her liver. And she walked around her bedsit like an
old woman, bent double with a pain no doctor would be
able to diagnose.

'*Will you be all right?*'

'What should I do?' she'd asked and Rose had said,
'Write it down,' so she tried. She lurched to the desk
and picked up her pen:

Will you be all right?
Will you be all right?
Will you be all right? . . .

'I won't do it!' She stood and walked to the door. 'It's
you or me, Gail.' The charge nurse had his head in his
hands.

'We could say no . . . ?'

'They'll do it anyway.'

'But if we all stood together . . . ?'

'And lose our jobs as well?'

'But . . . the Union?'

The charge nurse tried to laugh. He couldn't. 'Forget
it, Gail.'

She leaned her head on the door. 'They put you in a hole and then they say not only is there no way out but that you've also got to pull everyone over the edge with you. We might be able to climb back out, Jacko, but they never will. I can't do it. I just can't . . . '

Jacko slammed his hands on the desk. 'You've got to! Today it's your turn. Tomorrow it'll be mine, and the day after that it will be someone on another ward . . . not just here but everywhere, all over the damn country!'

'But it's like . . . '

'No it isn't! Be positive, Gail! Think of the social services, and the community psychiatric nurses, and the GPs . . . Those bed & breakfast places have all been vetted, and there'll be hostels . . . '

'They haven't even built the hostels yet.'

Jacko sat back and picked up his pipe. 'We have to be positive. They've got to go whether we want them to stay or not. Better it comes from us . . . '

The grey squirrels had all but died away. Johnny crouched on the path outside the ward kitchen window, breaking bread for the rest of them. Not that they'd come from the trees while he was there, they'd never be that tame, but he would watch with gentle delight from the kitchen window as they scrambled down the trees to feast on the ward offerings once he was inside. And drink the fresh milk from the bowl he'd left them.

They were his duty. His responsibility. Apart from working in the gardens, Johnny fed the squirrels. He never missed a day. Never. They depended on him.

Gail joined him on the path and crouched down beside him.

'Watch your feet,' he said to her. He arranged the bread in a wide circle, with the milk in the centre, so that they'd all get something.

Gail shifted slightly, then leaned back against the wall. She didn't think anything would ever be as hard as this. To be in such a position . . . to say what she had to say, was anathema to her, as it was – and would be – to all her colleagues. But it had to be said: the subject had to be introduced, and Jacko was right – better that it should come from her than from a stranger . . .

'Johnny?'

Johnny studied the circle of bread to be sure he had it right. There must be sixteen pieces . . . he broke the bread carefully, so that they would all have the same as each other . . .

'Johnny . . . There isn't an easy way to tell you this, but the hospital's got to close soon, so between us, you and I – and there will be others to help, but for the moment . . . you and I, we have to talk about your future . . . '

She could see his breath rising as mist in the cool morning air. He'd been feeding these squirrels long before she had started nursing: she always imagined that he would be here long after she'd moved on. This was his home. And now she had the task of evicting him. She knew how responsible he felt for these animals. She wished she could offer the same consistency of care to him . . . but nothing ever comes of wishing. You just have to deal with the here and now . . .

'Johnny?'

Johnny came to get better thirty years ago. They took away his clothes and gave him pyjamas tied with string at the waist. They sewed labels into his clothes and sent them to the laundry, where the trousers shrank to give that characteristic 'inmate style' above-the-ankle uniformity. They took him to the barber, who placed a basin over his head and cut round it. They gave him a locker without a key, a bed with a stained mattress and three meals a day followed by large white tablets the purpose of which they never fully explained. Johnny's hands began to shake from the tablets; he began to salivate. For a while he was 'acute', but after they'd hacked at his brain to curb 'violent impulses', after one hundred shock treatments to control his 'florid outbursts', after various 'therapies', another go with the surgeon's knife and BOTTLES and BOTTLES and BOTTLES of tablets, there was little more they could do and, well, look at him, he's a 'chronic case' if ever there was one. The leucotomies worked; he no longer fights. He does very little. The tablets – well, he's still on much the same as when he first arrived – once deposited on one of the 'back wards', Johnny was quickly forgotten.

He soon learned to follow orders from the nursing staff. Roused at six in the morning, he and his fellow 'inmates' trooped obediently to the cold washroom, where they washed and shaved under regimental supervision. An inmate cannot answer back, an inmate cannot argue, nor can he complain – who, after all, would be prepared to listen? And every barked command, every instance of being handled *en masse*, like a group of unruly sheep, served to undermine a little more of Johnny's self-esteem.

Johnny ceased to be a human being. Johnny was a patient, an inmate, a lunatic. Should he or one of his companions refuse, on occasion, to be 'managed', should they raise their heads in a frantic, confused and desperate act of defiance . . . should they prove themselves to be less than fully compliant, then additional doses of medication were always available, and heavy nurses ready to restrain. The incident would be duly recorded and the phases of the moon would invariably be blamed. An inmate must therefore be quiet. Get his head down and keep it down. Shhhh.

In those days the hospital was almost self-sufficient, so he worked on the farm. Later, when they started admitting milk and meat from the world beyond, he worked in the gardens, where he stayed. Often on his own, but he could still hear the voices, so he was never lonely. It was nice to feel the sun in the morning, and he liked to sweep the dead leaves. There are lots of dead leaves.

Years ago they talked about trying to 'rehabilitate' him, but there was nowhere he could have gone, so their efforts would have been wasted. What would be the point of building someone up – for nothing? So, for the past – oh – twenty years, Johnny has been on the same ward, with the same people, doing the same things day in day out. They never bothered him. He can't think for himself. Outside – out there – it scares him. At least there are people to talk to here. They never offered much, but in comparison to the outside world, it seemed safe and warm and companionable.

They're talking about 'guest houses'.

'Johnny, lift your head!'
They're talking about 'sheltered accommodation'.
'Look up, Johnny, look up!'
They're saying as how the home he thought he had
is being taken from him, as how he's got to leave, and
make his own way. He doesn't want it.
'Johnny!'
He doesn't know how.
'Johnny!'
People out there don't want him living next to them.
What'll happen to his friends? Oh Johnny, Johnny, they
fucked up your life all those years ago and now they're
saying 'have it back', and you don't want it! You don't
want it! You want to stay here, and be quiet, where it's
safe, until you die, like all the others died . . .
'Lift your head, Johnny, lift it up. We want you to
look up, now.'
In every psychiatric hospital throughout the country, Johnny must face the same ordeal. And there are
Sams, Arthurs, Walters, Josiahs, Freds, Miriams, Brendas
(Brenda's 'crime' was the birth of an illegitimate child in a
less 'enlightened' age) . . . The list is endless. 'Society' has
opted for a more progressive approach towards mental illness. 'With every change, there will always be casualties,'
said the priest at the closing ceremony.
The casualties number thousands.
If Johnny survives the trauma of being forced to leave,
if Johnny makes it to the day of his departure, a committed
and progressive young nurse will be standing at the door
to say goodbye. As he dons his coat, he might ask, 'Is it
cold outside today?' and if the nurse has any conscience,
she might turn her head away.
To the public, he should be in an asylum. To the
psychiatric service (currently) he should be in the community. His memories of hospital life revolve around a
semi-authoritarian regime. His experience of the community has been hostility, ignorance, prejudice. He inhabits
a void. Imprisoned by institutions, imprisoned by the
ignorance of those around him, imprisoned by suffering.
And suffering is his only crime.
For years, they told him the things he must not do.

Now he is told he must look to his own resources.

Above all else, he must be brave.

'Will you be all right?' she whispered. She couldn't help it. The truth will out. She felt scared for him, and ashamed of herself.

'Will you be all right?'

After thirty years at sea and many storms, he's suddenly dumped on dry land without being told how to make a fire. No use asking the natives. They don't want him. He's strange to them: they've always been afraid of the nautical life. At worst they'll hate him. At best they'll abuse his naïvety and exploit him. And it's no use the captains saying, 'Oh, a ship will come every couple of months to see how you're getting along.' That always assumes that the mother ship is still afloat. That they remember where he is.

In the meantime the natives will isolate him.

The nights will freeze him.

And he'll starve.

'I sailed that ship. It creaked and groaned under the weight of a thousand lies. I wasn't a captain, just one of the under-officers. I stood at the gangplank and saw new passengers on, then I saw them off again. And when that mass of flesh and steel came under new ownership, and the engines failed, I was one of those who routed people like Johnny from the forgotten quarters – the places no one used to bother with. I flushed them out, gave them their coats and waved them goodbye. Goodbye Johnny, I said, bye bye Brenda . . . It's a better place you're headed for, they tell me . . . bye bye, good luck, take care . . . '

She stopped and closed her eyes. Rose waited.

When she began to speak again her voice shook with emotion.

'Do you know what asylum actually means?'

'You tell me.'

'It means a place of safety: a refuge. Sanctuary. It once meant an institution for the care and treatment of the mentally ill, but it doesn't now. It's *obsolescent.*'

She laughed emptily.

'Where are you, Gail?'

'Will you be all right?'

The path outside the ward, the breaking of bread, the rustle in the trees, the cool morning air . . .

Johnny looked up at her.

'But who'll feed the squirrels?'

The Dark Territory

In the village centre, the shopping precinct, the place where they raped an orchard for a flat concrete surface; by the chip shop, just opposite the Post Office, squatted a black police van with wire mesh bolted to the windscreen.

The Uniformed Southern men, the protectors of peace and liberty, grown fat from an excess of overtime, lined the inside of the van. Relieved by more of their colleagues at the colliery picket line, the fat happy boys were having chips for dinner.

Gail stopped the car, wound down the window and inhaled deeply. This was The Country: an oasis. Hills rose above the rooftops in every direction. A cock crowed. Geese cackled. And if you took yourself to the village green, to where they shaved the grass for the grace of willow on leather, and looked back over the village – to the left of the grey carbuncular Welfare, where Sid and Renata performed Friday nights, bingo twice weekly – if you looked to the left, in the near distance, framed by a mountainous slag heap – grassed, in keeping with the countryside . . . If you looked, you could see the heart of the community, the headstocks, the towers of metal and winding gear, set to pull men and coal from the seams a mile below.

But the headstocks weren't moving. The heart wasn't beating. The miners were fighting, and the only people profiting from the existence of the colliery were the police, the country's massed constabulary, in their black vans with wire mesh at the windows. For in a spirit of free enterprise, in defence of liberty, they had been called to the Midlands from all over the country and really – although they would never admit to it, being the Law's Missionaries in a hostile region – but really, the strike could go on for as long as it liked: they were making a mint.

– Not that you could hear the strike from the village square, where she stopped. Sometimes you heard sirens – that was all. But in the village proper, you could taste the bitterness in the silence. The police vans were the colour of frustration. The very air seemed heavy with anger. Gail spent all that summer expecting thunder. And now the days were growing cold.

She drove on, through the dark colliery estate, past dark brick houses with dark muddy gardens and plumes of dark smoke rising into an already overcast sky; past miserable cul de sacs; past stray dogs that foraged in the hedgerow for scraps; past what the villagers euphemistically described as the 'nice bit' of the estate and on, ever deeper, to where the smoke billowed thickly from unswept chimneys and the sandstone brick terraces had been turned almost black with soot.

She passed a small concrete sign where dog turds piled unattended, and pulled up opposite a row of the blackest terraces on the estate, with dark alleyways that opened like toothless mouths between each rough front door. Her heart sank as she crunched through the latest coal deposits that hadn't made it to their respective coal-houses, unlocked the front door and went inside.

She leaned back against the door with a vague sense of relief. Inside the house it wasn't too bad. Albert wasn't home, just as expected. She went upstairs, undressed and fell into bed.

'I've had tea with me mum. You needn't bother.'

Albert turned on the ceiling light and she squinted herself awake. 'Glad to hear it.'

He opened the wardrobe door for no other reason than to slam it shut as loudly as he could.

'Thanks!' she muttered, pulling the bedclothes over her head, wishing he'd go away.

'Not that you'd be bothered if I hadn't eaten!'

'Go away, Albert!'

'Some bloody wife!'

'Oh, bugger off back to your mum's. Or go to the pub. Or something. And switch off that light!'

'Switch it off yourself!' He stomped out of the bedroom in fury, used the toilet and made a loud and spectacular occasion out of washing his face. She sat up in bed, rubbed her forehead irritably and lit a cigarette.

Albert returned, slapping a little aftershave under his chin.

'Have I got a clean shirt?'

'How should I know!'

He glared at her, stripped off his t-shirt, threw it on the bed and ransacked the wardrobe. She watched him. He had a nice torso: a very sexy growth of dark, fine hair that tapered almost to a point above his navel; strong, muscular arms – surprising for the little work he did – and a slim, athletic physique. His dark, shoulder-length hair was tied back in a slight ponytail. Very sexy. She remembered the gipsies that frequented her youth: something dark and romantic about them – and he had that look, that hint of mystery . . . They were married – he was right – she should do more for him. Oh bugger it, he should be working in that case! Nonetheless she felt slightly guilty.

'Try the chest of drawers,' she said.

Without responding, he walked to the chest of drawers and worked his way through each drawer in turn, flinging odd socks and knotted tights in all directions. He found a shirt.

'I've found one!' he said.

'Oh good.'

But the collar button was missing.

'It hasn't got a collar button!'

'Oh dear.'

'Bitch!' He took the shirt, stormed out of the room and down the stairs. A few minutes later she heard him leave.

Did he expect her to do it? Perhaps she should have done it. A proper wife would have rifled the sewing jar in a flash, but she hadn't got a sewing jar. She preferred not to sew. ALL RIGHT! SO IT'S NOT MUCH! BUT IT'S THE PRINCIPLE! THE PRINCIPLE! Oh bloody hell, why should she feel guilty?

Why should she?

She spent all evening feeling guilty.

Later she resolved to buy a set of sewing needles.

Albert returned stewed just after eleven, fell up the stairs and crashed into bed. She awoke at the National Anthem, turned off the television and followed him up, although not knowing (and not much caring) that he'd returned.

She couldn't sleep. However tired she felt. And she felt very tired – that much was certain, very tired . . . But she had done a terrible thing that morning. She'd said goodbye.

Nothing had prepared her for Johnny's suitcase. It was filled to the brim with hopelessness. It contained a spare pair of hospital trousers, two tight hospital jumpers, a hospital toothbrush and . . . that was it. After thirty years, that was it. And that really was it . . . poor Johnny. So how did she put that smile on her face?

Sometimes the past seemed inexplicably merged with the present . . . She felt haunted by the things that she never had the chance to say to her mum, and the nagging thought that perhaps her words would have made a difference; that perhaps words make a difference, but now it was too late anyway . . . for her parents . . . too late for Johnny, because she'd smiled and said goodbye and tried to tell herself it was okay because Christ in this job if you don't tell yourself things sometimes you'd crack up, go to pieces, fall apart and shatter . . .

But what hadn't she told her mum? She had been too young to know about depression then, she only knew the loss, and the anger, and . . . she rolled over and faced the wall. She never really cried and she wasn't crying now, only the pain of it welled up without release and took her breath away. Johnny might be okay, she told herself, you never know . . . but she could have said that she was sorry or something, could have told the truth for once, that she hated what the hospital was doing, and that it wasn't right to make him leave. She could have said that. But nothing makes it right ... If he believes the lies and reassurances at least he's in with a chance. Tell him what you're really thinking and he'd throw himself under a bus at the first opportunity.

Gail's eyes ached. She shouldn't have said goodbye. It was too final. And why smile when she didn't feel like smiling, why lie for the State, why pretend?

Albert muttered in his sleep. She turned to look at him. He had goosepimples all over his body: his young, lean, athletic body ... she wanted to touch him; trace her finger down the length of his spine, stroke the hair at the nape of his neck. But he was too drunk to notice the cold, or her fingers ... too drunk to notice anything. She got up, slipped on her dressing-gown and pulled the blankets over Albert's inert, sleeping body.

She shivered in the kitchen as she poured the whisky, paused, then poured a little more. The glass was half-full of bright amber liquid. She added water from the kitchen tap then drank, without hesitating, barely tasting, only hoping that it might wrap its heat around the place that hurt and stop it hurting. She wasn't even sure where the pain was. A gentle flame oozed towards her stomach and a sudden, glorious numbness travelled back up, through the spinal cord, towards her brain. She knew that her brain would protest in the morning, would expand and try to escape through her eyesockets, but for now she didn't care. She staggered slightly and put the glass on the cooker as she reached for the bottle again. Whoo ... perhaps not. Marvellous stuff! She floated up the stairs. She'd forgotten what had kept her awake. Albert snored beneath the bedclothes. She undressed and got back in beside him, pulled close and tucked her knees behind his, her hands around his waist, stroking the dense matt of dark hair beneath his navel. And then they were both out there, floating on the ocean of oblivion, and she fell asleep like that, holding tight, as though he'd keep her safe: but the ocean was

vast and treacherous, dark and endless, and he'd never
learned to swim, and no one could predict a change in
weather.

The Path Towards The Grave

'Will you be all right?'
  Are you still out there?
  I don't think you died.
  I don't think so.
  Did you find the squirrels?
  Did they comfort you?
  Was it too cold for you?
  Was it too cold, Johnny?
  Was it too cold?
Gail sat back and lit a cigarette. She wanted them back, all of them. She wanted to resurrect the dead.

But the dead won't return.

Dead's dead.

She rested the cigarette in the ashtray and rocked back and forth in her chair.

You can't mend the past. It won't mend. Rose can't mend it either. You have to come to terms with it. You have to mend yourself. Be the instrument of your own resurrection.

'Oh Christ,' she whispered, interlocking the fingers of both hands.

'Oh Christ.'

Somebody was talking about the weather. Somewhere red. Who gives a fuck about the weather. Somewhere north of Watford ... bound to be. Bet it's shining in London, shining shite.

'Switch it off,' grunted Albert.

Someone had died on the picket line, said the radio ... not ... but ... Gail couldn't hear. Dead anyway. Dead's dead, wherever you are.

'Switch it off!'

'You switch it off!'

Morning. A cold car. She couldn't do it. She rolled over and pulled the bedclothes higher.

'Watch out for roadworks on the M25 this morning . . . '

'Yeah, sure,' muttered Albert irritatedly. 'I've never bloody seen the bloody M bloody 25. I've never bloody been to bloody London and I don't bloody want to go so they tell me about the bloody traffic on the bloody motorway. I don't even drive a bloody car . . . '

'Just switch it off,' Gail mumbled from under the bedclothes. She closed her eyes tightly. It didn't work.

Albert fell out of bed and attacked the alarm clock. 'We should have had a ringer.'

'I didn't want a ringer.'

'The least you could do is switch it off, seeing as it's yours. Instead I always do it.'

'You're nearest.'

'Aren't you supposed to be at work?'

'Christ!' She sat bolt upright and squinted at the soft red digits on the clock.

'I'll be late! I promised Edith . . . '

First Gail was there, then Gail was gone. No warm embrace, no tender sighs, no morning charm between her thighs ... First Gail was there, but Gail was gone. He went to put the kettle on.

The car protested violently against being woken at such an ungodly hour, spluttered and turned over again and again before finally, just when she thought the battery was dying, grunting into life. She pulled the choke out as far as it would go and spluttered down the street, through the colliery estate and out into the country, heading for the river, taking the back-door route to work. With one hand she wound down the window then lit a cigarette. Once in motion, the driving was almost automatic, she knew the route so well. But when she crossed the bridge and turned down the lane that ran parallel with the river, something else took over: a tormenting, obsessive urge to turn the steering wheel away from the road, through the hedgerow and into the water.

The city greeted the morning with a rumble of traffic. The shell was filling with sand from the ocean. Down the Embankment, a hundred cardboard shelters fidgeted as the occupants began to rise, stiff and cold with the river's mist. An old man pissed against a tree. The cardboard, now too damp to be used again, was discarded, carrier bags were collected. Someone rose from a lake of vomit, looked down at the mess confusedly, belched and vomited again. The others left him to it. In non-communicating ragged groups they crossed the busy road.

Johnny awoke to the sound of coughing, scratched himself in a hundred places then almost fell out of bed in his rush to use the toilet first. The urine covering the floor should have dried by now. Relieved by his good fortune, he re-entered the bedroom – for ever dark from the massive wardrobe that obscured the large bay window and substituted for a curtain – and stumbled through piles of dog-ends and empty bottles towards his bed – the third in a row of six, all occupied, mirrored by another six along the other side, in a room half the size of a modest public convenience. Separating each bed was a locker, although many of the doors were broken and those that weren't were always unlocked as no one had a key. Most of the men slept with their belongings under their pillow. Most of the pillows had no pillowcases. Most of the beds had no sheets. The mattresses were dubiously stained. The blankets were grey and lousy with fleas. Sometimes you stepped on a cockroach or two. Or a patch of vomit. Or worse.

The rats in the back yard scattered when the landlady arrived. She locked a cigarette between her lips and fought with the back door to get in. You couldn't just open it, you had to turn the key and push. Sometimes she kicked it.

Johnny was worried about the squirrels. He'd always fed the squirrels. And when he thought about the squirrels he thought of breakfast in the dayroom, of taking tea in the patients' canteen, of the comforting metal trolleys and Mr Jackson dispensing his morning medication.

Johnny should have taken his medication himself to-day, but the bottles had disappeared overnight from his bedside locker. He closed his eyes tightly. Perhaps, when he opened them again he'd be back on the ward. The voices in his head returned, quietly persistent. He kept his eyes tight shut. Sometimes, if you close your eyes and just pretend, things go away.

The Butterdish

'I was born on the day they launched the Dreadnought submarine. Which doesn't make me old – just nuclear.

'My Gran had a butterdish.

'The butterdish lived in the pantry, along with the cheesedish and breadboard. I can't remember much else being in there. Partly because they didn't have much money but also because – only having a pantry – you bought on the day what you'd cook on the day. When you lifted the lid of the butterdish the butter always seemed to be sweating, light drops of perspiration – but it wasn't off. Granny's butter was never off. It was perfectly golden and perfectly delicious. The cheesedish had a crack running from the mouse's tail down to the edge of the lid – it was dropped long before I was born. Drop something now and it breaks.

'Within a couple of days the cheese went hard with a thick crust that galloped towards the centre. Then it cracked. You chewed cheese at my Granny's. Granny draped a damp cloth over the bread and it stayed fresh for two days, then she made a bread-and-butter pudding with what was left.

'The pantry had stone shelves and a tiny air-vent in one corner. It smelt of butter, cheese and bread. One of the few things in my life that felt real was Granny's pantry. Which was why, when one of the old Lodges at Anydale went vacant, I wanted it.

'The Lodge was built at the same time as the hospital,

nearly a century ago. It had thick wooden banisters, an outhouse, a coal shed, a proper cupboard under the stairs, three bedrooms, a front room and what I suppose could have been a dining-room that led into a tiny kitchen with a sink, a counter and one cupboard with a cracked plate in it.

'The back yard was walled. I could have hung washing in the back yard. We could have dug up some of the gravel and made a little garden. It had a thick, tall wooden gate with a latch near the top. Safe for children. I thought of children then. I thought that Albert and I could move here – we could perhaps start a family – Albert could get a porter's job: I could leave work for a couple of years then go back on nights, or part-time, or something. I thought families then, but not in the dark mining village. At Anydale, at the top of the hill, I felt safe. I loved Albert. In those days it was possible to dream.

'It also had a pantry. A proper pantry. With stone shelves just crying out for a butterdish. The more I nursed, the more I longed for somewhere quiet to sit and – however illogically – I needed to sit in that pantry, on the tiled floor, with cool shelves overhead and the thick wooden door shut tight. Somewhere real. Somewhere that I believed in. It's easy to get lost as a nurse: sometimes you get to wondering where you finish and other people begin. And it's the same with marriage – well, it was with Albert. Sitting alone in that pantry I could have reclaimed myself, examined my hands and feet: reintroduced myself to myself, remembered that the mind inhabits a body and that the body separates one human being from another and that therefore, if you can distinguish your own body, you can keep your mind.

'I disappeared into the pantry while Albert examined the broken toilet in the outhouse, by which time we had already toured the rest of the Lodge together before wandering off in different directions. And when we met up, it was in the kitchen: I came out of the pantry in case he came to look for me and he came out of the outhouse to complain about the broken toilet. We met in the kitchen. He opened the cupboard door, we both saw the broken plate; he shut the cupboard door. The door fell off its hinges. He looked at me. I knew what was coming.

'"We haven't the money."

'"They'll rent it to me. I work here."

'"We haven't the money to do it up."

'"It doesn't need much!"

'"The toilet in the outhouse is broken!"

'"There's a perfectly good toilet upstairs!"

'"Just look at this kitchen! Where will we put the fridge?"

'"We've got a pantry. We'll find room for the fridge. It's solid, Albert – look at those banisters . . . "

'"Yeah. And look at the outhouse! We need carpets . . . "

'"I'll find carpets . . . "

'"Sweetheart," (he said that sometimes) "Look love," (he said that as well) "I know you want this house, but be realistic. I mean, look . . . "

'He took the broken plate out of the cupboard and held it up to me, as though it said everything. I smiled.

'"At least we've got something to eat off!"

'He turned his head to one side and eyed me comically, then he laughed and put his arms around me. I loved him for that: I thought, "This is how it happens when dreams come true. The man puts his arms around you and concedes to your foolishness. He laughs at your foolishness but he loves you. He puts his arms out to protect you. Then dreams come true."

'Albert made love to me against the kitchen wall. Smooth and golden. He led me out to the car where I dozed, still fluttering, while he took the key back to the office. Then he drove us home. I felt warm, slightly melted, and safe in his care.

'When we stopped outside the house – the dark house, I asked him.

'"What did they say?"

'"What do you mean?"

'"At the office. Did they say we could have the house?"

'"I told them we didn't want it. Someone else was interested. I said you weren't bothered."

'Dark men have dark thoughts. They don't know about butterdishes. They know how to lie.

'It wasn't much of a row. I felt too wounded to argue. He'd caught me off guard, he made me believe that he wanted it too, he turned what could have been something tricky for him into something sly against me. What exploded was my love for him. And of course it went on, when we got into the house, it went on, but he just took my anger, because he knew he'd won. I hadn't known we were having a battle. That's how much you can know someone. I didn't know a thing about him. And I hardened towards him, like the cheese in Granny's pantry, I grew tough at the edges and as time went on that toughness edged towards my heart. I went stale towards him. He wouldn't touch me like that again.

'So if you think that perhaps I seem cold when I talk of Albert, remember that it was Albert who turned off the heat with the ice in his lies. Remember that. I thought I'd married a real man. I later realised that I should have looked for a good man instead. Or maybe just not look. Leave them alone. That's what he did to me.

'I was born nuclear. The deaths of my parents split the atom. Then Albert fused the casing.'

Wormwood

The morning's clouds promised yet another wintry day, as Agnes Wormole stood in the hallway, putting on her anorak.

As she unfolded her scarf she surveyed with a thin smile of satisfaction the spidery handwriting that covered her calendar. Not that she particularly needed to, as her days were organised with military precision, but she liked to feel that she led a full life, and therefore referred to the calendar every morning. The calendar was in the hallway, in a position of prominence, to (subtly) inform potential visitors how busy she was, and how lucky they were to find her in. Not that she had many visitors.

Mrs Wormole lived what appeared to be a full life. There was the Church and associated functions. And the Women's Institute. And her voluntary work. All very laudable. And proper. But beneath this outer, brittle crust of respectability nothing good endured. Mrs Wormole's social life was rather like a nice shortcrust pastry covering a maggot pie.

Mrs Wormole baked for the Women's Institute. They couldn't stop her. Blackened scones that, if bitten into, would necessitate immediate dental treatment. Stunted fairy cakes with hideous green icing. Sponges: flat and leathery, smelling slightly fungal.

She cleaned the Church. She was an excellent cleaner. The brass gleamed, there was never any dust anywhere,

and the tiled floor was scrubbed so vigorously that the
colour had started to fade.

She was Mistress of the Mop, stunning with a chamois,
brilliant with the Brasso and a dedicated duster. Her own
home was thoroughly orderly, and had that remarkable
quality of lifeless cleanliness that so befitted a woman of
her stature.

Her voluntary work involved hospital visiting. Long-
term patients had been known to cover their heads with
a sheet upon her arrival. Short-term patients, after an hour
in her company, were generally anxious to leave as soon
as possible. In her own small way, Mrs Wormole helped
to reduce the waiting lists. She particularly enjoyed visiting the lesser-known diseases: the more unpleasant the
better. Amputations, however, were her favourites. She
had a talent for being able to 'give out' an enormous
amount of gossip at the same time as gathering a fresh
stock . . . if the input was a little bare and unimaginative,
she'd fabricate. She remembered names only if those
concerned lived in her neighbourhood – otherwise the
patients were dehumanised and grouped under headings. She had known quite a few cancers, lots of heart
failures, several attempted suicides, diseased livers and
gall-bladders. She believed that all men with 'prostrate'
trouble have only themselves to blame, for indulging in
carnal sins.

The God she admired would issue divine thunderbolts
at a drop of the trousers, and smite with disease those
whom she, Agnes, felt deserved to be smitten. When she
heard of another AIDS victim she would nod approvingly:
'Vengeance is mine, saith the Lord.'

All praise to the God of pestilence!

Almost unbelievably, Mrs Wormole was married to
a man who loved her. Agnes Trotter, aged eighteen,
was quite pretty in a way: pretty enough to fool Henry
Wormole into marrying her. Henry, a kind-hearted young
man, saw in the young Agnes a faint vulnerability, and
attributed the pursed lips and severe expression to her
brutally religious upbringing. Her father, a large Non-
conformist minister, battered his congregation verbally
and his wife literally. His daughter accompanied him to

every sermon, and detested her mother's weakness. She never doubted her father's honourable veneer, and fitted herself comfortably into a life of Bible doctrine and the ever-present risk of hell-fire and damnation like a sharp, square peg into an equally sharp, square hole. Until Henry came along, that is, and offered her a life so completely opposed to the one she'd known that the prospect appeared temporarily attractive, and she agreed to marry him.

She soon discovered her mistake. First there was that 'business under the bedclothes' on their wedding night. Agnes, utterly disgusted, quickly put a stop to it. Then there was her husband's liberalism; more inclined to discuss than condemn outright, Henry seemed to her a weak, spineless individual. In her mind she held the two men side-by-side, noting her father's fierce upright-ness and her husband's smiling sagginess: there seemed no contest. From that point on she nourished her disap-pointment vigorously, adding, at frequent intervals, new grievances. Henry snored. Henry smoked a pipe. Henry didn't argue. Henry agreed to everything for a quiet life. Detestable.

Poor Henry survived for twenty years, clinging des-perately to a deluded impression of the woman he'd fallen in love with; accepting her insults as deserved admonishments, resolving always to be better, to try to please her. When she insisted that he put a portable stove in the greenhouse and sit in there to read his paper, he agreed. After all, his feet were always dirtying her floor. He accepted the need for separate beds after two months of marriage, as he couldn't quite resist stroking her in the night, and it upset her so. The move to separate rooms also seemed the best thing, really, as she couldn't bear his snoring. This constant acquiescence only served to fuel Agnes's rage: a better man would have beaten her, like her father beat her mother. To attack Henry was like hitting blancmange; no resistance. Consequently all the bitterness she felt towards him festered and seethed in a little tureen of malice, with no release.

Mercifully, Henry died. Painlessly, in his sleep. She'd found him, cold but with a hint of a smile upon his lips

. . . which in itself was annoying; that he should have had anything to smile about. Nevertheless, his death proved to be convenient to Agnes: now she had cause to be perpetually jaundiced towards life: widowhood became The Great Excuse for bitterness and misery, and The Great Defence against possible attack for her heartlessness. Henry had become, in retrospect, in 'grief', a great man, whom she loved deeply and missed terribly. She invented a 'Henry would have said . . . ' stock of phrases to conjure sympathy when required. And his passing added another item to her calendar: every Tuesday she donned a black arm-band and took fresh flowers to his grave, sporting a sad-but-proud expression that she had cultivated carefully.

No one noticed how she wielded the scissors she used to weed his grave; no one saw how she would thrust them savagely into the air above her husband's plot; no one heard her curses as she stabbed at his memory.

She liked to believe that her neighbours whispered to each other, 'See how she struggles on, without him . . . ' Being herself void of fellow-feeling, she never realised what the neighbours *really* said.

So stood the woman, studying her calendar. There was no hint of Henry left; she had scrubbed all traces of his presence from her life many years ago. And yet, beside the calendar, in the hallway, beneath the ostentatious wooden crucifix hung a photograph of the couple on their wedding day – 'for the benefit of visitors'. But no one ever called.

'You miss Albert, don't you?' Rose asked.

Gail didn't answer.

'For a while we were forced to live with his mother. She had a face like a sucked lemon and a very broad Midlands accent. Living in Newcastle had done nothing to change that, and Albert seemed to inherit his mother's tongue. On Sundays she dressed in black and went to Church with Agnes Wormole – an evil little woman who lived over the road from us when we moved to The Terraces . . . If I'd known, I wouldn't have bought the house, but in the end we were desperate to get away . . . '

'Give us a kiss, lady!' Albert knelt in front of her.

'I'm watching *Coronation Street*!' Gail was curled up on the settee, absently twirling her hair round her fingers.

'You *were*.' Albert turned the TV off. 'Give us a kiss!' He closed his eyes and puckered his lips. She leaned over and pecked him on the cheek.

'Is that it?' He opened his eyes in pretend surprise.

'It's all you deserve!' she laughed at him.

He fell on to the carpet and put his hand to his head. 'I'm comin' down wi' something. Nurse me!'

'Oh, like what?' She left the sofa, rolled him on to his back and sat astride him. He opened one eye and looked at her.

'It's deadly,' he whispered.

Her hands moved to his chest and started undoing his shirt buttons.

'It's called "Not being kissed o'mania".' He grinned.

'You poor thing . . . ' She bent forward, her hair trailing across his face. He put his arms around her and pulled her to the floor with him.

Then they heard the back door open. Gail jumped up. Albert fumbled with his shirt buttons as he turned the television back on. When his mother entered the living-room the couple were sitting quietly on the settee. Albert nodded at the television: '*Coronation Street*,' he told his mum. She scrutinised them both, not entirely convinced. 'Aggie's here. You two goin' out?'

Albert sighed. 'Yes Mum,' he said resignedly.

Gail clenched her teeth. 'I don't much fancy . . . ' she began, before Albert stopped her. 'Let's just go,' he said.

Gail was telling Rose: 'She and Agnes got together twice a week to play Pontoon. She drank three pints of milk stout a day and complained about her "internals" – flaccid bladder, knotted ovaries, constipation, "various veins", piles "like plums" – incessantly. "Woman's troubles" she called them – the after-effects of childbirth, she inferred.

Something we must all suffer as women: our martyrdom
to the great fertile cause which, through suffering, con-
fers upon a woman the right to *own* her offspring – what
woman, in the form of Mother Marsden, had created, let
no other human on the face of the planet have a share
in! Albert had caused her piles, veins, knotted ovaries,
bladder and bowel problems. She loved him for it and,
by God, the lad was hers! So whenever she spoke to me
about Albert she described him as "my boy" and the
look in her eyes said, "Don't go gettin' ideas that he's
yourn!" She charged twenty pence a bath to cover the
cost of switching on the immersion heater and, despite
our paying board and lodgings, she never kept any food
in for the three of us. I couldn't do a thing right as far as
she was concerned. When Albert was on his own with her
she cosseted him, but when I arrived home from work she
virtually chucked us both out . . . '

'Didn't you ever try talking to her?' Rose interrupted.

'There was nothing to say. She made it quite clear
that I'd taken part shares in her property – Albert – and
that she couldn't stand me. She was enraged that I took
"that contraption" (the Pill) to stop myself "catching"!'

'What did Albert think?'

'Of what?'

'The Pill?'

'He didn't, at the time. When we moved to The Terraces, I think she put pressure on him. That's when he
really started to change.'

Mrs Marsden peered through the missing slats in the
gate as Gail stood in the back yard, pegs in her mouth,
hanging up the washing.

'*Seen our Albert?*'

Gail ignored her. She should have knocked at the
front door, but didn't. Gail knew that she wanted to
see what she hung on the line. Let her wait.

It was a dull, overcast day, threatening to rain soot.
She didn't care. Everything spoiled round here. Except
for Nellie next door. She liked Nellie. With a wall between
them they'd shout to each other, or Nellie would stand
on a crate to lean over the wall to talk to Gail. They'd

talk about the weather, or the telly, or Mrs Wormole's twitching curtains, or her Alf (upbeat), or Gail's Albert (vaguely hopeful) and the prospect of either of them finding a job – which in Albert's case was impossible as he didn't want one, while in Alf's case it was just unlikely, there being so few jobs available and him so close to retirement age. The house on the other side had been vacant since she and Albert had moved in.

Alf and Nellie had moved to The Terraces from Beckwood Green, a housing estate on the edge of the city. The Terraces were ex-colliery, with not enough work to draw new colliers to the area, and too little work to keep the previous residents from moving back to South Shields. The Terraces were therefore vacant and for sale at rock-bottom prices. So Alf, who'd spent thirty years as senior checker at the old cycle factory at Beckwood, used half of his redundancy money to buy 'a place in the country' – i.e. the house next door. And Gail had just enough financial security as a staff nurse at Anydale, together with enough money for the deposit, to buy theirs.

Albert was all for it at the time, as Mother Marsden often tutted about the risk if Uncle Alf in Bournemouth found the two of them living with her. Uncle Alf wasn't beyond upping the rent, particularly if he knew Gail had a job.

'Seen our Albert?'

The dark house had a back yard, about eight feet by six: just enough room for the dustbin: '44's NOT YOURS' scrawled over its battered belly in red enamel – Albert's masterpiece of domestic creativity. He grinned like a child when Gail came home from work that day: he wanted her to see it. And thereafter, whenever she mentioned housework he'd say: 'I did the bin, didn't I?'

The back yard also had a coal-house. Not that they ever had much in it. They kept a small fan heater in the living-room and a paraffin stove in the kitchen. On the day they moved in they bought a sack of coal to celebrate. Albert stole a couple of old pit-props which he chopped up with his dad's axe, raked the fire out, layered it with rolled-up newspaper and small pieces of coal, then larger lumps and finally a chunk of pit-prop.

It was the finest fire Gail had ever seen, although they
had to put the fire-guard up, as the wood was full of
nails that spat out of the fire occasionally like bullets
from a gun. She made spaghetti bolognese that night.
They drank a couple of bottles of red wine. He brought
the quilt down from the bedroom and laid it on the carpet in front of the fire. She remembered the glow from
the heat, and the perspiration from their bodies, and the
wine glasses on the hearth; their movements silhouetted
by the fire and their mingled shadows dancing on the
living-room wall . . . They used up a whole pit-prop that
night: by morning there were eight blackened nails lying
on the hearth.

'Seen our Albert?'

The back yard had an off-yellow wooden gate, blackened like the walls, like the grass, like the mud on the
colliery estate. Gail had put all of her savings into the
house – the house was in her name – so they couldn't
afford a washing machine or tumble dryer. They had a
small spin-dryer that someone had given her as a belated
second-hand wedding present: one of the dinner ladies
in the staff canteen at Anydale – a small busy woman
called Brenda who did a bit of part-time work helping
the domestics in the nurses' home. She followed the
progress of Gail and her friends from raw students to
qualified nurses, with maternal eyes, helping them out
whenever she could – either with extra chips at dinner or
bigger things when she heard they were setting up home.
And of course they were all always broke and extremely
grateful for whatever was offered. Brenda wasn't the only
domestic who helped the nurses out, but she had a neph-
ew 'in the trade' – selling second-hand household goods
– and she got a few things free.

The spin-dryer had a couple of castors missing and a
bit of rust round the lid – which had to be jammed shut
with tissue paper – but otherwise it worked fine.

Living in at the nurses' home had spoiled her: there
were huge rumbling monsters on the ground floor that
took three hours to wash, but at least they did the work.
Now, with Albert, she was back to washing for two by
hand again, suds up to her elbows in the large porcelain

sink, and anything – *anything* – that offered a little respite earned her undying gratitude.

She lodged a couple of copies of *Exchange and Mart* under the dryer to compensate for the missing wheels. It screamed relentlessly at full power and thumped from side to side slowing down: the whole block knew Gail's washing days.

The back yard led on to a muddy back lane that split them from the opposite row of houses and similar back yards by about eight feet – just enough room for the dustbin lorry to rumble through once a week, but too uneven and mucky by far to be used as the main entrance to the houses. So everyone used their front doors and the only people who used 'the lane' were the dustbin men, kids who needed somewhere quiet and dark to sniff glue, and the village 'hostesses' who did their business by car and needed the same environment as the glue-sniffers for a shag and a fag with someone else's husband, ten quid a go. So for Mother Marsden to be standing on the other side of the gate, her citric face peering at Gail through the broken slats, there had to be a special reason.

'I knocked at the front but you wouldn't come!'

'I didn't hear.' She carried on pegging.

'You're doin' it wrong. You'll get bumps in the shoulders. Hang 'em upside down.'

'I'm happy doing them like this. I've always done them like this.'

'Hmm. 'Ave you seen 'im?'

'I thought he'd be with you.'

'Hmm. Yo nossin' today?'

'I'm working nights this week.'

'Hmm. Well I'll have 'im 'ome, then.'

'You might as well.'

'Tell 'im, then, will you?'

'You'll probably see him first.'

'Hmm.' And then she was gone.

The special reason, she later discovered, was an old girlfriend of Albert's called Sheila. The wicked old bat was playing barbed Cupid. But she hardly knew anyone in the village. The whole village could have told her. Mrs Wormole – who knew everything, could have told her. Nothing would have given her greater pleasure. But for reasons of personal distaste Gail kept a guarded distance from Agnes Wormole, and was therefore never treated to the glorious scandal of Albert round the back of the Philistine Arms with Sheila pushed up against the toilet wall. Mrs Marsden, ever the caring mother, found Sheila's knickers in Albert's jacket pocket and silently disposed of them. Let the boy sow his oats, she thought. The boy was living in a barren field.

Through The Tunnel

On a cold, wet, miserable Thursday evening in January, the front door to a dark terraced house in the industrial arse of the Midlands burst open, illuminating a small patch of rain-soaked path, the kerb and the busy gutter. The curtains twitched and flapped about uneasily as the breeze shouldered its way in and caught hold. The door banged once, twice against the outside wall and then, pushed by icy hands, slammed shut.

To the left of the door stood an archway, between numbers forty-two and forty-four: a black tunnel stretching the depth of the houses, leading to the back yards. At the end of this tunnel could be heard angry voices – at first muffled, then another bang, then the clacking of heels marching swiftly along its cobbled stones, followed by another pair, less steady, running.

A young man emerged through the archway, heaved a battered brown suitcase on to the pavement, stopped to straighten his sweatshirt, shivered once, then pulled up the lapels of his jacket. Finally he reached into his jacket pocket, pulled out a cap, and, slicking back his hair, put it on.

The running feet had stopped: now they clicked more slowly along the passageway. Gail emerged in a long blue terry towelling housecoat: the towel that had originally been wrapped around her washed hair was now draped unhappily over her shoulder.

She looked up the street – a few curtains twitched.

The light in Mrs Wormole's front bedroom came on, then dropped back to darkness as a pale face peered eerily out of the window. She sighed.

'The whole street'll know about this in the morning.'

'Let them know.'

'Where will you go?'

He laughed dully. 'I'm not telling YOU!'

'Well, you can go to hell, for all I care!'

'Too right – for all you care! The truth is, you don't bloody care. Never have.'

'Tell me another story. You're stuck on this one.'

'Oh balls! I'm going!'

'Go on then!'

'Go to hell!'

'What will I tell your mother, when she asks about her "little boy"?'

'Tell her ... tell her ... No, don't tell her. I'll bloody tell her.'

He heaved up the suitcase and walked, a little lop-sidedly, down the street. Gail ventured further into the path, folded her arms and watched. As he began to turn the corner she shouted: 'You're going home to Mother, then?'

Albert stood, rapidly turning crimson, his whole body stiff with rage. She knew he wanted to hit her. She almost wished he'd try: just let him try! But being Albert, he refused to look, stared straight ahead, put one foot in front of the other, began to walk, march, then break into a trot.

She stood watching the corner for some time, then, noticing the rain soaking into her gown, she went inside.

For once the front room was warm. Albert had built a fire with what was left of the coal. And she thought ... He didn't give any indication otherwise, so she rushed upstairs to take a bath.

She'd been late home. When she came downstairs after her bath Albert had his suitcase ready on the settee. And the marriage certificate in his hand. Which, when Gail came in, he threw on the fire. She wanted to laugh at him for being so theatrical, but they shouted instead. He told her about Sheila. Shocked and angry, Gail threw open the front door and ordered him out. He took his suitcase off the settee and stormed out of the back door. She stormed after him. When she came back there was nothing left of the certificate.

The following morning she deposited her wedding ring in the grate. He took it, and left her his key in its place. She took the key and, wondering if she should be strong and clear his clothes out, went through the chest of drawers, wardrobe, bathroom, spare room, downstairs toilet, kitchen, front room and coal shed that night, particularising and removing every Albert-item from the house. Which she then dumped unceremoniously in the back yard. Except for his spare cap.

She put his cap in the fire and burnt it.

Kilns

'In the long summer holiday between the end of primary school and the start of grammar school, Mum's GP twisted a few Council arms and managed to move us to some flats near the centre of town.'

'How did it feel to move house?' Rose asked.

'At the time it was exciting. Celie had gone to stay at her grandmother's in Halifax, but we'd both passed our 11-plus and knew we would see each other in the autumn.

'We felt like royalty. The whole street turned out to watch the removal men load the van. I kept running in and out of the house, getting in people's way, until one of the removal men picked me up, slung me over his shoulder and asked Dad: "Do you want this one to go as well, or shall we put her in storage?"

'Dad said: "We'd better take her with us!" and they all laughed. He stood me in the van and gave me the ignition keys: "To look after, or I'll surely lose 'em!"

'I felt very important, standing in the van like that, and I thought that removal men were the loveliest people in the world, as they all winked and patted my head as they loaded the furniture in.

'Billy came to say goodbye, and his mum stood at the garden gate with her new baby in her arms. I waved and she smiled. Billy wanted to play in the van but when I said he couldn't he got bored and disappeared. Mandy's mum was poorly so she was helping her dad wash and peel the potatoes for the chip machine.'

'What about Patrick?'

'He'd gone a long time before. He and his brothers and sisters were put in care after a Welfare Officer visited and saw how drunk his dad was.

'Anyway, we moved – it was closer to Granny's house as well. Our block was joined to a second that looked exactly the same and a third at right-angles to the first two, so that we had a courtyard to play in.'

'We?'

'There were a lot of boys in the courtyard. I joined their gang. The long, high wall of the Corporation Yard formed the third side and a large electrical warehouse just beyond the garages completed the rectangle. It felt like another world, inhabited by an alien species . . . neighbours rarely smiled or said hello, the people seemed private, restrained and unwilling to communicate.

'At that time, the town's horizon was marked by the strange roofs of malt kilns, and the rich scent of hops filled the air. Down by the river there were other smells: of rotting leather and bones for the glue factory, sewage . . . It all depended on the direction of the breeze. There were a number of kilns around us; one on the opposite side of the courtyard, used as a warehouse, one just over the road from the end block of flats, two more near my gran's, that they turned into warehouses, and several more near the river. You could see them all – other than the one at the end of the flats – from my bedroom window. The warehouse opposite had an alarm that, due to some fault in the system, burst into life at two o'clock in the morning on a fairly regular basis throughout the summer. It was impossible to sleep through, so I'd kneel on the bed and open the window, inhaling whatever the breeze decided to blow my way. I'd look out: at the other flats, and the rooftops, and the malt kilns silhouetted against a background of orange street-lighting. Sometimes there'd be mist coming from the river and a smell so sweet and full of promise you could almost imagine yourself living in the country, with green fields stretching away in front of you.

'Kevin's mum was a vast, heavy-limbed aberration of the female species; whose Neanderthal physique would have seemed better harnessed to cart, or barge, rather than motherhood. Playing in the courtyard, we were warned of her impending arrival by the squeals of mechanical protest as she neared the corner. We'd vanish, and watch from a safe distance the incongruous sight of this immense, violent creature pushing at the pedals of the bike with spade-like feet attached to great trunks of flesh ... puffing, panting, heaving, cursing, she'd emerge between the garages then stop, red in face, plant both feet solidly on the ground, and shout for him: "Keviiiiin! Keeevinnnnn! C'mere! C'mon, yo bogger! Keviiiiin!"

'She wore, always, a huge bell-tented black mackintosh, belted at midriff, and black plimsolls. Her calves, thick, blotched and hairy, remained naked whatever elements prevailed. Her eyes were like two small slits in a paunch of spotted dough. Her thin mouth, set tight in concentration as she pedalled, opened to reveal a cavernous blackness, dotted here and there with stumps of yellow. Her voice had an effect similar to that of a nail down a blackboard. Kevin, in contrast, was thin, sallow and a little small for his age. His hair – dirty blond and curly – was so completely the opposite of his mother's flat, short, mucky brown covering, that it gave rise to certain inevitable speculations.

'Summer holidays in the courtyard were generally hot, dusty times; made pleasant by occasional dips in the local swimming-pool – but the water was cold, and some days it was impossible to take to the idea. When the sun shone brightly for a few days together, the water felt tepid, and the days spent there were a joy. But some days the sun refused to shine and we lacked the money, so we looked for something else.

'The cattle-market was held every Wednesday, tempting us with the thought of seeing the sheep, and cows, and the pigs ... but the abattoir was next door and the animals were terrified ... it was hardly the sort of place you could enjoy. The sold cows were led through a metal trap, where their ears were punched. They emerged shitting, the blood trickling down their necks, with eyes wide and full of fear. Kevin's eyes would look like that, whenever he heard his mum approaching.

'We could go to the town locks and watch the narrow-boats sit patiently, descending with the water level, then chugging away from us when the heavy black gates opened for them. On one occasion we found a dead pig, lying in the stagnant water close to where they repaired the barges. Bloated and unmoveable, it remained there for months, slowly rotting away. We could go to the Castle, but the little of it that remained was uninspiring, so we saved it for the really dull days. We could follow the canal beyond the locks to "Parnham's Mill", where it met the river – or we could go to our bit of river, near Kevin's house, just past the scrapyard, and while away a couple of hours breaking the patches of oil floating on the surface, making rainbows. Down there the river looked like deep dark treacle, and the fish glooped unhealthily. In the evenings the water-rats would appear; their brown heads bobbing above the surface marking a more sinister part of the day, when we'd leave the river, suddenly afraid of the shadows. At about this time Kevin's mum would also appear, calling Kevin to look after his younger sister while she and her husband went to the pub. I believed, for a while, that she emerged from the depths of the polluted water each evening; covered in slime that dried to form her mackintosh, with the rats and her husband at her feet. Now I know that people like Mrs Frost are real and unchanging. They flourish in an unhealthy climate and stain future generations. Kevin's sister was, in comparison to Kevin's emaciation, a bulbous child of nine or ten; in every respect her mother's daughter, and spoiled. What love the sour woman could offer was lavished upon this miniature replica.

'Kevin appeared to serve his adolescence as handy punchbag and babysitter, and seemed as afraid of his sister as he was of his mother.

'Further downriver stood the glue factory, and to reach the weir – another haunt – we had to cross the railway lines and pass through a yard piled high with bones and leather to the right, and a large derelict kiln to the left. Peering through its broken windows and rusted iron bars we could see rats: huge, fat rats, shuffling through the debris, waiting for the night to come. I suppose they must have lived off the maggots coming out of the bones. They certainly flourished – as did the maggots. There are maggots under the flats that were built on the site of the kiln facing the end of our block. Over the years, loose grains of malt had fallen into the basement and when, after the fire, they excavated to prepare new foundations, they discovered a writhing mass of pupae. Not knowing what else to do, they dumped concrete on top of them – or so the story goes. Some years after the fire and following her husband's death, Mrs Frost and her daughter moved into one of the flats.

'Kevin's mum kicked him out every morning with a warning not to return until pub opening time. Most mornings I'd finish my breakfast and look out of the window to see Kevin sitting on the swings, waiting. After a while Ken would join us, a couple of other lads would turn up, and we'd plan what we were going to do. Or rather Ken would plan, and we'd agree.

'Ken liked pulling the legs off bluebottles. He liked ringing doorbells and scarpering. He liked spitting. He liked to go fishing and race maggots off the end of the concrete parapet at the weir – lining up three or four, holding a lighted match behind them, then laughing delightedly as they twisted and curled their way to the edge, before finally plopping insignificantly into the water. He liked when particularly bored to play tricks on Kevin, because Kevin took it as a mark of friendship and generally came back for more. I suppose, considering the way his mother treated him, Ken's "games" were tame in comparison, but they must have hurt. Kevin was called a "loony", and Ken condescended to include him in his gang almost solely for the fun he would have teasing him . . . You see, Kevin spoke incoherently and rarely – and when he spoke, spittle would gather at the corners of his mouth, blowing little bubbles that popped and streaked his chin with saliva. It was impossible not to notice the bruises on him, and on the one occasion he came swimming with us, we could see little burn-marks peppering his stomach and legs. His left ear was a mess; his mother had bitten off the lobe in a fit of violent temper. And big green and purple bruises covered his back.

'Kevin would vanish for several weeks at a time, only to return under a different persona. Perhaps he was being fostered ... whatever the reason for his disappearance, he always came back, and the torment continued as before. His father – a thin, stooped little man, seemed barely to exist and took off to the bookie's at the first hint of discord. Discord being plentiful, they never had much money. His father did not play to win. And what with the pub, the daughter's chocolates and Mrs Frost's cigarettes, she barely had enough left over for food, let alone Kevin. So he scavenged the local dump for clothes, and tried desperately to find a disguise that would alter his situation.

'Once he turned up with a flick knife, cursed like his mother and scored little holes in the stairwell banister. Ken confiscated the knife and cut the back of Kevin's hand as punishment. On another occasion he arrived in psychedelic jeans and t-shirt, and chalked "Peace" slogans on the dustbin shed walls. Ken pushed him over the first-floor banister rail and held him there by his ankles until his face turned blue. Finally he arrived as a salesman, with a briefcase that looked as though it had been pulled out of the river. What he called his suit had a lapel missing and a tear from the left shoulder to halfway down his back. His shirt was filthy and lacked a collar button. Ken made him stand with his back to the wall in the concrete stairwell, told him to close his eyes and pulled his legs out from under him. To Ken, Kevin was much more entertaining than the maggots, because Kevin cried, and Kevin bled.

'The last time I saw Kevin was on the day we found the dog in the Corporation Yard. Ken had scaled the fence to retrieve the football and we followed because getting into the Corporation Yard was something of an adventure. It lay in the middle of the yard; a stiff black-and-tan mongrel cadaver, left by the dustmen who had picked it up on their rounds and had been unable to think of what to do with it. We had to take a closer look, because you don't see a dead dog every day. Its mouth was drawn back as though grinning; it was as rigid as a piece of wood. It was collarless, filthy with neglect and the bare

patches on its coat suggested fleas. We kept our distance
because Ken said the fleas might still be there, but Kevin
touched it: he knelt down and stroked its forehead with
a gentle, soothing motion. Ken called him a dirty sod and
said it could have been Kevin's dog, it looked so scraggy.
Finally he threw the ball at Kevin in frustration, and Kevin
rose.

'He followed us slowly and by the time he reached
the fence the lads were already playing football on the
other side, whooping and hollering. I sat on the swings
feeling strange, as though I had witnessed a tragedy, but
felt unable to quite work out what it was. Kevin climbed
the fence and let himself drop down the other side. I
watched him pick himself up dejectedly and walk past
Ken, who was still calling him names. Kevin's face looked
raw, somehow. I wanted to say something, but nothing
would come.

'The connection with the dog I made much later: I
was young at the time and it was the dog that made
the greater impression, not Kevin. But I remember the
fire like yesterday: all the fuss, and the flames lighting up
the sky, and the smell of burning. I remember the firemen
rolling huge canisters of gas away from the building and
the thud and the clang as they rolled them, one after
another, against the wall of the flats. I remember the roar
of flames leaping high, and the crash of falling masonry. I
remember thinking how funny it seemed, that people who
had lived in the same area for years without speaking suddenly fluttered about, offering tea to the firemen, showing
consideration to their neighbours, chatting animatedly –
as though the disaster had brought them suddenly to life.
Women in dressing-gowns and curlers, men in braces –
for a few hours the neighbourhood seemed different, as
though we were all living under the same roof – and I
remember Kevin's mum standing there, just looking, with
a fag in her mouth, her evil pock-marked face shining out
with every fresh burst of flame, then receding into the
darkness. And her husband, thin and bent, searching his
pockets for a match to light his wife's cigarette.

'They caught Kevin and locked him up. The kilns
dropped from the horizon one by one, after several more

nights of fire, but no one ever really knew who to blame.

'Sometimes, when I look back, all I see is heat and ashes. From that point on. But I burn when I write to you, as well. Sometimes I'm so wild I don't even know what I've written. The words just come, and I burn. But it's a good kind of burning, isn't it?'

Rose nodded.

'It takes me away from where I've been, and forward in the direction I need to go. It hurts, Rose, but I'd rather have the burning than that hollow ache of despair.

'But I know two kinds of burning. And the other is Kevin's kind: expression through a desperate, dangerous act of destruction. It didn't mend his life; it resolved nothing, but it relieved his situation.

'I remember that night so vividly. I remember how the flames danced and roared, exposing, beneath the ash and debris, the mass of maggots, rendering them finally impotent – and I wish that could have been the way for Kevin's life. But nothing ever comes of wishing. I remember the rats in the derelict kiln: the sleek fat rats. Wherever there's decay, they come to feed. It's happening now.

'I try to understand. That summer, to me, was like leaping from innocence to awareness. But in the chasm that I managed to avoid lies Kevin: grieved for in retrospect, understood in retrospect, but suffering in silence. And I know what makes me burn, and what Kevin set alight.'

Refuge

Albert sat in the comfy armchair untying his shoelaces, one leg crossed over the other. Mrs Marsden watched the flickering screen, smiled as the show's compere smiled, laughed when he laughed . . . and out of the corner of one eye watched her son, settling himself in as easily as he had before he married – as though he'd never been away.

'She's got no heart.'

'Took you long enough to find out . . . all that contraption business!'

'She won't listen to me.'

'Ooh look, she's won them saucepans!'

'She's allus on about her job . . . '

'You should have wed your Sheila!'

'She's not mine, Mam!'

'More's the pity.'

Albert leaned his head back and groaned at the ceiling.

She thought she heard him and looked his way, then back to the screen at a sudden flash of red: 'Ooh! Look at that car!'

He'd asked and she agreed. Mothers always give in to their sons. She hadn't even questioned . . . not yet, at least. Plenty of time, she knew. He knew she knew, the way she weighed his case as he dropped it in the hall. Whatever he wanted to say didn't much matter. Things were panning out just as she'd hoped. He assumed that tomorrow she'd mention how he'd tied the knot and should be more responsible. Mother Marsden had no such intention, but Albert wasn't to know. So he thought balls to responsibility! He'd had enough. He didn't care about Gail. Already a memory. He wouldn't care if Gail cared, but, as she didn't, it didn't matter. No, he'd already forgotten her. Sitting there in the glow of the gas-fire, already feeling liberated . . . we all make mistakes. Albert's biggest mistake was marrying the bitch. So he'd come home, after his moment of triumph with the marriage certificate, and he'd just go on living: him and his mam and bollocks to anyone else!

The following morning was bright but cold. Nellie stood at the sink, pounding Alf's smalls to surrender with Omo and elbow grease. Alf took one last drag from his Woodbine, dropped it into his saucer and supped, noisily, what was left of his tea. Smacking his lips he stood, pulling up his braces. Without looking at Nellie, he demanded: 'What was that racket about last night, then?'

Nellie continued pounding and answered stiffly: 'Gail next door. Albert's gone and left her.'

This called for another Woodbine. He reached behind his ear, took the cigarette, lit it, inhaled and sat down again.

'Well, if that in't a bogger.'

'I know. Poor Gail.'

'He'll be back.'

Nellie pursed her lips. 'If she wants him!'

'Like that, is it?'

She turned to face him, her hands foaming. 'All I know is what I'd do, in her position!'

'It's a damn shame, though.'

'No,' Nellie whispered into the sink, 'it's not much of a shame at all.'

Alf checked the time by the kitchen clock, whistled vaguely, and without speaking, left for the 'Stute.

The library was situated a few streets away. Part of the Working Men's Institute – the 'Stute – a small red-brick building with the title carved in stone over the door, providing the local men – whether working, retired or – like Alf – unemployed – with a meeting-place and somewhere

to read the morning papers. Alf arrived, removed his jacket, pulled up his shirt cuffs, grabbed the nearest tabloid
newspaper and sat down. A fresh Woodbine nestled
comfortably behind his ear, ready for the morning break.

Alf, like many of the other men, timed himself. He
arrived at 9 a.m. each weekday morning, read until 11.30,
then stopped for a tea from the machine and a smoke
on the steps outside. Then, back in the library, he and
the other regulars exchanged papers, read a little more
and packed up at 12.15. On the dot. If there had been
a machine, he would have clocked himself in and out.
Back home, Nellie would have the dinner on the table . . .
a bit of meat, plenty of mash . . . then back to the Institute
in the afternoon for a chat with his mates – maybe a walk
– until 4 p.m., which seemed just about the right time to
go home, settle down and get ready for an evening before
the telly. He managed the pub once a week, and Nellie's
bingo accounted for her leisure . . . two evenings' worth,
as she didn't smoke.

By 9 a.m. Gail had already been on duty for two
hours. The patients were washed, dressed and having
their breakfasts. The beds were almost made. If she
thought about Albert at all, it was with a rising tide of
anger and disgust. All she could see was Mrs Marsden
peering through the broken slats of their back gate . . .
'I'll have 'im 'ome, then,' she'd said. Mother Marsden
had known. She'd probably arranged his meeting with
Sheila . . . Well, good riddance. They had never been
suited. She had a car, full time work and a social life
beyond marriage. She'd do more than survive without
him. She'd bloody well thrive.

'Bear me a child!' he said.
'I think it's time to procreate!' he said.
'Gi's a babby!' he said.

After the dinner party
After the CND Branch Meeting
After the piss-up

They had sex.
They made 'beautiful music'.

He fucked her, roughly.

They had a son.
They had a love-child.
They had a babby.
He planned for public school.
They discussed creches, multi-ethnic primaries . . .
They didn't think about it.

He grew up rich, undisciplined, took to drugs.
He became an accountant and joined the Territorial
  Army.
He left school too early, couldn't get a job, married
  young.

'I don't want a child!' he thought.
'Have I time for a child?' he thought.
'Gi's a babby!' he said.

Gail said no: that was the trouble. If she'd said yes, he
might have bothered looking for work to support them
both. But she said no. He couldn't assert his manhood.
He told his mum.
  When at last he got through to her, she puckered
her lips and sat back thoughtfully.
  'I'd no choice, our Bert,' she said after a pause. 'When
me and your dad got married, he did just what he liked.
On and off me all the time. Then you came along, me
ovaries got all knotted up . . . Still, you should have
forced her. I don't know what your dad would have
made of all this . . . '
  Agnes Wormole was in a rush that morning. She'd
seen it all! Hss! She took her big wicker broom out on
to the front path and managed to sweep the pavement so
hard that she dug up the dandelions emerging tentatively
between the paving stones. At six-thirty, when Gail left
for work, Mrs Wormole was there, leaning on her broom,
to see her off. Mrs Wormole saw Gail, she saw Gail's suitcase, and Gail's unhappy expression as she drove away
. . . Oh joy! Oh rapture! Wouldn't Mrs M be pleased! So
she swept the dandelions into the gutter and scuttled off,
broom still in her hand, to break the glorious news.

Reflections

The Philistine Arms was an honest if dilapidated city pub: the landlord, in his potbellied wisdom, had steadfastly refused to tart it up as a fun pub, stripped-pine traditional pub or even – given its close proximity to the mining village – an olde world rural pub.

It began life as a working man's pub, bordering the city and the country, close to the industry through which the city flourished. As the city flourished it grew, spreading out like spilled paint in all directions, and the Philistine became a suburb pub – if such a term exists. And when the small agricultural valley just the other side of the hill sprouted headstocks, it became the pub where the miners retreated in droves 'to get away from the wife'. In time, as the village's population changed and the village landlords, aware that inherent snobbery towards the miners was like shooting themselves in the financial foot, opened their doors wide to allcomers, the Philistine's popularity diminished. Why the men altered their desire for 'escape from the missus' and chose instead the open log fires, timbered ceilings and corduroyed inhabitants of the village pubs instead has proved to be one of life's mysteries. Perhaps the miners didn't really want to leave their wives at home. Perhaps a new way of life beckoned them. They were still rough as stubble down the pit, still blunt, outspoken and principled, but it was as though they were breathing gentility in the damp country air ... Miners are born deep. As obvious as the winding

gear on the surface, but inside, they go down a long
way . . . Never try to analyse a miner. They'd wallop
you.

Albert, on the other hand, was not a miner. And the
Philistine Arms was his favourite pub. Mostly because
the landlord was Albert's idea of what a landlord should
be.

'A pub is a pub,' said the man. 'You sup your ale, talk
if you're sober enough, fall down and throw up if you're
not. Me dad ran this pub, and I keep it the way he'd've
liked.' A dartboard, yellowed paint, dominoes, full ash-
trays and no juke box. The landlord was not popular with
the brewery, but refused to budge. His only concession
to the changing times was the absence of credit – the
slate had gone, together with the jobs: 'Don't sup what
you can't pay for,' said the man.

When Albert had paid board to his mam (a meagre
amount – 'She won't tek much!') he still had a tidy sum
left over: enough for fags and ale, a flutter on 'the hosses'
and Saturdays on the football terraces. Everything to do
with the house had been in Gail's name . . . she could
sell the house for all he cared, so long as it took nothing
from his pocket.

Several months had passed since their separation and
Albert repaired his wounded pride – 'What would your
dad have said?' his mother delighted in reminding him
– by slagging Gail off at every opportunity. Which was
what he was doing at the bar, to a similarly dressed young
man whose cigarette hung comfortably from the side of
his mouth, dropping ash in his ale every time he reached
for his glass.

'Thinks she's better than me!' said Albert; a white
froth from the latest pint settled happily on his upper
lip.

'Pah!' said his mate, farting disgustedly.

'What can you do with a woman like that? What
did we get married for, if it wasn't to 'ave a family?'

Meanwhile Gail was telling Christine: 'I would have
had a family if he hadn't lied to me about the Lodge.
I could have got him a job here . . . '

'I could have got a job just like . . . like that!' Albert

waved his hand in the air. 'But she wouldn't 'ave it. Oh no. Likes 'er job too much!'

Christine asked: 'Then why did you marry him?'

'I don't know. I fancied him. He seemed so normal. He reminded me of . . . '

'Who?'

Gail laughed. 'A normal person!'

Christine grinned. 'You wouldn't have had much luck with the Lodge anyway. Not if we're closing down.'

'True. Perhaps it's for the best, then.'

'And who wants normal, when you could have a nurse?'

'Any wine left?'

'We've drunk it all. What will you do now?' Christine asked, peering down the spout of the empty green bottle.

'Start again. Move on. Get a divorce first, sell the house, make a vast profit and enter the stock market.'

'Doing what?'

'Selling shares in the Health Service.'

'Can I be your accountant?'

Gail giggled. 'We could be anarchists!'

'What do anarchists do?'

'Not sure. Rebel, probably.'

'Sounds like fun. What else could we be?'

'Christine, we are women of the eighties. We can be whatever we want to be . . . '

'Except nurses.'

' . . . Do whatever we want to do . . . '

'Except nurse.'

'We could go down to the pub and proposition men!'

'How many?'

Gail pursed her lips. 'A dozen at least.'

'Each?'

'Each. Then bring them back . . . '

' . . . And bonk ourselves silly!'

'But no normal men?'

'Definitely not normal men!'

'No nurses?'

'NO!'

The room went quiet, then Christine picked up the paper. 'Shall we see what's on the telly, then?'

Albert's mate leaned across the bar to him: 'Why'd'you get hitched, then?'

'She was alright. It was those magazines givin' her fancy ideas. I tried 'idin' *Cosmopolitan* but it did no good. I flushed 'er pills down the toilet but she wouldn't let me near 'er without a johnny on . . . ' 'Johnny on, Johnny on, gotta putta johnny on!' hummed his mate into his beer, thinking about the AIDS warnings. 'You should've slapped 'er around a bit!' – beating a wife, according to the Philistiners, was a sure way of keeping her in check. Albert's mate wasn't married. 'Well that's no way for a wife to be. If she won't 'ave a babby she can't 'ave me!' Albert slammed his glass on the bar. His mate looked up, then farted again.

'You should be a poet – if they weren't all such poofters!'

'Pah!' said Albert.

'Pah!' said his mate.

They ordered another round.

'Men!' shouted Christine at the television screen.

'Men!' Gail replied in kind.

'Men!' she shouted at Rose. Rose lifted an eyebrow.

'Men!' she shouted at the crack in the bedsit ceiling. Martha tapped lightly on Gail's door: 'Don't knock 'em so loudly chuck – I've a living to earn!'

Later still, Gail sat in Nellie's kitchen, nursing a cup of tea. 'They're a nice young couple, Nellie. He works in a bank. They love the house. They're a bit trendy, but otherwise . . . '

Nellie took Gail's hand and patted a few times before clutching it conspiratorially: 'Me and Alf, we could never . . . Not that I'm sorry, but sometimes I wish . . . You're like a daughter to me, lass. I'll be here, whatever happens . . . '

'It's much cheaper at the nurses' home, and I've got enough now for a decent car . . . ' Gail felt guilty. Nellie looked at her.

'By the sound of it, you and Albert will be better apart and, well, I was young once, and what I wouldn't have given to wipe the slate clean and move on.'

Nellie's kitchen, with its steam and fading fruit-pat-
terned wallpaper, had an atmosphere of rugged, grim
determination and warm earthiness. Nellie had endured
three decades of baking bread, cooking, cleaning, mend-
ing, making do, ironing, washing and complaining only
to the dough she kneaded because . . . because . . . That
was the way Nellie's mother had taught her, and her
grandmother had taught her mother. But Alf's unemployment gave Nellie's life as well as his own a sense
of futility. Their routines were the same, their perception
of life much the same, but what had once been the core
of their married existence was now absent. The structure
continued, but the reason had ceased to exist.

Alf, who had been sitting in the front room watching television while the two of them talked, came to
the door with Nellie to say goodbye. As they shut the
door, Nellie leaned against it for a moment, listening to
Gail starting the car and driving away. Motherhood had
been an unspoken subject during the long years since her
miscarriage. These days she had no choice but to accept
that all chance had gone. Admitting her maternal feelings
towards Gail had been difficult, and now the admission
made her time of life even less bearable. She stood until
she could no longer hear the car's engine and then, a
little more wearily than usual, returned to the kitchen to
prepare Alf's dinner.

Having already moved what was left of her belongings
and arranged to sell the house with furniture *in situ* (let
someone else fight with the spin dryer!), Gail unlocked
the car door with a sense of profound relief and an
aching love for the plump, unhappy woman who had
just hugged her goodbye. She looked up at the row of terraced houses, with neighbouring houses in neighbouring
streets looking, she knew, just the same, and it seemed to
Gail that the whole estate had the air of a prison. For a
moment she even felt sorry for Mrs Wormole – although
the vicious little woman created her own cell. The Terraces changed on Agnes's side of the road. They looked
almost the same, but Agnes had a big back garden. And
a greenhouse. Where she deposited things she hated, like
her husband, when the man was alive. Nellie had told her

that. Nellie had said, 'They should have given everyone gardens. I've never had a garden. I'd love a few roses to look at.'

She frowned as she settled into the driver's seat and turned the key in the ignition. It felt good to indicate and pull out: good not to be caught here . . . She shuddered at the thought that, had Albert had his way, she'd be in the same prison, looking out from behind those invisible bars.

She sped out of the village and into the country, hardly aware that she was driving the car. She really saw through him now. Just a child, with a child's irresponsibility, posing as a man while still locked in his mother's arms . . . Wanting her to bear his children just as his mother bore him; slipping into his father's role as if by magic, as though starting a family on *his* terms would make everything right! Liking the fact that it was Gail's money that paid for things, but not liking the fact that those things were in her name. Refusing to help in the house because 'That's woman's work!' The horror of it. But he could be gentle at times, and that was what she felt unable to reconcile. If she could only have described him to herself with just one word, she would have felt less confused – she could have coped with his memory. But Albert refused to be categorised. How could someone so immature, irresponsible and ridiculously boorish be gentle as well?

Back at the hospital, she parked her car and then stood on the forecourt, looking down to the road at the foot of the hill and then following the road westwards towards the city, bathed in orange fluorescence. The breeze felt cold but refreshing: as it pushed back her hair she felt herself flying, and stood, grateful for the sensation.

By now, Nellie would have wiped down her kitchen tops for the last time, put the lid on the peeled potatoes she had prepared for tomorrow's dinner, turned out the lights and followed her husband upstairs to bed. The street would be silent. Across the estate, Albert would either be snoring in a drunken stupor, or somewhere else – some dark alleyway no doubt, with Sheila in his arms again.

The bastard. Gail lit a cigarette and blew smoke into

the darkness. Was she jealous? Of *that*? Of Sheila? She'd
never met the girl. She'd only ever heard of her from his
mum – an ex-girlfriend, who Mother Marsden pointedly
referred to at every opportunity, just to register her dis-
approval of Gail. And always in front of Gail.

'I saw your Sheila outside the Co-op today, our Bert.'

'She's not mine, Mam.'

'More's the pity!' she'd say, looking at Gail.

I bet Sheila's got a head like a solid potato, Gail thought
angrily, throwing her cigarette to the ground and scuffing
it out with her shoe. She'd have to be a real potato-head
to want him . . . But then I wanted him, didn't I? Fellow
potatoes then. I hope she's all he ever wants, and he's all
she ever hoped for. And I hope she's fertile. That'll be all
he ever wants her for. She might be pregnant already –
well, good luck to her. She might like prisons.

And then she felt ashamed of her need to place Albert,
sod that he was, into some kind of category that would
negate his gentleness and make him somehow easier to
cope with. She, Gail, had known Albert as both a rough
and gentle lover, and at the time either approach would
have excited her. Before the Lodge incident, at least. He
could be charming, funny, and at times his defiant irresponsibility could be very endearing. She missed him. So
why try to bundle and parcel and tidy him away, just
because she'd lost him? Because she didn't understand
him? She of all people should be against doing such
a thing. She – and her colleagues – had been trained
to educate the public, to encourage people to *try* to
understand, rather than dragging life to a lower level
of comprehension and labelling it. So what was she? A
hypocrite?

Then she thought of what her father had once said
to her as a child, when she was helping him to dig the
garden. He'd pulled up a clump of misplaced grass from
behind the daffodils, shaken the soil from it and handed
the complex, delicate mat of roots to her. 'All that for a
few blades of grass, Gail. Makes you think what you're
doing when you walk on it!'

He took the trowel and continued weeding, while
Gail sat cross-legged on the path, stroking the dense,

gently fibrous underside of something she had always taken to be so plain. She tried to imagine each fragile little root pushing its way into the soil and tangling . . .

Gail half-smiled, half-winced at the memory, climbed the steps and unlocked the large front door. It wasn't a perfect metaphor but it would do. For now, at least, Albert as a clump of grass would simply have to do.

His Ring

Midnight in the nurses' home.

Christine lay in the bath and thought about David.
She dipped her head beneath the steaming water's surface
and thought of David. When she came back up for air
the thoughts of David hadn't gone away. She wondered
if taking the hostel job was like following his memory. She
thought it probably was, although there were a thousand
other reasons too. But it was David, mainly David, probably, painfully and persistently David who had caused
her to apply.

She thought of the park on a bleak, rain-stricken morning. She'd arrived late, breathless from running. He had
been waiting for twenty minutes. She attempted a greeting. He grunted and walked towards the café. She hurried
to keep up with him.

At the café David took her coat without speaking,
removed his own, bought two coffees and seated himself
opposite her. Both concentrated on opening the packets
of sugar and stirring. Apart from a white-haired vagrant
who insisted on dipping bread in his tea, the place was
deserted. The woman behind the counter disappeared
into a back room.

Nevertheless they spoke in hushed voices: 'Did you
bring it?'

'It's in my bag. Do you want . . . ?'

'No, it can wait a minute.' He struggled to find words.
'How are you?'

She had been pleased to see him, but now she felt bitterness rising like bile in her throat. She fought to contain it. 'Better than you expect, I should think!'

'I'm sorry. That was stupid. I just don't know . . . '

'Then don't!'

An awkward pause.

'How's work?' he asked.

'I've just taken the exams.'

'How do you think . . . ?'

'I might have passed. No thanks to you!'

'You can't blame me for everything!'

'Can't I?'

'You made it worse for yourself!'

Christine turned to look out of the window. She saw nothing. 'Have you any idea how hard this is?'

His voice softened. 'I'm sorry.' Then, 'I keep apologising!'

'Good.'

'I didn't mean to hurt you!'

She looked at him: 'But you did.'

In the ensuing silence Christine noticed the old man sliding the sugar-bowl to the edge of the table and surreptitiously emptying the packeted contents into a carrier bag.

David worked in the voluntary sector. He was an inherently kind man. 'So much hypocrisy!' he'd explode, when plans for housing projects failed to materialise due to public hostility. 'They shout and protest when they hear of our plans,' he'd say. 'They think that anyone leaving a mental hospital is criminally insane, or perverted, but it's their attitudes that are perverse! They label people "inadequate" that they haven't even met! They have our clients confused with people from Broadmoor or Rampton. Or they call them "mentally handicapped" and when I say that they're mentally ill they look at me with such venom and spit: "Well? It's all the same, innit?" You just can't get through to them; they don't want to understand!'

Unlike many of his colleagues, however, David persevered. Continued hoping. Patiently cleaned the hostel walls of the graffiti that regularly gathered there: things

like 'MADHOUSE' or 'LOCK THE LOONIES UP!' Spoke quietly
to the groups of children who, urged on by their parents,
gathered outside the hostel to laugh and jeer at the residents. Worked long hours without complaint. Eternally
optimistic, bright and willing to listen to the problems
of others, he seemed to Christine to have some deep,
unsullied nugget of humanity lodged deep inside. When
they met and she fell in love with him, she felt that she
had stumbled upon a rainbow, and found gold.

And he had loved her. He had loved her. She stirred
the coffee again. She couldn't look up. One morning in
early June he woke her with coffee and urged her to
dress. Outside it was half-light; the first birds had only
just begun to sing. She became slightly irritable with his
constant attention until he held her close and whispered
quietly.

They walked through the mist to the river's edge and
sat down side by side to watch the sun emerge above the
trees on the opposite bank. He reached into his pocket
and produced a small blue box, coughed nervously then
spoke: 'This belonged to my mother, her mother and my
great grandmother . . . ' He opened the box and produced
a plain gold ring. 'For our eternity . . . ' He took her left
hand and slid it over her finger. The mist had cleared and
the sun shone brilliantly. She felt she would die with love.

Then one night she went to him and he wasn't alone.

'How many people did you give the ring to?'

He smiled at her. 'Only you.'

'But now you want it back!'

Now it was his turn to look away. 'I *need* it, Christine.
It's all I have!'

'Will Tom get to wear it?'

He met her eyes directly. 'Yes.'

She reached into her bag. 'So take it!' She passed
him the box. For a moment it sat on the table between
them. Then David picked it up and, without looking, put
it in his inside pocket. He stood up to leave. His clothes
seemed to hang from his body. His gaunt, yellow-hued
face forced through the painful blur of her emotions. A
creeping realisation came upon her.

'David?'

He opened the door and was gone.

Christine submerged herself in the bath again. The underwater echoes of the home's plumbing had always fascinated her. She stayed under for as long as she could. She didn't hate him. She loved him. She loved him so much that she had a ton of ready-mixed cement delivered to his house and dumped on his driveway while he was at work. She loved him so much that he was forced, in the end, to change his telephone number to ex-directory. She loved him so much that she had once even chased him down the street. She had humiliated herself through loving him, but she didn't hate him. After that day in the café she almost went for the test, but decided against it. If she was HIV Positive she didn't want to know. The Pill had never suited her, so she'd always insisted that he wear condoms – in the days when condoms simply meant not getting pregnant. She'd thought about having an IUD fitted but her doctor advised against it. And diaphragms looked like baby's swimming-caps, so she had always used condoms, and thought that she was probably safe. Probably. And he had loved her. Probably. Until she made such a fool of herself. But that's what love does to you.

By the time she returned his ring he had moved house. When she phoned the hostel they'd said he was ill and off work – she tried to be proud and not ask for his new address but she asked in the end. They said they didn't know. It was a lie. And if she saw him, or tried to find him, or contact Tom, it would only hurt her again. Love and foolishness and humiliation. She was scared he might be dying, and it was *so hard* to think that he wanted nothing more to do with her.

Now the hostel was due to be reopened and she had applied for the job. What's 'eternity' after all? A life-span? It was like a stone on her heart. Life had become almost arithmetical. It hurt her so badly that she spoke of it to no one – not even Gail. Despite every rational explanation she knew that taking the job was like following him. She lay in the bath and stared at the finger where the ring used to be. She stayed in the bath 'til the water went cold.

Amusements

Nellie jumped and clapped her hands together with a childlike delight as the machine chugged and a seemingly endless cascade of pound coins fell, delightfully, into the winnings tray. Behind her, the queue of middle-aged women muttered to each other: 'She's got the jackpot! A hundred pounds!'

'That's the first time she's had a go. It int right.'

'What about us regulars, putting money in every day?'

'Would you believe it?'

The woman whose turn it had been before Nellie, looked on with nausea.

'That's her first fifty pence on the machine!' someone cried.

'Cow! Comin' in here with her one bingo card and 'avin a go on our machine! There's no justice!'

Nellie, meanwhile, heard none of this. She stared with joyous incredulity at the growing mountain of gold that seemed reluctant to stop. She thought the heavy chugging of the machine's winning mechanism was probably the most exciting sound she had ever heard in her life. She couldn't believe her luck.

One of the bar staff helped her to gather up the winnings. Nellie lifted and held the front of her skirt as the woman shovelled handfuls of coins into the temporary hammock. She offered Nellie a bag to put it in, but Nellie, who had never held so much money in her life before, wanted to hang on to it, savouring every moment.

'Would you like us to change it for you?' the assistant asked.

'No! Well . . . yes, you'd better.'

So Nellie, weighed down with a bulging skirt, her slip showing, not caring, waddled carefully to the bar and watched, amazed, as the assistant counted the coins in bundles of tens and the girl behind the till placed a ten-pound note beside each carefully constructed column.

After she had treated herself to a rum and black at the bar, and the saucy young man calling the numbers had announced the second session, Nellie floated back to her seat and tried to concentrate on the last three games. The woman opposite with a spare pen behind her ear, her phosphorescent yellow highlighter poised over the six cards she was simultaneously marking, took every opportunity to tut and cluck as Nellie, with her red biro, prodigiously circled her numbers. When someone behind her called 'House!' and the hum of voices broke the tension, Nellie noticed that all the women seemed to be staring at her, averting their eyes whenever she looked up. The elderly woman sitting next to her patted her arm and whispered, 'Ignore them, duck. They're only jealous.'

But it was hard to ignore them, and Nellie was relieved when the last 'House!' was called and she could leave.

She hurried to the bus stop, anxious to get home and tell Alf. She had already decided that they would use the winnings for a bit of something nice in the front room: Alf would agree, she knew – this was luck after all, and they would need something to remember it by. A carriage clock for the mantelpiece, perhaps – she had always fancied a carriage clock. And yet, even as the bus was rumbling homeward, another idea was forming in her mind: or rather a temptation was being aroused. By the time she reached home the desire had become overwhelming and she felt giddy with rum and excitement. She rushed into the house.

'Alf – I've won something.'

Alf started up from the armchair and looked eagerly at his wife.

'How much?'

'Fifty pounds!' Nellie shouted, so gleefully that she

almost believed it herself. Alf's anxious face formed a smile that grew broader by the second.

'That's grand, lass! That's grand!' And it was. Very grand.

It was rather like a spring, held down by years of hardship. When the hardship lifted – even temporarily – the spring jumped up, and it was difficult to push it back down again. Nellie was experiencing the first thrill she had had in years, and the first opportunity to buy something other than necessities.

But it was more than that. Nellie really believed her luck had changed – and, God knew, she needed some good luck. She could change nothing in her life ... Watching Gail walking out of an unhappy marriage, she couldn't help but feel envious. Her periods had stopped, reminding her of all those empty, wanting years, when a missed period would have filled her with unutterable joy. The one life they had conceived had simply fallen from her in blood, pain and grief.

It wasn't that she thought about leaving Alf ... she still loved him, in a gentle, practical sort of way. Only it would be nice if life could be a little easier and they weren't always forced to count the pennies. She wanted release, but not from Alf – just a little freedom from the burdens they were forced to carry. She didn't dream much – only for the child they had lost – but it seemed unfair not to have the right to dream. Now she had a chance – an opportunity – to make something of her good fortune. Heady with unexpected wealth, she wondered if it would work again, her luck.

On a more fundamental level, she wanted to hear that glorious chugging sound again; she wanted the excitement of winning. For years she had avoided playing the fruit machines, had kept herself to one card per bingo session and had won only a few groceries. And so it was, with quiet determination, lacking in her usual common sense, she resolved to keep the other fifty pounds a secret and spend it on herself.

The following day she treated herself to a cream cake and coffee in the city centre, did a little window shopping, walked into the Rat Alley amusement arcade, bought five pounds' worth of change and set to work. Many of the machines let out harsh, brittle tunes; many cost twenty pence a go, but she opted for a ten pence machine, like the ones she and Alf played at Skegness. It seemed strange to be standing in the city centre, playing – these amusements were linked in her mind to sand and sea, but it *was* a kind of holiday . . .

Ten pence, twenty, fifty – a pound. The machine gobbled up the coins, gave a few brief seconds of excitement, then waited. Two oranges, two bells, then a cherry on the first line . . . She won ten pence. Which the machine gobbled up again. After two pounds had disappeared in as many minutes, she began to wonder if it was such a sensible thing to do. Then she won fifty pence, which removed all doubt from her mind and set her ploughing silver into the little slot in a state bordering on frenzy. Then, after four pounds' worth of silver, she won a pound, and it all seemed worth it. She couldn't help but notice that a youth of fourteen or fifteen was hovering in the background, and remembered the tales she had heard about 'professional' players, who waited until some poor amateur had filled the machine with silver then stood to play, inserted their ten pence and won the lot. Well, that wasn't going to happen to her. So she stood, rooted, her purse emptying fast, but bolstered by the occasional coins that dropped into the winnings tray.

After thirty minutes her money had gone, but she had fallen on two bells again, and the machine might hold them there on the next go. She couldn't leave it like that. So she waved to an assistant, who changed her second five-pound note. As the man walked to the kiosk for the change, Nellie looked around. The youth was still hovering, and she could see several more leaning against various machines. A woman of about the same age as herself, but much thinner, was exchanging the last few decimals in her purse for one more go on the machine. A man in his early fifties stood at one of the more complicated machines; the kind that burst into life with a hundred flashing lights and jangling tunes every time a coin was inserted. And there were others, none of them

looking as though they had two pennies to rub together, playing the machines with a fanatic concentration,
ploughing more into them than they could possibly win
back, but not stopping until everything had gone. Nellie
scratched her nose and smelt an unpleasantly metallic
odour on her right hand. Holding it up to the light from
the fruit machines it looked dirty – soiled with the coins
she had handled. She frowned in the dim, reddish light
and decided to leave, but the assistant returned with her
change and asked if she would like a coffee. She looked
again at her machine . . . She just couldn't leave those
two bells . . .

The coffee was scalding hot and tasted of dishcloths.
She rested it on top of the machine as she played. She
had resolved to spend no more than another pound, but
she won two pounds on her penultimate go and couldn't
help but feel that she was close to something big, so she
continued.

The woman who had emptied her purse stood weeping silently by the door, but Nellie hadn't the time to
notice. The machine took control and would not let go.
It became easier and easier to insert the coins, and the
longer she played the more reason she had to continue.
She wanted her money back. But the winnings went,
and her second five pounds dwindled to fifty pence,
then thirty, then nothing. She remembered her coffee
and, to her surprise, discovered that it was stone cold.

She walked out of the darkness and into the street.
It had grown cloudy, and everywhere seemed grey and
drab after the lights and colours of Rat Alley. But her
clothes smelt of stale cigarettes and her hands were dirty.
She was forced to concede that losing ten pounds was
enough for one day.

She passed young Frank Watkins, who seemed to be
heading in the direction she had just come from, but he
didn't notice her and she felt relieved. In truth, it wasn't
just her hands that felt soiled . . . it seemed to be inside
her, this overwhelming sense of dirtiness, and guilt, and
shame. A week ago, the ten pounds she had frittered away
would have seemed like a fortune in her impoverished
hands. But today it had gone, just gone – disappearing

in an hour of vague excitement. And she had lied to Alf
. . . She felt close to tears and dreadfully ashamed. She
walked to the bus stop with her head bowed; afraid that
people would see the sin of wastefulness written all over
her unhappy face. She remembered Alf's smile and his
words of the night before: 'That's grand, lass!' Her chest
heaved. How could she do this to him? The clouds
seemed to press down on her, enveloping her in shame.

That night she cried a little and Alf, who didn't
understand, put his arms around her for the first time
in years and tried to comfort her.

'Look,' he said, 'what you need is something nice!
I'll tell you what we'll do: we'll have a look through the
catalogue and find that clock you were saying you'd like.
And if it costs more than we've got, we'll put the money
for the telly licence towards it, and I'll cut down on me
drinking to save up for it instead!'

He thought it would cheer her up. He couldn't understand why she seemed to be crying harder than before,
so he just held her, and blamed it on the change.

The following day Nellie didn't treat herself, nor did
she window shop. She went straight to the Rat Alley
amusements, changed a ten-pound note and set to work
on a different machine. It had taken her money: well,
she would damned well make it pay it back. She felt
refreshed after a good night's sleep, and Alf had been so
gentle . . . So she was here for a reason, she told herself.
She wanted her money. She tried to ignore the little thrill
of excitement as the first ten pence disappeared and the
reels started rolling . . .

Ten pounds lighter, she left. The day seemed even
darker than the day before, her hands dirtier and the pit
in her stomach more empty and more overwhelming. She
thought she would die with shame. 'That's the last time!'
she told herself firmly.

But it wasn't. She was hooked. All the shame and guilt
in the world couldn't prevent that tingle of anticipation
as she entered the arcade. All the love she felt for Alf –
and she felt it more keenly now – couldn't prevent her
hand from inserting the first ten pence, then the next,
then the next . . . All the common sense she could

muster couldn't match the awful allure of the loud, brash, gobbling machines.

And so the money disappeared in a week.

In a sense, it was easier when it was gone. She had not told Alf: she could almost pretend it hadn't happened. It was just a bad dream, a very bad dream, and it was over. The money had been hers . . . well, she'd never had so much. It wasn't real. Once it was gone, the urge to spend also vanished. But she avoided walking past Rat Alley from that moment on. There was something in the atmosphere outside the place that seemed enticing. The noise, the red-shaded darkness, the clatter of coins . . . and the smell. More than anything, the smell . . . A distorted, vicious, thieving, grabbing, stinking transient utopia.

Dirty money.

A journalist emerged from her trendy little flat in Fulham and took the tube to St Pancras Station. Sat, feeling gradually more and more depressed as the train travelled northwards. It was a long journey, she felt – measuring distance by counting the backs of miserable little houses in grey, ex-industrial wastelands. At the appointed destination she alighted, visited a seedy-looking hotel close to the station and gulped down a dry Martini, 'for courage'. She braved the Ladies', and produced a disposable paper cover for the toilet seat before she sat, gingerly, to perform her natural functions.

Back outside once again, she boarded a taxi and demanded to be taken to a sprawling scene of inhabited desolation, five minutes from the city centre. She was wearing her 'slumming' clothes – black slacks, fisherman-knit beige jumper and grey anorak. She discarded all jewellery before leaving the flat; all credit cards (except one) from her purse. She removed all but the spartan necessities of life from her roomy leather shoulder-bag: toilet seat covers, soft toilet paper ('they use the shiny stuff up North,' a friend had warned her), a notepad closeted between the covers of her Filofax, a cassette recorder, an anti-mugging alarm and spray, spare rolls of photographic film and a camera

slung around her neck. She was 'on safari'. She came
prepared.

She arrived at the flats and ordered the taxi-driver
to cruise a little. He whistled quietly through his teeth
and warned her that 'cruising' in this area could easily
be mistaken for kerb-crawling. An interesting point: an
angle her editor hadn't mentioned. She jotted it down in
her notepad. But insisted nevertheless.

Some flats demolished; walkways leading from glass-
strewn, functionless parapets to the stricken, littered
earth below.

Some flats still standing: windows boarded and covered in graffiti, other windows with shards of broken
glass still hanging from the frames. Incongruously, one
yellowed lace curtain flapped half in, half out of a broken
window. The carcass of what was once a family home. A
good image. She focused and clicked the camera.

Some flats inhabited: drab, dusty faces peering over
walkways – bleak and impressive. Good shots. She
clicked the camera rapidly and expeditiously, the two
spare rolls of film ready beside her on the seat. A black
youth saw the camera and shouted obscenities: she
focused on the angry gesticulations and recorded on film
what, she knew, would make a good header: 'The Black
Side of Britain', she'd call it. The editor would like that –
so soon after the riots. Apt. She smiled with satisfaction.
She noted his curses on her little pad, adding a few of
her own to touch it up a bit, then pointed the camera
again.

They rounded a corner to where, close to a row
of boarded-up shops, a child sat on a paving slab, her
back to a couple of acres of recently demolished factory
rubble. The girl's jeans were ragged but clean. She wore
a t-shirt with 'I [love] New York' emblazoned across the
front. She was playing, absorbedly, with a doll's head, a
brick for the doll's body, and lots more bricks for the
doll's house.

'Stop the car,' the journalist demanded the driver,
'and wait for me!'

Using years of hack experience, the woman encouraged the girl to talk; carefully focusing, now and again,

on the most effective backdrop of waste ground. She
instructed the girl to hold the doll's head by the hair,
and to look at the rubble behind her. The image wasn't
quite working . . . she gave the girl a pound coin and
asked her to roll in the dirt – rub a little on her face. That
was much better. The girl was getting used to journalists,
as she told the woman: ' . . . An' I was on the telly.
That's what made Mum cry.'
  'Why?'
  'They was comin' down on the Tuesday, an' Mum
said that we ought to look smart, so we got to wear
our Sunday Best . . . '
  'Sunday Best?'
  'Don't you have no Sunday Best? Our smartest clothes.
Mum says we're the smartest kids in the world in our
Sunday Best.'
  'I see. Just turn your head slightly . . . there. What
happened then?'
  'It was these *World in Action* men that come to film. They
filmed Mum talkin' wi' lipstick on. She did look nice. An'
we all sat beside 'er on the settee. Then I walked our dog
down to the "rec", an' they filmed me. I'd got my very
best dress on, that Mum bought from the Mail Order not
long back – all pink an' lace round the neck. I think it's
the prettiest dress in the world. An' a new pair of white
socks. An' black shiny shoes, wi' buckles.'
  'Why did it make your mum so upset?'
  'Well, it was what this lady wrote in the paper. About a
week after it was shown. It was dead good seein' ourselves
on the telly. But she spoilt it, an' made Mum cry.'
  'What did she say?'
  'She said we looked as if we didn't need any 'elp,
bein' so smart. That's why Mum cried. She said it wasn't
fair, an' were we supposed to dress like beggars for the
camera? She said it int right, 'ow they don't leave you
no pride.'
  After what she felt to be sufficient time exposed to the
rough side of Britain, the journalist gathered energy for
her return journey with steak – rare and bloody, and a
tolerable red wine from a provincial but adequate top city
hotel, paid for by credit card – to be claimed on expenses.

Travelling back to London in darkness, she had time to reflect on her day. A hundred selling images captured ... That little girl in the factory site, and her account ... enough to make you want to cry ... She turned to the black window, grinning, and her reflection grinned back.

'That'll do nicely!' she whispered. The train thundered on.

Albert, true to his image of being able to ''old 'is ale like a good 'un', stalked carefully out of the pub with a back so straight that he seemed encased in a steel corset. Once outside, he breathed deeply the night air, walked carefully to the nearest garden wall and vomited, copiously, in a rose bed which, due to the owner's despair that all his efforts were generally sicked upon by the Philistiners, was left untended and permanently overgrown with weeds. Once he had finished heaving and spluttering, he sat down on the wall and lit a cigarette, patiently waiting for the street to right itself and the two street lights before him to merge into one again.

Young Frank Watkins, who had just parted company with a group of youths after sharing out certain items that were hastily stuffed down trouser fronts, in deep jacket pockets and up jacket sleeves, noticed Albert sitting on the wall and, after checking that the street seemed clear, sauntered across to sit beside him.

'How'ya doin', Bert?' said Frank, looking slightly amused at his friend's pale complexion and dishevelled hair.

'Eh? Uh – oh, it's you, Frank. Got a match? Me ciggie's gone out.'

Frank reached into his pocket, carefully avoiding several small objects that nestled there, and pulled out a box of matches. Striking one, he relit Albert's cigarette with difficulty, since Albert found himself unable to focus on the fag-end and consequently kept missing the flame.

'Ta!' Albert, drawing heavily on the cigarette, had apparently exhausted his conversational ability with the one word, but Frank felt quite content to sit a while: for one thing it gave him an alibi. It looked better to chat with a mate than it did to arrive home at the same time as his companions opened their front doors – not living too far apart, you could never tell who might be watching . . . So he sat, patiently, as Albert swayed and groaned, quietly.

Frank liked the night. He liked the dark, empty streets and their shadowy corners. He liked the space in which to run; he loved the feeling of exhilaration as he belted through quiet neighbourhoods in darkness, his mates keeping pace, breathing heavily but grinning from ear to ear as they ran, proud of another conquest, another successful mission, another never-to-be-resolved crime – for that was how it felt. They'd done six houses so far and no one was any the wiser: they felt uncatchable, sharp as ninepence, safe as houses – a good joke, that one! And if one of them got collared – so what? Frank knew that his friends' fear of him would ensure their silence. Oh, but they were good: prowling like tigers, stealthy, careful what they nicked, and fast as the wind getting away. Dodging and weaving, climbing fences, through back alleys . . . always careful to do a different area each time, and never on their own doorstep. Then the next day they'd meet, looking clean as a whistle, at the Rat Alley amusements, and Trevor would tell them, quietly, what he planned to do with the stuff they'd taken, and when . . . for they weren't daft, and left it a while before they got rid of the loot; giving it time to cool down – and anyway, Trevor nearly always arranged it so that they'd be a job in hand: so they always had money coming in . . . Worked out just nice, it did. Just nice.

Frank patted his pocket with satisfaction. Worth a few bob, this lot . . . pity about the old slag, but they didn't hit hard, just roughed her up a bit . . . Some of the ones they'd done were just stupid, like the daft old bogger with over three hundred quid under his mattress . . . they never learn – well, it's good they don't – finding cash like that is always the best, as they don't have to bother with Trevor and his cut for fencing, they could just share it out and spend it . . . except for the big notes: the fifties and twenties – better to share out the smaller stuff then ask Trevor to change the larger notes, as it always looks bad in their neighbourhood, brandishing big money when most folks only have the dole coming in . . . suspicious, and you never know who to trust. You'd think we'd all be in the same boat, thought Frank, but we're not. Some sods are as poor as church mice, but vote for the Tories come the election . . . Well, they're all pratts, all of them: I'll not vote – it just looks like you're taking whatever they dole out . . . ticking bits of paper does no good . . . me, I'll vote with me jemmy, and give the 'V' to any berk in a suit who comes telling me what to do to change things. They never change things, anyway, so why should I bother? They're all arseholes, sitting in their little palace chucking words at each other like it makes a blind bit of difference . . .

'Frank?' said Albert, and Frank, halted in his reverie, looked up at his companion who seemed even paler than he did before.

'Help me 'ome, will you? I need to get some kip, an' if I stay 'ere much longer I'll never make it.'

Frank allowed Albert to put an arm round his shoulders and half-walked, half-carried his friend over the hill to the now quiet smog-filled village, where the one light remaining shone out from the Marsdens' front-room window . . .

'What you doin' here anyway, Frank?' asked Albert.

Frank smiled. 'Just visiting,' he said.

'I thought I'd see you at The Philistine tonight. Ted was there. He asked after you.'

'No, not tonight. Do you fancy meeting next Friday in town?' asked Frank. 'We could meet in The Fusiliers and go on the rant. I've not seen you in there for ages, not since Gail . . . '

'Yeah, well . . . '

Mrs Marsden had gone to bed hours before, but left the light on to guide her son home just as she had done, years before, for Bert's father. Albert struggled with the keys, then opened the door.

'Thanks, Frank!' he said with a hint of gratitude. Frank smiled and walked down the path, calling back, 'If you can't 'elp your mates . . . ! See you next Friday, then?'

'Aye, maybe . . . ' returned Albert, unenthusiastically.

Frank, shutting his friend's garden gate behind him, stepped into the street rubbing his hands: 'Now then, who's going to tek me home tonight?' He looked at the decrepit saloons parked along the street and selected one.

Mrs Marsden, not quite deaf enough to miss her son's return, waited until he'd made it to bed, then nipped downstairs, dropped the latch, and switched off the light.

Falling By Degrees

The snow was falling thick and fast, the fields were white and deadly cold, and Johnny was searching fruitlessly for squirrels.

Johnny had found fields. He remembered fields. There were fields all around where he used to live. And trees: where the squirrels lived. On a hill, he thought. Find some fields, look for a hill and then find the trees: that's where the squirrels were. That's where he belonged. When the farmer spotted the small figure kneeling hopelessly in the snow Johnny was close to death, and no nearer the place that he needed to be. These were the wrong fields, on the opposite edge of the city, but Johnny wasn't to know.

The farmer called the police. The police took him to hospital. The hospital asked Johnny for his name. Johnny muttered 'Jebediah'. Jebediah had no history, although the hospital staff tried every avenue of exploration. Those avenues that were left. Jebediah was a problem to the hospital, but Johnny had no intention of staying anyway. After two days he disappeared, together with a hospital blanket and a small piece of bread for the squirrels.

Johnny had left hospital in June the year before. How Johnny had survived so many months in the community was impossible to fathom. Life can be persistent, if nothing else. On his first night in the bed & breakfast someone had stolen his tablets and sold them round the guest house, one cigarette a pill. Despite the apparently thorough aftercare preparations, the harried community

nurse had visited once to give Johnny his monthly injection and, as he hadn't been there, was never able – due
to pressure of work – to visit again. The landlady cashed
and pocketed his Giro, conveniently forgetting to give
Johnny his personal allowance. His suitcase was stolen:
now all that Johnny had left were the clothes he went to
bed in.

One of the few kindnesses that the landlady offered
was to allow new tenants a couple of days spent in the
house before pushing them out, as she did with all the
other tenants, at ten o'clock in the morning. So Johnny
spent two days in bed – more or less undisturbed, as
the room was rarely cleaned. He slept as much as he
could. When he woke he didn't know where he was,
so he rolled over and tried to sleep again. He listened to
his voices and thought of the squirrels, as the voices told
him to. On the third day he left, and never returned. The
Giros continued to arrive: one of the administrative ironies
during a decade of 'parasite'-bashing. Over one hundred
and fifty pounds a week was what the Government paid
to salve its collective conscience. The landlady had no
conscience. As far as she was concerned Johnny was
still resident – his name was on the books at least. The
money came in handy.

Where Johnny went during that time was a mystery.
Gail saw him once, sitting on the kerb with his shoes
off, shouting at the cars – but she was part of the traffic,
caught in a no-parking zone behind a loud red Porsche
whose owner kept straining his head out of the window
to see if there was any way to beat the deadly slow crawl
of traffic inching towards the city centre. When the driver
looked back in her direction she recognised his face – she
was sure of it – as Billy Foster's. But she couldn't imagine
Billy Foster dressed up like a dog's dinner, sitting behind
the wheel of a Porsche, so she dismissed the idea as idle
fancy. She turned left at the traffic lights – the Porsche
had turned right – and parked outside a hi-fi shop. She
hurried back on foot to the place where she had seen
Johnny, but he was gone.

A friend of Christine's who worked in one of the
city centre building societies described Johnny fairly

accurately one night at the pub. They were talking about the closure, which was now only months away, and she said that there was a tramp who came in asking about squirrels or something . . . The manager had pushed him back out again – the tramp had smelt *foul* and they'd just been refurbished . . . bad for the image. I mean really, she said, you can't tell me people like that can't get a job if they'd only clean themselves up a bit. The truth is they can't be bothered to help themselves she said, they make me sick she said, sponging off honest working people.

This girl's favourite phrase was: 'God helps those who help themselves.'

The girl was a fool, Christine later said, but she had stated a fashionable view at that time. It was a kind of governmental absolution from responsibility for the welfare of others. It tripped from the collective tongue very easily and *most* conveniently. No need to feel guilty, it said. Absolutely no need to feel guilty whatsoever. You are here to look after your own interests. God says so. Or at least the Government said that was what God had always meant. It fitted the prevailing attitude of self-interest like the critical piece of a jigsaw reshaped with a penknife and hammered into place.

But Gail remembered God. She remembered Sunday School. And what she remembered most clearly was the label on a treacle tin, with a dead lion surrounded by bees.

'Out of the strong came forth sweetness,' the caption said.

William's Progress

Once upon a time there was a young boy – a *strong* young boy – whose even younger brother had a train set. A brand spanking new train set. And wouldn't let his brother play.

'It's mine!' he said.

'I should have it!' his older brother whined.

'It's mine!' the little boy repeated, and still refused to let him play.

So the older brother, not wanting to cause a tantrum and get a smack, went into the garden and plotted.

Later, as the younger boy was trying to get the station master through the first carriage window, his brother came in and sat beside him on the floor.

'I've got something,' said the older brother nonchalantly.

The little brother stuck his tongue out of the corner of his mouth in concentration over the station master, and ignored him.

'I've got something very special.'

The little brother tried hard not to be curious.

'In fact it's so very special I'm not going to tell anybody but you.'

The little boy looked up from his train set.

'What is it?' he asked.

'Ah!' said his brother.

'What?' said the little boy.

'Well . . . ' said his brother.

'Go on, tell me!' the little boy insisted.

The brother appeared to relent, looked around conspiratorially and whispered: 'In the garden!'

'What is?'

'Behind the strawberries!'

'Can I see it?'

'Only if you let me play with the trains!'

'I don't mind. We're brothers, me 'n' you. I don't mind if you tell me what's behind the strawberries!'

'I want the train set first. I want you to give it to me.'

'No!' cried the little boy.

'I won't tell you what's behind the strawberries!'

'I'll go and look myself!'

'How will you know what to look for unless I tell you?'

The little boy considered this and being very young, agreed.

'Look for a pebble,' said his brother.

'A pebble? That's not worth my train set!'

'It could be a diamond!'

'Coo!' said the little boy, running out.

The older brother smiled and set to work on the station. He wondered if they sold toy coffee machines and toy hamburgers. He discarded the trees and the shrubbery. He yanked the pipe from the guard's mouth and wondered if he could get hold of some suits to put the passengers in. After a while his little brother returned, weeping.

'This is a pebble!' he cried.

'Yes!' said his brother triumphantly.

'But you said it was a diamond!'

'I only said it could be.'

'But you lied, and I gave you my train set!'

'No. You believed me, and you deserve the pebble!'

From *The Hutchinson Encyclopedia*, eighth edition:

> . . . (The cuckoo) somewhat resembles a hawk, being
> . . . bluish-grey and barred beneath . . . It is a 'brood
> parasite', laying its eggs singly . . . in the nests of small
> insectivorous birds. As soon as the young cuckoo
> hatches it ejects all other young birds or eggs from

the nest, and is tended by 'foster parents' until fledging.
Cuckoos feed on insects . . . which are distasteful to
most birds.
    . . . Its foster parents will have to work hard to feed
the cuckoo, which will quickly grow to several times
their size.

Was William born, or did he simply arrive? Dropped
on unsuspecting parents, he demanded his way through
childhood and adolescence, leaving Peter, his younger
brother, with only the dregs of maternal energy and attention. Their father was a poorly educated man who wanted
more for his children, and worked endlessly to provide
his firstborn with a private education. They couldn't
afford the same for Peter – a pale, thin, sparrow-like
boy with mousey hair – so Peter accepted whatever the
State chose to offer and watched his brother's triumphal
progress with proud, loving eyes.

The love was not reciprocated. His family doted on
William: William had little time for his family. William's
eyes were fixed firmly upon the future. So he took what
his parents could give him without thanks, studied prodigiously and at eighteen, armed with 'O' and 'A' Levels,
made for London. Peter left school at sixteen, worked for
two years with a carpet firm, attended evening classes at
the local technical college and at eighteen applied to train
in social work.

By the time Peter started his social-work training,
William had already established himself in the City and
was doing well. He owned a flat in a converted warehouse by the Thames, and it was here that he received the
telephone call. It was his mother about Peter. He received
the news solemnly; told his mother that he would try to
attend the funeral, but was so busy he couldn't promise.
He put down the phone and sat back thoughtfully.

Trusting to the last, his weak, foolish brother. Peter
had been visiting an elderly couple on the fifteenth floor
of a vast block of flats in Middlesbrough, when he was
thrown off the balcony by a burly middle-aged man with
a deep-seated hatred of social workers, for taking his
children away.

'Got a light, mate?'

'Oh – sure . . . hang on . . . ' And over he went,
one hand in his pocket, the other clutching his diary.

. . . William sent flowers . . . but that night, stalking
London's nightlife in his bright red Porsche, he couldn't
help but feel as though what had happened was instinctively *right*, somehow.

William was an extremely attractive young man. His
blond hair was cut short and meticulously groomed. His
eyes were hazel, his face a little pale and his lips a little
thin, but as these features suggested a hint of vulnerability
they worked for, rather than against him. He wore suits of
fashionable blue and grey, with pale blue shirts and white
collars, cuffs and ties.

Rather than admit to his working-class roots William
had constructed a childhood in Berkshire, but told colleagues and girlfriends that his parents were dead.

When the stock market crashed in the late nineteen-
eighties William, feeling suddenly rather insecure, decided to pocket the money he had made and head for the
provinces. Just as he had been shrewd enough to avoid
personal disaster when the City crashed, he was obser-
vant enough to recognise the potential of investing in
property, and confident enough in his abilities to move
to the Midlands without so much as a backward glance.
The nation was changing under his beloved government;
the provinces were becoming an ideal investment opportunity. Buying houses – nay, blocks of houses – in those
areas where railway lines were undergoing electrifica-
tion almost guaranteed a sizeable profit as commuters
flocked north for cheap housing. So he bought himself
an apartment in 'Upstart Quay' – a fashionable riverside
development, and applied his lack of scruples to the
booming property market.

In the early days of his first year in the Midlands,
William began his personal collection. 'This one, this
one, and that one!' he would say to the estate agents,
'Subject to surveyors' reports, obviously.' But behind the
bravado lay a period of shrewd and careful consideration.

William bought, and bought, and bought. Terraced
houses in smart back streets just aching to become

trendy, new developments in converted warehouses, cheap property in villages close to the towns, within a ten minute drive from the railway station, and so on. William was not alone in seizing the opportunity. Through their representatives, anonymous businessmen bought considerable chunks of property without even leaving their smart London offices. Young executive couples gazumped locals in their determination to move to the provinces and commute. Two-up, two-downs close to the station – which had always been viewed by the locals as noisy, gritty and not very appealing, were rapidly becoming desirable residences.

William dipped his fingers in many pies. And he had ten fingers – that's an awful lot of pies.

When a pit closes, nature takes over. Roofs cave in, tunnels fill with water. You can't reopen a pit when the need arises. When it's closed, it's gone for good. When a hospital closes, you'd imagine that there might be a chance for reprieve, but just as rapidly as a pit fills with water, big business takes over. Big business likes land. Lots of it, preferably somewhere nice. And when big business sees, it buys. No argument. Pitch money with people and money always wins. If Johnny's on the street that's okay: Johnny's where he needs to be, for money's sake. And Celie's husband, Jack – or Alf, Nellie's husband – if they've lost their jobs then that's the way it has to be, for money's sake. Money likes land. It eats land, then regurgitates shopping malls or superstores or leisure complexes or yuppy museums or blocks of offices rising high in steel and concrete or nice little housing developments that only the rich can afford to buy . . . and all of these things make money. It breeds itself, and shrugs off the detritus of unprofitable humankind.

Anydale was one of William's 'pies'. He joined the army of suits wandering the corridors with clipboards in their hands, doing God knows what . . . measuring wards, talking into their portable telephones – while the old patients shuffled down the corridors with bin-bags of clothes and personal possessions, being shunted from ward to ward as part of a supposed 'rehabilitation programme'. When little George went to his locker to check that he had left nothing behind, there was a note taped to the foot of his bed. 'LOT 43.'

'What does that mean?' he asked the nurse who was with him.

'It means that somebody likes your bed,' the nurse replied solemnly.

He paused for a moment, then looked up at her: 'I'm dead. Where do I go?'

She hugged him.

Gail saw William often now. Sometimes she heard him from a distance. William didn't care where he was or what he was doing. He had no respect for feelings. So even when driving his Porsche carefully over the ramps on the hospital's perimeter road, he turned the stereo up as loud as his ears could stand – which was louder than any of the patients could stand. He subjected the entire hospital to the Bee Gees: 'Ah ha ha ha staying alive . . . ' Once an old woman threw a clod of earth at his windscreen. William jammed on the brakes and leapt out, his normally insipid smile turned into a scowl of rage. The old woman shook with fear but put her hands on her hips and faced him. He took a step towards her, his raised fist promising violence, then caught himself. The anger retreated. It wouldn't look good to hit a patient. Best not to excite the natives. They wouldn't be natives much longer anyway . . . the sooner this site was cleared of bodies the better. So he restored his insincere smile, leaned across and simply flicked the earth away with a tissue, which he let fall on to the road. Then he returned to the car, turned the music up louder than ever and drove carefully away.

William was a child of the seventies but a disciple of the eighties – hence his taste in music. Playing it loud was his way of celebrating life – the hospital was forced to endure it because the hospital hadn't any life, as far as he was concerned.

Gail no longer had any doubt that William was Billy Foster. Although he had trained his voice and developed a clearly upmarket tone, he couldn't change his facial expressions. As he stood against the corridor wall, clipboard pressed to his chest, to let the ranks of bemused patients be herded from one place to another, there was no mistaking the look in his eyes. It was Billy Foster watching with excited delight as the ants he'd poked with a stick ran in all directions. And Gail had seen his eyes struggling to recollect who she was as she passed him, even though his smile never once wavered. She had no intention of helping to remind him. He was loathsome. She kept away from him as much as she could. But it was Billy alright. The lad she wouldn't let on the removal van, that day they'd moved house, all those years ago. Now he was into the removal business on a massive scale. He made her flesh crawl. They were bitter times: times when William and his fellow suits pulled out the chocks that kept the roof from falling in, and the corridors became tunnels rapidly and irreversibly filling with money.

There are Porsches and Porsches. White, blue and yellow Porsches. Porsches with and without accessories: spoilers, fancy hub-caps, sun-roofs, tinted windscreens. Porsches that – like William's – announced their arrival by the blast of rhythmic, pulsating music issuing from their interiors. Second, third and fourth-hand Porsches. Porsches with a black trim jutting from their squatting rear ends. Porsches in growing abundance – beetling symbols of opulence.

But William's Porsche was new and not an average sort of Porsche. William didn't believe in averages. He had a 160mph listed edition 944 Turbo, the brightest, most dazzling pillar-box red you ever saw. A front-engined, four-cylinder, 250 brake horse-power, turbo-charged lust machine. Sporty, powerful, aggressive and *extremely* expensive: to see William's Porsche was to know William.

Sexually William liked to believe he had a certain image, and took much pleasure in reinforcing that belief. He was a Zorro of the bedclothes, a swordsman of ill-repute. A buccaneer, a penile swashbuckler, a bandit of sexual encounters – the original 'smoking gun'. He and his Porsche went well together.

But his days as a young buck left their legacy. For he screwed a woman who screwed a man who screwed a man and something passed between them all. Something that knew no morality and had no concept of sin. Something that thrived on promiscuity, regardless of sexual orientation. Something that was introducing itself to William by a small purplish lesion on his thigh, and was keen to become better acquainted.

Good Copy

It seemed that the winter would never end. The country
trudged on.

One particularly bleak morning, in a trendy flat in
Fulham, a painfully emaciated, weak and pale young
woman walked unsteadily into her pine-panelled kitch-
en, opened the fridge door, stared at the contents and,
swaying a little, shut it again.

It wasn't that she didn't want to eat, particularly. Wanting or not wanting didn't really come into it, as she could
keep nothing down. Hunger seemed academic. She knew
she ought to try. The doctors told her to try, but it wasn't
the thought of the food, it was the actual physical effort
of having to prepare something – even cereal – and then
the energy required to chew and swallow. It just didn't
seem like a pleasant proposition.

In a while, the voluntary worker would be in to help
her – make her a drink, get her to take her medication
. . . it all seemed very pointless, very tiring. She fell
into the nearest armchair, not even feeling capable of
drawing back the living-room curtains. Her whole body
seemed to ache – a curiously non-specific kind of ache.
If she could isolate the pain, it'd be easier . . . but it felt
as though the ache was in her bones, somehow, seeping
out and affecting everything else.

It was getting hard to breathe.

In the dark, stale room there seemed no hope to the
morning. The morning was simply an extension of the day

before, and the day before that. Sometimes the sickness seemed worse, and some days slightly improved. Whatever – it made no difference. Nothing really changed . . . just her body growing weaker by degrees . . .

Ultimately death. All roads leading there, no way of turning out of the area and moving on, just watching the time pass, and waiting.

She appears resigned, but she isn't. She's more stunned than resigned, more angry than accepting . . . but she's weak, very weak, and she doesn't have the strength to scream.

The district nurse will come. The home help will come. The volunteer will come. Someone will change the soiled bedclothes; someone will help her wash; someone will hand her her pills while she sits, a passive recipient. And if they talk, they'll ask her how she feels and she'll reel off a new list of bodily complaints. She no longer has a mind. The body's in control, with its aching – and the disease controls the body.

In time, they'll carry her to the general hospital and she'll lie there, declining – and maybe the friends who don't visit her now will visit her there, in sterile surroundings, where the disease is more like a proper disease and less ugly than this fetid darkness. And maybe they'll kiss her, because she'd like to be kissed, but they'll kiss her forehead, or her hand, or they'll just hold hands, because they're not terribly sure of the ways they could catch it. Or maybe they won't come at all.

Perhaps they're pretending she's already dead.

They'll be relieved, she thinks, when it's over, because they won't have this pretence to keep up. Miffy sent her a bowl of oranges via the volunteer, with a little card saying, 'Warm wishes, will visit soon . . . ' but Miffy was standing outside her front door, just waiting for someone else to go in. Mark sent carnations, and a card with a heart on the front . . . and a few others, this and that, all carefully avoiding the 'get well soon' comments – short, guilty messages . . .

The editor came to visit her, to tell her that they'd been forced to find a replacement. 'You know how it is . . . ' he'd said. She knew. She tried to write letters, but it took up too much energy. She tried phoning people, but her old friends had started avoiding her calls. Her parents were dead. Her brother lived in Australia, and couldn't leave his nine-month-old son, he said.

A fellow-journalist had visited, brought grapes, then asked if she'd agree to being photographed, weekly – as a kind of serialised ongoing documentary . . .

'It's good copy,' he said, 'the public should know!'

She refused.

Decline

Slowly and inexorably comes the malady,
Slowly, slowly we watch our disintegration:
The shadows fall, and we become the shadows.

Terraces on the left and on the right, more terraces, multiplied in kind throughout Beckwood Estate. At the edge of the estate, large, bright and ultimately concealing, a vast DIY superstore. Deposited in the centre, nested like a cluster of tall, thick grey warts, stand the tower blocks; cracked, infested, stinking legacies of unbalanced architects from a previous generation. A little further on, there's a factory that no longer thrives. A factory which, in fact, no longer exists ... Note the rubble, the rusted iron bars, the bits of lathes scattered and fragmented – barely recognisable. Chip papers, old crisp packets, used condoms, broken bottles – muddied and desolate in the relentless winter storms. Between the remains of industry and the DIY superstore runs a road – an arterial route to the city – crammed with commuters in bright comfy cars, heading for work.

A young woman sits in her Renault 5 – brand new – so new that she has not had time to run it in – and checks in her purse, as she waits at the traffic lights, for the credit cards she dare not leave home without.

A young couple, in their Montego, also waiting, are

chatting casually about the colour scheme in their living-room. Tracey wants humus – a living colour, she feels, and original . . . Roger prefers grey, to complement the tubular steel and black of their Habitat furniture.

A middle-aged man in vest and jeans, sitting in the cab of his lorry, checks the time on his digital water-proof watch, turns up the radio and glances again at the 'fantastic tits' of the bird on page three; then thinks about the latest case of child abuse . . . 'Bleedin 'orrible bastards out there,' he thinks to himself.

Arnold the insurance man, once a walker and tapper of doors, now sits comfortably in his company car and wonders to whom he might offer a secure future today.

Back on the estate, many of the local inhabitants would jump at the chance of a secure future.

The estate belongs to the council, although a few of the houses have been bought. The council would like to sell all of them, but most of the occupants cannot afford to even think about buying. The occupants would also like automatic washing machines, dishwashers, videos and compact discs, but poverty prevails.

These terraced houses, half a century ago, would have witnessed the emergence of young men in uniform heading proudly to war. Some returned, but not all. Until recently, the sound of the factory siren calling men to work would have pierced the wet morning air as men, both young and old, emerged from the ginnels and walked proudly if unwillingly to the factory. Only the factory does not exist any more, the men are no longer proud. The women are struggling. The flats' occupants wonder just how bad the damp must become before the council rehouses them. The children sell drugs and don't think about the future . . . The older men wonder what in God's name they fought a war for, climbing filthy stairs because the lifts are always broken.

On the radio, a president insists, courageously, on the establishment of human rights in the Soviet Union. A prime minister agrees, wholeheartedly. Freedom of speech, freedom of choice – particularly choice, they chant. How wonderful she is. How British; how damned British. Fly the flag.

The young woman knows all about choice. She – and her credit cards – live in a wonderful age: exciting, stimulating, dynamic.

The young couple know all about choice. Currently, despite the news, their immediate attention is drawn to a choice between humus and grey.

Arnold knows all about choice. Which policy to take, which investments are sound . . .

And the lorry driver, also, knows about choice. He also carries credit cards; his wife has a dishwasher, his children a computer. He doesn't belong to a union – the companies get away with it these days – but Rod doesn't particularly mind. If not belonging to a union keeps him in work, that's fine . . .

Young Joe Watkins, however, doesn't understand what people mean when they talk about choice. He is sitting on what remains of a wall on the factory site, watching the fine cars pass him by. He wishes he could just sit in one of those cars and go to wherever they are going. He doesn't want to live here any more. His dad has gone funny and speaks to no one; his mum is tired all the time, and his Uncle Frank stays out most nights, up to something. He should be at school, but can't see much point. He is thirteen years old and wishes he had a cigarette. So he waits on the wall, because sometimes people throw them out of the car windows and he can still manage a puff or two from what they have discarded.

They met at the Wimpy.

'Two coffees, please . . . do you want anything else?'

'No, coffee's fine.' Celie took off her coat and sat down opposite Gail.

'Do you think you'll get back together?' Celie asked her friend.

'No. I'm sure of it.'

'It's a pity though, with Jack and Albert being so close.'

'Celie . . . ' Gail took her hand. 'Do you ever feel as though you got it wrong?'

'Got what wrong?'

'Life. Your marriage?'

'Gail, we're just about the same age, you and me. You could be anything you want to be. You're independent.

I've got two kids, stretch marks, no money. I could have stayed on at school – remember? Instead I met Jack and fell in love. With the way things are now – I don't know . . . but Jack needs me, and the kids, and it's my life. I don't think it can be wrong.'

'I expect you're right. I mean, for you I know you're right. I think you've managed much better than me.'

'I didn't have the sort of things you had to contend with when we were young, Gail. I think it's screwed you up a bit.'

Celie stood looking in the window of the Job Centre: scanning, a little vaguely, the 'latest vacancies' . . . She'd try homeworking again, but Jack had put his foot down over that a long time ago, and refused to discuss it now. 'It's slave labour. And if the DHSS get to hear about it, we'd only be in a worse position,' he'd said. 'The kids were neglected last time, with all the work you had to do – and look at the state you were in! No. I'd rather get myself run over for the insurance money than let you go through that again!'

He was right, of course. The kids *were* neglected that year . . . when was it? Glueing silk linings into little jewellery boxes all day every day, until she seemed to live, eat and breathe little pieces of purple silk, and boxes everywhere; stacked on the sideboard, piled up in the corners . . . she earned three pounds fifty for a gross of completed boxes . . . one hundred and forty-four little boxes to be lined painstakingly . . . glue getting everywhere, threads of purple silk tangling in the vacuum cleaner. It took her a day to earn that amount. She tried to enlist the kids, but Frank refused; Cindy, then aged five, glued everything except the bits she should have glued, and Joe, aged eight, decided it was a game and stuck the silk in upside-down when he grew bored. And Celie snapped and cursed, because she knew they would dock her wages for every mistake. Sometimes she didn't even get paid: the man would load the boxes in the back of his Mini, tell her he'd send a postal order, and then conveniently forget to pay. She couldn't prove that she had done the work, so she'd no way of complaining.

She didn't tell Jack the first time this happened, but on the second occasion she felt so upset she had to tell him: which was when he insisted that she gave it up.

Celie moved on, jostled out of the way by a huddle of job-seekers gathered behind her. She walked into the square and sat on the bench beside the fountains. The sound of the water soothed her anxieties a little, so she remained and watched the people passing by. To her right a man sat huddled behind a bright blue-and-yellow stall, shouting at frequent intervals, 'Een Po! Een Po!' She smiled, and remembered how Jack had pointed this out to her once on a shopping expedition. Since then she had listened to the shouts of the paper-sellers, dotted among the city's streets, and tried to visualise the actual spelling of their chants. Little things that kept her sane.

She watched a bright glint in the sky's deep blue, and the vapour-trail that followed slicing a narrow path through the heavens before dispersing gently into puffy white cloud, fading slowly . . . She tried to think about the plane's destination, but her imagination felt scarred with too much reality these days. A poster . . . blue sea, palm trees . . . no. She frowned and tried again. Nothing. She dredged up place names, names of fabulous cities . . . Rome, Venice, Cairo . . . but no images settled before her, just nouns: Rome – Pope; Venice – canals; Cairo – camels. She tried to imagine sitting on a camel: what sound does a camel make? A moo? A grunt? – yes, but what kind of grunt? What does the camel look like? Brown . . . and a hump . . . It didn't work. She shook her head and looked up again. The plane's glinting pin-prick of light had gone, the trail broken, the puffy white clouds dispersing . . .

She stood, wearily, and decided to head for home. School would be over soon, and Cindy would be waiting for her. She wished things could be easier. As she passed the knot of drunks in the square, she thought of Jack, and wished again for an easier life. She had never imagined marriage could be so hard. She didn't know how to cope with him. Sometimes she felt so frustrated at his moods, she wanted desperately to take him by the shoulders and shake him back to life. It was like living with a 'vegetable' sometimes. It took all her strength to get him

down to the DHSS to sign on. He didn't speak; he barely
acknowledged her presence. Only in the evenings, when
the sky darkened, did he seem to come alive. Dr Fawcett
had prescribed antidepressants, but they didn't seem to
help. What he really needed, she knew, was a job, but in
his present state of mind it was pointless to look for him:
he wouldn't make it to the interview.

Responsibility for the family's welfare seemed heaped
upon her shoulders and she hated it. Young Frank looked
perpetually sullen and disappeared every evening with
mates who looked similarly jaundiced; returning home
after midnight whether she protested or not. He needed
Jack; he worried Celie. She felt in her bones that he was
up to no good but she knew there was no point in asking,
as he wouldn't tell her. It seemed only a matter of time
before some kind of crisis would descend upon her –
possibly a visit from the police – and she had no idea how
to prevent it. She had tried, of course, but the attempts
were little more than precipitants to yet another row;
yet another session of door-banging, shouts and abuse,
and her heart constricted when she thought of Cindy's
wide-eyed, tearful confusion, not knowing where to run
from the storms, sitting outside her father's bedroom door
plucking at the strands of loose carpet, as though hoping
that being close to her dad would somehow make it right,
without daring to open the bedroom door and break the
illusion. And Joe quietly slipping out of the back door at
the first signs of an argument; returning a couple of hours
later smelling of tobacco smoke and refusing to answer
her questions.

Celie was losing control, she knew. What once had
been a family now seemed to her to be a nebulous
organism with a slippery texture that somehow she
had to hold on to but couldn't seem to get to grips
with. She had to try, for Cindy's sake: for and because
of Cindy she held on – yet it was through Cindy's total
bemusement that she felt the predicament most clearly
and painfully. She listened to Cindy's childish chatter
on the way home from school, and held her little hand;
nearer to the flats the chatter would die away, lapsing
into silence, and the little hand would grip hers more

tightly as she unlocked the front door. But what could she do?

It seemed hopeless, utterly hopeless sometimes, but she struggled on in the dim hope that there would be some kind of resolution – that nothing bad could last for ever. As she trudged up the street to the bus stop she noticed a flash of red, and stopped to watch the brightest car she had ever seen turn the corner and throb its way towards the Market Square.

Jack was once a proud man. Now he walked with head bowed, despairing, to the Benefit Office. He was obliged to accept the dirty street, the grimy building, the hostile faces. He pushed open a side door and entered the arms of the State. He tried to think, but his thoughts seared like acid: 'Once there was a city. Once a factory or two. Once a populace, in heavy but dignified labour.

Once there was a country: a flag, a kind of unity.'

bury the flag

'I seem to remember . . . but can I be sure? I seem to recall . . . was there a war?'

this is what we give/ this is what was meant for you/ this is your reward/ a token of gratitude/ get in the line/ get to the back/ bury your dead/ bury your concern/ avarice reigns/ bury the flag

'I try to tell myself that it'll be for the better. I can see how we change. I can feel the changes. I try to tell myself that it'll improve.'

bury hope

'I try to tell myself that they care, really. They look as though they care, when they speak. But I've come to assume that all contact between soul and gob is lost. All contact lost.'

Once inside the Benefit Office Jack tried to shut out the tired, fraught faces, the voices raised in anger and frustration behind the screen that hid the clerks and ticket-holders from view. He walked along one of many rows of red plastic seats with steel frames bolted to the floor, until he reached the grimy window. Staring out at grey, inhuman offices towering above him, he could not see the sky, but knew it would be cloudy. Overhead the

fluorescent lighting flickered with a white, formal glare,
illuminating dirty jackets, tattered trousers, screaming
babies, weeping mothers, little impersonal tickets, forms,
and more forms. One-time workmates in degradation;
gathered together like cogs in a machine, subject to the
excuses and inquisitions of sour-faced officers, dependent themselves for pen-wielding power upon a government whose presence was felt in the clogged, unhealthy
atmosphere and as a dark, oppressive shadow in the hall.

Jack, you're living on a pittance. You're a beggar, Jack.
You're crawling in the dirt for your dole, and they want to
push you further down. You're living in misery, your children
have no clothes, your wife's on tranquillisers to help her cope.
You've been unemployed for two years now. Go – get a job.

But Jack was defeated. It wasn't as though he hadn't
tried. At first he thought it would be easy. But he didn't
have the qualifications – only the experience. Experience
meant nothing. The employers chose the pick of the crop.
And Jack couldn't bear the thought of another rejection:
he couldn't face the bludgeoning despair. He couldn't
face the looks these people gave him. He couldn't face
people. He couldn't face his wife, his children, his parents. Each day stretched before him like an endless,
intolerable vacuum of failure.

Pick yourself out of the gutter, Jack.

Jack was sitting, but not really thinking. Thinking
stopped some time ago. It didn't help to think. But
he couldn't stop the taunts, the sneers, the jibes that
came to him through the fog of his consciousness. The
days passed through sitting. He sat at the window and
watched the grey banks of cloud gather overhead. He sat
in vacuum. Time passed. The days passed as unwelcome
breaks between sleep and sleep. It's no use asking where
he was. He wasn't anywhere.

Scrounger. Parasite. Leech on the belly of society. Inadequate.
Only half a man. Pathetic. Get a job.

Some evenings, before bed, he felt more hopeful. In
the night's blackness he imagined a gap in the clouds.
He saw a way ahead. He remembered that he was a good
worker: punctual, well presented, conscientious. A man
of integrity.

With the curtains drawn, and the gas-fire's comforting warmth, he felt safer. It didn't hurt so deeply. Plans and ideas formed in his mind: he resolved to be more positive in his outlook. The ideas became grandiose, exciting. He couldn't sleep – his mind raced. Tomorrow would be better. He'd get up, bathe, get dressed . . . he'd go to the Job Centre and a job would be there, just waiting. He'd impress his prospective employers at the interview. They'd pay him well, give him a position of responsibility. At the end of each week a bulging pay-packet would come to him. He'd take his family on holiday. The children would nestle close to him as they used to do, before the darkness. They'd ask his advice. They'd tell him their problems. They'd feel safe and secure, next to him. The lines of worry would vanish from his wife's face. She'd start to smile. There'd be no more arguments. He'd be the breadwinner again: proud and in control of his destiny, and his family's. He'd write a polite but formal letter to the DHSS, telling them that he no longer required financial assistance. He'd itemise every complaint, every difficulty, every injustice he'd suffered at the hands of the acid-faced clerks in the Benefit Office – but with detachment. He'd look down, from his position of superiority, at those uncaring officials with their endless rules and regulations, their endless forms, their endless excuses, and he'd tell them exactly what he thought of them, individual by pen-pushing individual. His spine would straighten; he'd walk tall. And no one would hurt him or his family like this again.

Sleep came, finally but fitfully. He dreamt of crooked hands, of fists and broken glass. He dreamt of a mountain rising before him, that he must climb, but each time he climbed, a little pin-striped man pushed him to the bottom again. He rocked in his bed like a ship in a storm. He cried out, then woke, alarmed, to face a dim, shadowed ceiling. Four a.m. Celie slept in the children's room. The bed was damp with his sweat. He didn't move. The ceiling crouched overhead. He didn't know how to move.

At 4.30 a.m. he decided to take a bath. At 5.30 he heard his wife rise. At 6.30 she brought him a coffee, shook his arm, and left the room without speaking. He heard cupboard doors in the kitchen being opened and closed, the sound of cutlery being removed from the drawer. He heard his wife enter the children's room at 7.30: the muffled voices as the children were woken, sounds from the bathroom, the kitchen . . . He couldn't move. His eyes were fixed on the ceiling. Sleep wouldn't come. At 8.30 he heard the rustle of coats in the hall and muffled voices again, as Celie left to walk the children to school. He knew Celie would go to the Job Centre on his behalf, and a tight band constricted around his forehead. He frowned and closed his eyes. It didn't help.

He rose with difficulty – his limbs felt heavy and aching with fatigue. He visited the bathroom and, with vague recollections of the night before, ran a bath. The water was cold. He emptied the bath and turned on the immersion heater. After fifteen minutes he turned it off again. The water was lukewarm. He bathed and washed his hair. This made him feel a little more alive. Towelling himself down, he returned to the bedroom, took his wife's hairdryer, and sat on the bed to dry his hair. The mirror faced him. The heat from the drier warmed him. The face in the mirror didn't belong to him.

At 12.45 Celie returned with the children and, leaving them to settle, came into the bedroom to find her husband, naked and cold, staring at the mirror. She asked if he wanted dinner and, receiving no response, decided to put it in the oven and warm it up for him later. She took his clothes out of the wardrobe and helped him to dress. Her mouth was set in grim determination. Returning to the kitchen, she made another coffee and took it to him. She knew he wouldn't come out while the children were there.

To Joe and Cindy, it was like living with a loved stranger, but without a father. They didn't understand, but over the months grew used to his fluctuations in mood. They chatted to each other. Celie heated the stew and set it before them, with plenty of bread.

At 1.30 she left with the children again and Jack, growing a little more aware, ventured into the kitchen. Made yet another coffee. Ate a slice of bread, which he tore into pieces and pressed to a doughy consistency in the palm of his hand. Looked at the paper, but digested nothing: not even the bread, which he chewed slowly and gulped down between flushes of nausea. Sitting at the table, he stared out of the window at more grey concrete. At 2.30 he rose, feeling suddenly and oppressively tired, and returned to bed. He laid his head upon the pillow like a child nestling against its mother's breast and drew the covers around him for comfort. Sleep came gently, like a welcome friend.

Parasite. Leech. Beggar.

At 7.00 his wife woke him. He could smell his dinner warming, so he dressed in ragged jeans and jumper. In the living-room his children argued in front of the television. In the kitchen Celie was at the stove, patiently stirring his stew. The children had already eaten. He walked to his wife, put his arms around her from behind and leaned his head upon her shoulder to watch her work. They didn't speak. Her body stiffened, then relaxed, then shook gently as she wept. He held her, his eyes smarting, unable to speak. She turned to him and there, in the kitchen, amidst the steam of the cooking, with the noise of the television in the background, they held each other tightly for a while.

He ate the dinner willingly, tasting little, but enjoying the heat from the food on his tongue. He drank the hot, sweet tea with relish. He helped Celie with the dishes and, once the dishes were done, joined her in the living-room. His children looked up anxiously as he entered, then averted their eyes to face the screen once again.

Some game show. The adverts came on. Granite watches or something ... crisps ... then beer ... Then a man in a car, driving through the country – dark, dark clouds overhead – passing horses, startling birds ... a man sitting at a table – in the background the sea – opposite a sophisticated woman, drinking wine – champagne – something ... Always, always, an educated masculine voice intoning: 'It probably wouldn't surprise you if we said it would do wonders for your love life ... '

Jack looked at his wife, who stared at the screen: lost

in some private fantasy. The band around his head grew tighter.

Then the final scene. The man parked his car on the forecourt of some country house, raised the boot . . . The voice, subtly superior, concluded: 'But if we told you that this car costs less than a dozen sets of professional golf clubs, we think you'd be pleasantly surprised . . . '

The tears no longer came.

Parasite. Leech.

The tears were dead.

Beggar. Inadequate.

Anger was dead.

Can't feed your children!

Words didn't help.

Get a job.

Nothing helped.

Get off your arse!

A deep, deep ache.

Scrounger!

He didn't know how to stop the ache . . . Despair clouded his vision. His world had become an infected wound. So there, in the living-room, in the shadows beyond his children's faces, his wife's quiet, escapist absorption, there, in the shadows, he considered how best to burn the pain away.

Shouting At The Wind

The charge nurse picked up his coffee and walked to the window. There was nothing to see but walls. 'I'm sure it was him,' Gail said.

He sipped at his coffee. Without turning he replied: 'And what if it was?'

'There must be something . . . '

'Was he causing a disruption?'

'He was swearing at the cars.'

'And you say the landlady doesn't know where he is?'

'She says he comes in now and again, but that it isn't her job to keep track of them all. I don't believe her anyway. She just wants his money.'

'So he's not there?'

'I don't think he's been there for months.'

'You think we can do something?'

'I think we could try . . . '

'I think you'd be shouting at the wind, Gail. No one wants to know. We've enough of a job shifting the rest, without worrying about Johnny.'

'But at least we could . . . '

'At least what? I tell you, Gail, NO ONE WANTS TO KNOW!'

'Then what are we doing here?'

'Keeping our pensions.'

'And that's it?'

'That's it.'

'When I started training, Jacko, I respected you.'

He didn't turn. 'I think it's time you moved on, Gail.'

163

'I thought you were a good nurse . . . '

'Sister Lane wants you on female admissions. Humber Ward. You'd be dealing with transfers, not discharges.'

'You want rid of me?'

He turned to her. 'I want you off my back, yes.'

She stood up. 'I'll see her today.'

'Good.'

'Right.'

'And Gail . . . ?'

'What?'

'Perhaps if you were my age . . . '

She turned back to him. He'd always been a tall man. He seemed to have shrunk. She wanted to stay angry. She *was* angry. She wanted to say that, even at his age, she'd still want to be able to live with her conscience, but looking at him, she knew he was only doing what he felt was right. He looked so defeated. They all did – all the old nurses. So defeated . . . so old.

'I'm sorry, Jacko,' she said, 'you're probably right.'

The elderly died on nights like these; with the storm buffeting the window panes.

They died while the Government pondered over the paltry supplemental heating allowance, and took pains to withstand many a heated political exchange. The hot air floating wastefully from the Commons might have saved lives, could it have been collected. But like all hot air, it simply drifted away. And before the Government decided, for political expediency, to relent to the wishes of the Opposition, many old people died . . . In small, dark rooms where the sun's warmth never seemed to reach. Huddled in blankets, sleeping on sofas to be close to their inadequate fires. Wrapped in three layers of clothes that prevented circulation, wearing woolly hats, or perhaps another blanket, around their head and shoulders; wearing three or four pairs of socks to keep their feet warm, but desperately cold nevertheless. Sleeping fitfully, starving themselves rather than leaving the comparative warmth of their bedclothes. Wishing for a nice cup of hot, sweet tea as their mouths became parched and their lips chapped from lack of fluid. Lying there they seemed like small, frail islands, unable to risk abandonment of this imagined heat to venture out into the cold room beyond.

As the dampness from the cold houses seeped into their bedclothes, they slept. As the coldness spread insidiously from their feet upwards, they slept more. As civil servants emerged from their centrally heated modern houses into a bright frosty morning, noting the sunlight and thinking – 'It isn't cold enough today!' – they slipped the final cords of life; their bodies as cold as the blankets that covered them, as cold as their rooms, as cold as bureaucracy.

Celie tossed and turned: she could hear Jack moving about and although she had grown used to his behaviour, tonight it seemed different. She went to him, but he turned from her.

'Go to bed, Celie.'

'But won't you come?'

'Later. You go.'

So she checked the kids and returned to her bed.

Something was wrong tonight.

She didn't like the storm.

In their earlier years, nights like this would have held them close. Jack's strong arms would have been around her, whispering words of comfort. If the children had cried, Jack would have gone to them.

She tried to stay awake, but tiredness won.

Jack's hands were shaking as he balanced the note for Celie on the mantelpiece. He zipped up his anorak and stuffed into his pocket a bottle of pills he had taken from the sideboard drawer and a box of household matches from the kitchen. The wind howled through the gaps beneath the doors, rattling the window panes and moaning between the tower blocks, shaking empty streets, quiet towns, deserted cities to a state of frustrated neurosis. It raged violently within Jack, denying comfort, preventing rest: harsh, cold and intolerable it drove him out of the flat and into the night. It laid waste the past. It made him wild, numb to emotion; with all his energy and intent focused upon one final act. He would go south. It was all that was left to him. He would make his protest and find release. He was beyond pain, beyond hope, beyond reason . . .

The storm will blow: there is nothing you can do.

On Upstart Quay, the canal had risen considerably with the constant downpours and the young executives quivered with excitement as they watched, through their living-room windows, the heavy black clouds thundering overhead. Some, after waving to fellow-executives across the courtyard, wrapped themselves in designer jumpers and overcoats, and ran, laughing, to join a group of fellow-Upstarters in a night's wine-sodden vigil. At number thirteen, however, William was too preoccupied with himself to notice the storm.

He had woken in a sweat, his sheets soaked with perspiration, and had decided to take a shower. As he showered he noticed that the lesions seemed to be popping up all over his body. He didn't understand what was happening. Apart from the night-sweats that had become frequent recently, he felt fine. But these lumps . . . there had to be a reason. For some time he had avoided thinking about them, but something was wrong, he knew. Only last week he had received a letter from a colleague in London, telling him about an old acquaintance – a journalist – who was dying from AIDS. The colleague seemed to imply something . . . but William was having such a good time that he had refused to think about it.

He switched off the shower and, towelling himself dry, walked into the bedroom. He replaced the wet sheets and climbed back into bed. He lay, growing comfortable again, and thought of his sexual conquests since moving north. Then he thought of the conquests he had made in London, the endless round of partying and screwing . . . and he thought of the journalist: she had been particularly good in bed and, being of similar natures, they had spent some time together.

As he tried to count the number of women he had slept with over the last few years, a kind of coldness entered his consciousness: a shadow that seemed to creep towards him however hard he tried to keep it at bay. He sat up, switched on the light and reached for a pen; listed names, dates and numbers . . . The figures grew larger and larger, becoming slightly ominous . . . He had always been proud of it before, proud of the number that he had bedded – proud of his sport but now, now . . .

For the first time in his life, William felt afraid.

Celie awoke with a start at one in the morning, the bedside lamp still switched on. The violent night had not receded; in fact it seemed to have grown worse . . . outside a milk bottle chinked and rolled, pushed by heavy gusts.

She listened. Apart from the howling and rattling, she could hear no movement in the front room. Had he fallen asleep on the sofa? . . .

An icy blast from under the front door caught her nightgown and she shivered, rubbing her arms as she padded across the hall. The lights were still on but the room was cold. He wasn't there. He had left her a note on the mantelpiece.

> 'It's impossible, Celie. You'll all be better without me. I've nothing left to offer. Take care, angel, and please try to forgive me. All my love, Jack.'

She gripped the back of the settee. He hadn't called her 'angel' in years. Seized by a sudden fear, she rummaged in the sideboard drawer for the new bottle of sleeping tablets she had received on prescription only the day before. They were gone.

Arnold the insurance man particularly enjoyed driving at night. The roads were clear; he could put his foot down, turn up the stereo . . . There was a kind of beauty to the night – no scenery to note, no hold-ups; just a clear stretch of motorway and darkness. Time to think, to contemplate, to balance the accounts in his mind . . . It isn't a bad life, thought Arnold: business meetings in London, all expenses paid . . . he had a regular booking in a hotel close to the company offices. At any rate, he thought, it could be worse . . .

The headlights picked out a figure on the roadside, walking with arm outstretched, thumb in the air ... A wild night to be out, thought Arnold and, feeling rather generous, he indicated and pulled up. Through the rearview mirror he watched the man hurry towards the car: his jeans, anorak and training shoes illuminated by the red glow of the brake lights. He leaned across and unlocked the passenger door, pushing it open.

'Going far?'

'London.'

'Hop in.'

The man settled into the passenger seat and shut the door. Arnold indicated and pulled out. 'Miss your last bus?' he asked. The figure beside him didn't answer. 'I said – been on a day out, have you? Missed the last bus?'

'No.' The man spoke quietly and looked at him. At least a response, thought Arnold. Maybe there's hope for a conversation.

'Only I noticed that you haven't any luggage.' The man didn't answer and turned to face the road again. Arnold sighed. Some people just aren't grateful. 'It's going to be a long journey!' he thought wearily, wishing now that he hadn't stopped.

He dropped the man off close to St Pancras, grateful to be rid of him, and made for his hotel. The man had said he would walk from there.

The garage forecourt attendant would later regret her decision when a man in jeans and anorak asked to borrow a petrol can. But he looked so tired and upset she couldn't help herself. His car had run out two miles back, he explained ... He filled it with petrol, bought a small bottle of lemonade and left. What a fool she had been to believe him! The boss gave her hell and told her he would dock her wages. That was what she regretted.

He didn't bring it back. You just can't trust anyone these days.

With the petrol can concealed inside a large plastic carrier bag, Jack joined the thousands of commuters in the morning rush for work. Over Westminster Bridge, past the Houses of Parliament, half-walking, half-carried up Whitehall towards the Cenotaph. He and Celie on their honeymoon in London had been as eager and excited by the city as any tourists, proud to be walking through what had seemed then to be the very heart of democracy. Now Jack was aware of nothing, felt nothing, saw nothing as he struggled through the jostling crowds. He had nothing profound to say, no statements to utter; all that remained in his life was to reach his destination and have done with it. He was afraid, but his fear was a cold, detached numbness kept distant by the sheer physical difficulty of achieving what he felt he had to do. By the Cenotaph he broke free of the stream of pedestrians, found a quiet recess in one of the buildings and turned his back to the endless flow of city suits. He emptied the bottle of sleeping pills into his mouth and washed them down with the lemonade. He unzipped his anorak, took the petrol can from the carrier bag, unscrewed the top and began to douse himself with petrol, holding the can carefully to avoid wetting the outside of his coat. The pungent fumes filled his nostrils but already the pills were starting to work, so he dropped the can, zipped up his anorak and pushed his way back through the crowds to Downing Street. As he felt in his pocket for the box of household matches, his mind wandered vaguely over the fact that his kids wouldn't get a cooked breakfast today.

A small huddle of tourists had already gathered at the end of Downing Street. Two policemen chatted quietly as they stood guard behind the barriers: 'I said you can't wear *that*: what in God's name did you buy it for!' said the young policeman to his colleague.

The latter was about to make a joke, was just thinking up the joke, when they heard shouts and a scuffle, saw a man standing a few feet away screaming, 'Keep back!' and striking a match from a large household box with violently shaking hands. For a second they weren't sure, but a Japanese woman shrieked and turned her face away.

'Can you smell . . . ?' said the older policeman, but the youth was already climbing the gate and reaching out to snatch the flame away as the man touched the match to his jeans and burst alight.

Others were also dying. Watched from above, the millions of small flames that signify life flickered and danced in the previous night's storms; in a wind that, for some, seemed to renew their energy and for others, seemed intent on snuffing them out.

So they died. Not through choice or accident, but because of a sickness.

The child, whose frail battered soul, whose weak and emaciated little body had been tenuously gripping the very edge of life for weeks; locked in a cold, dark, loveless room, tensing in terror at the sound of the key turning . . . The child whose round, dark eyes had seen too much pain, whose bruised limbs had never known the joy of play, whose bewildered mind had been closed to comfort and love, whose broken ribs made it difficult to breathe, gave out one last, tiny whimper and expired.

An old man fell in Hyde Park from a stroke and lay face down in the mud for two hours before a passer-by bothered to look. By then it was much too late.

The journalist from Fulham gasped out her last few breaths strapped to an oxygen machine in an isolated sideroom, away from the main ward. No one was with her.

And closer to home, if the owners of the old merchant's house in the now exclusive area of the city had looked out of their window during their dinner party, they might have seen a small figure dragging cardboard down the street towards the railway sidings. Apart from the cardboard and a stubborn determination, all that this figure possessed was a small lump of stale bread. Which he kept for the squirrels.

There were many, many more. Small flames fading unnoticed. And it was part of the sickness, this not noticing. Seen from above, the millions of small flames burning below should perhaps have lit up the night: but not so. Each flame burned stubbornly, but seemed to burn for itself alone. Each illuminated nothing, and gave no light to the darkness.

Confrontations

'Joan?'

The gap beneath the window was three inches; enough room to breathe the air, but not enough to jump through.

'My name's Gail. I'm the staff nurse on this shift. I've been talking to Christine. She says you haven't spoken since you came in . . . '

Joan didn't move from her position at the window.

'Sometimes it's easier not to talk, isn't it? When words feel hard.' She sat back in the chair, far enough to see Joan's face. Although some twenty years younger, Gail could see herself in Joan. Joan's face was empty. But Gail knew more than that. She could sense it. Joan was *there*, but she wasn't letting anyone in. The slight flickering of the older woman's pupils informed her that Joan was thinking; thinking hard. 'I think you can hear me. I know it doesn't help you now, but I promise that this time will pass. That's why you're here. It means you can relax a little, give yourself time to heal. Whatever hurts you now will ease soon. Are you thinking that can't be true? It's hard to imagine the pain stopping, but it does. I've seen it happen.'

I know where she is, Gail thought. I know where she is.

She left her chair and knelt down beside Joan at the window, her back to the dayroom. They were well staffed for once. She had time – these days it seemed a precious commodity – to spend with someone. She could do the thing she felt supremely qualified to do, which the institution seemed to bend over backwards to prevent her from doing, by inundating her with far more practical tasks. She could *reach*. 'I'll just stay here with you for a while. Is that okay? I won't try to make you talk – all I want is for you to understand that I'm here. I'm not a mind-reader, but I know that depression is much the same for all of us. If it's any kind of help, I've been where you are now. I know how bad it is. If I could climb inside and hug you, where you are, I would. I'd take your hand and face it with you. I could show you other ways out than those that you're currently considering . . . '

Joan turned to face her. The expression on her face didn't change, but she was listening. Gail's heart skipped a beat. She'd found her.

'Try not to act on your thoughts for a while. Trust us. They'll pass. You may think you're alone, but we're all with you – doctors, staff – and many of the other women on this ward who once felt as bad as you do now. They recovered, and so will you, I promise. If you feel you can't fight for yourself we'll fight for you. We won't let you go.'

Whereas a general nurse spends the day on her feet, never idle, constantly changing drips or cleaning bedpans or taking physical observations, a psychiatric nurse seems, at first sight, to be doing nothing. A good mental nurse uses every sense to observe. She is receptive to every movement, expression, sound and gesture. She listens to her instinct: 'gut' feelings that tell her when something is wrong, or about to happen. She becomes sharply perceptive: she has to be. And she must be articulate, infinitely patient; a good listener.

She knows that when someone turns their head slightly, in the absence of company, he or she might be hearing voices. So she watches. She knows that a suicidal man needs only seconds alone to kill himself, so she stays close. She knows that people confide more easily in each other than to a figure of authority, so she eavesdrops. She watches, follows, listens. A nurse sitting in the dayroom is busy, despite her casual appearance. She is there for a reason. And very, very tense.

More often than not, through the demands of a ward full

of people, her time is spent in observing from a distance. The physical limitations caused by staff shortage and the 'open' ward environment demands that she remains precisely where she is, watching ten or more people at once, until she is relieved by another nurse. It sounds simple, but it's much harder than you think. The satisfaction in such a situation is confused: she will only know that by being there, she is helping to avert a catastrophe. Generally however, she feels like a jailer without a key. The real satisfaction is when she sits alone with someone – when she has the chance for real contact, then all the skills she has had the experience to refine, all the emotions she feels for the person she is with, all that she knows, all the resources she has, all the humanity that brought her into nursing in the first place, merge and join forces. Then she stands at the edge of her neighbour's darkness and reaches in.

Bigots know the answers to everything: she has no answers. Fools make assumptions: she is not a fool. Those ignorant of the nature of mental illness barge in with blundering boots of advice. She goes barefoot, to feel the texture of the ground. And if she is not afraid, she walks into the darkness, she works her way around the boulders of resistance, she *feels* her way forward until she reaches the place where her neighbour stands alone. She stands with them, to see what they see, neither judging nor alarmed, because she knows that the most she can offer is understanding. She believes – although she cannot express it fully – that every life is a link in a greater chain of humanity, and when the chain is broken something precious falls away. So she walks through the darkness to retrieve that link, because it was beside her, and then it was gone. She struggles to reach because she misses what was lost. She misses that person. Human beings have the capacity to reach great distances, once they recognise that the distance exists – once they realise the honesty of love.

'It's all bullshit,' Gail said to Rose without warning.
  'What is?'
  'Everything. Everything we do, or say. Because in

the end they're just words, aren't they? Just words.'
She pushed the chair back and moved to the far wall,
where she crouched as though something had scared
her. 'Words. They didn't stop Jack from setting himself
alight, or Johnny from . . . or my parents from dying. Or
Joan . . . '

'Or you?' Rose interrupted.

'Or me what?'

'You know.'

'You overestimate me. I don't know anything. I couldn't
save my marriage. I can't even save myself. Everything
comes to nothing in the end, because nothing means anything . . . it's all just words. You can't live on words. What
are they? Dead on arrival. Dead once they're admitted.
They go nowhere. They touch nothing . . . '

'So why are you afraid?'

'Because I'm not in control.'

'Not in control of what?'

'Anything. My life – their lives . . . I don't know!'

'I think you do.'

'Fine. You take over my head for me, then. I don't
want it. I don't want any of it any more . . . ' She put her
head in her hands and faced the floor. She didn't see the
carpet, she saw herself walking through a small pathway
beside the church, that led to the nurses' home.

He was waiting for her. She hadn't anticipated this,
hadn't thought that he might visit. She felt shocked and
uncertain . . . he had been sitting on the steps. He stood
as she walked towards him.

'It won't take long. I just thought you should know.'

Had he been crying? He saw the concern in her
eyes and looked away.

'It's cold,' he said.

'Bitter,' she agreed. 'How did you get here?'

'Taxi. I'll walk back . . . '

'It's too far. You could stay . . . '

'I need the air.'

'Well at least . . . ' Gail made towards the large front
door.

'No!' There was a clear note of desperation in his
voice. Not cold, but simply defensive. He looked lost

and confused. It had been raining but his cap was in his pocket. Little droplets of rain fell from his sideburns and travelled erratically down his neck, beneath his upturned jacket collar. She loved his neck. Funny the things you love about people. Just under his ears: it was there that she sensed the child in him. She wanted to reach out and touch him – catch the droplets and brush them away.

He reached into his pocket for a cigarette. His hands were shaking. He couldn't seem to hold it in, whatever was wrong with him. She didn't know what to do. All she could do was stand there.

Albert took a deep drag on his cigarette, coughed and began to speak.

'Jack's dead . . . Don't say anything. I think I might hit you.'

He stopped. Jack.

'Oh Christ . . . '

'Shut up. Just shut up and listen. He went to London, took some sort of drugs and set himself on fire. They did what they could but he'd covered himself in petrol and was so badly burned they couldn't pump his stomach, couldn't give him injections or whatever the fuck it is they do because he'd no skin left. They couldn't even hold him. He died in agony. Screaming.'

He moved as though to strike her but pushed himself away, as though he knew he wasn't safe. Gail couldn't move. She tried to tell herself that it was real, what was happening, but it didn't feel real . . . Albert was shouting at her. He wanted to attack her, she could see it, but it wasn't real. It must be a nightmare – what he'd said about Jack – she almost wanted to laugh, it was so absurd . . . then her legs gave way and the crack of her knees on the cold forecourt brought her back, roughly, to reality. And Albert was still there. She could have been crying. She wasn't sure. It was difficult to see clearly.

Albert put both hands to his head, as though it felt about to explode. 'I can't stop him screaming. I can hear him all the time, and I can't stop him. If he'd only said something . . . I could have gone round . . . but I wasn't to know, was I? He's still burning up inside me; he's still screaming. Christ! But you don't realise, do you, until it's too late, what you could have done. And maybe I wouldn't have known what to say . . . perhaps that's why I didn't go round, but I could have been there for him . . . I might have made a difference. Do you think I could have saved him? Do you?'

He walked agitatedly towards Gail and knelt down in front of her. He took the hem of her cape and felt it between his fingers. He was openly weeping now. He couldn't stop. She had never seen him like this. 'I think you can just love people, can't you? Even when you don't know why, or it doesn't feel right, you can still love them. I wish I could have told him that, but it doesn't make any sense, what you feel, until after the moment's gone and you realise you were never brave enough . . . '

'Come inside, Albert.' It was said instinctively and immediately regretted. He fell back on his haunches as though shot, then staggered to his feet.

'Just who the hell do you think you are? I'm not one of your patients. You can't take me inside, leave me on a ward and then walk away. I've been inside *you*, Gail, you can't turn me off like that. I'm real – remember . . . ?'

He lunged forward, thrust his hand between her legs . . . 'Remember?'

She screamed, suddenly alert with fear. She tried to stand upright, to get away from him.

'We never really mattered to you, did we? None of us . . . '

'That isn't true!'

'Then why weren't you *there*? You talked about your job all the fucking time, you could have done something . . . '

'Like what?'

'You could have talked him out of it!'

'I didn't even know . . . !'

He backed away from her then.

'You should have known! It's your job!'

'I . . . I haven't seen him . . . '

'Some nurse! Some *friend*!' He spat the words out.

'Jesus, Albert, don't blame me . . . '

'Oh, I blame you all right. Can't you take it? Shoulders not big enough?'

'Go to hell!'

He punched the air.

'Don't you ever listen, girl? *I'm there already!*'

He turned on his heel and ran from her.

Christine, after she'd handed over the ward to Gail that afternoon, had retreated to the male hostel for a few games of cards. When they gave up cards they turned on the television, as there seemed nothing better, in their collectively miserable state of mind, to do. After *Coronation Street* they got drunk. At about 11 p.m. Christine returned to the nurses' home, nowhere near as drunk as she wanted to be, and found Gail sitting on the steps. The next day all she could remember, through a blinding headache, was that her friend was cold, and sitting on the steps when you're cold didn't seem a good idea, so she ushered her upstairs. She didn't remember Gail speaking. And Christine was so half-drunk and utterly pissed off that she didn't – couldn't – ask her why she'd been sitting there.

Christine stayed with Gail that night, sleeping beside her in the armchair. Too much seemed to be happening at once for all of them. She went to her room to collect the bottle of whisky she kept for emergencies. This seemed like an emergency. By the time she returned Gail had climbed into bed fully clothed and was asleep. Christine understood the need for sleep. At least Gail was warm. They could talk about it tomorrow.

Christine drank a large glass of whisky and settled herself down in the armchair.

Sometimes it seemed as though the world was about to end. Christine had to remind herself that it was only a hospital closing, not the approach of death. But the way things were, the way people felt, it could have been.

She reached for the whisky again and this time, ignoring niceties, she drank from the spout. Then she wondered absently if she was becoming an alcoholic – it was her second bottle that week and it was only Wednesday ... no, it'd be Thursday now, after midnight. She felt glad that Gail was on in the morning – she'd have time to sleep this off – and it's cinema in the recreation hall on Thursdays ... I wonder if anyone will want to go ...

no, they shut the hall down last week, didn't they? Ready for the closure ... Ah shit ... She swallowed another mouthful and let it dribble down her chin on to her nice, smart, useless fucking uniform ... They used to have a laugh sometimes at the cinema ... they always – not her, but the older ones – they always sent the blind patients to the cinema and the deaf to musical appreciation in the library ... She snorted. Something in that ... And the door handles opened the wrong way throughout the hospital, and the hospital was arse-about-face anyway, with the main reception at the back ... Heh! Who's the more mad?

She took another slug as she considered the fact that she couldn't afford this extravagance. And another mouthful when she realised that her monthly pay, when it finally arrived, would only cover her overdraft ... And that's how they get you, she thought vaguely. You can't protest about the closure because your job's on the line and you need the money. Simple as that. They get you by the balls, metaphorically speaking ... that's a long word! If I think it, can I say it? 'Metaph ... phantasmagorically!' She cheered, giggled and waved the bottle at the ceiling. 'And some have only one ball, while some have no balls at all ... ' She took another slug.

Then they neuter you. Because you don't say they can't. They make you into an instrument, rather than a victim, of the hospital's closure ... Oh, fuck 'em!

She swirled the amber liquid in the bottle, took one last mouthful and replaced the cap. She'd meant to mention to Gail about the hostel job – they'd take her like a shot, and it'd be nice to leave for something else together ... Well, it would have to wait until tomorrow, or whenever ... Something had happened tonight. She tried to remember what, but couldn't, so she pulled at her cape until it covered her body and was tucked snugly beneath her chin, closed her eyes and was gone.

The nurses on night duty wished that they were asleep. The dark hours had always been bad, but with the prospect of imminent closure they had become bleak. The world had shrunk to a temporary collection of hospital buildings. It did not revolve. No room for movement left. Only grief, in anticipation of the event . . . Only memories stirred the dark night air. Soon even the memories would be gone; obliterated by those last hours spent at the bedside, mourning the death before it was too late even to mourn.

The bottle fell from Christine's hand and bumped to the floor as she and her colleague drifted through the unconsciousness of failure. Only the sound of the boiler room, the steady 'thuk thuk thuk' disturbed the institution's silence.

It sounded in the distance like a heartbeat only noticed in the hours before its cessation, because suddenly you know what it is, what it means, how much you need it and how frightened you are of it *not being there*.

'Ratting'

On hearing about his brother's death and unable to face Celie, Frank sought refuge in the house of one of his mates and hid from his grief behind bottle after bottle of whisky, supplied by the proceeds from his last robbery.

Then the news came. His mate burst through the front door in a state of blind panic.

'Frank! Frank! For Christ's sake, Frank!'

'What's up?' Frank roused himself with difficulty from the settee where he had been sleeping off his most recent binge.

'Oh fuck, Frank, they're on to us!'

'Tell me later . . . ' slurred Frank as he laid back down.

His mate, white with anxiety, took Frank by the arm and shook him awake.

'No, damn you, wake up!'

'What's 'matter? Get off me!'

'Frank, you've got to wake up and listen. Trevor's gone off the rails. He gave himself up to the police this morning. His girlfriend said he couldn't cope with what your Jack done, and said he was goin' to make a clean breast of it. That's what his girlfriend says. Are you listenin'?'

Frank was awake now, alert with adrenalin, eyes wide, staring at his friend.

'Are you sure?'

'Fuck yes! She told me herself! Said she couldn't stop him!'

Frank stood, rocking slightly. 'Shit. I . . . What are you going to do?'

'Well I'm not bloody hanging about to get nicked!'

'No, nor me . . . '

'I know someone who'll lend me a van for past favours. Take me a couple of hours. You stay here, I'll be back!'

With that his friend dashed out. Frank rubbed his hair, reached for a cigarette and sat down on the edge of the settee. If Trevor really meant it none of them had much time, and hanging around for two hours might be leaving it too late. What if his mate was setting him up? What if he was going to the police as well? No, keep calm, Frank, he won't do that. If he'd meant to do that he wouldn't have woken you up! Would he? But he'd always thought Trevor was trustworthy, and if Trevor isn't, who is? Two hours. Two hours. Is it too long to wait?

'Yes it fucking is!' whispered Frank. He stood, reached for his parka, gathered together his belongings and left rapidly through the back door.

Deliverance

something's got its claw in the brickwork
something's jammed in the doorway
something stops the window closing
something's coming in.

The night-sweats were a nuisance. He went to see the doctor. The doctor examined him thoroughly and noticed several small purplish lesions on his legs, his back and neck. Now, said the doctor, the two might be totally unrelated, but we ought to take you in for a while and have these lesions investigated. Best to see a specialist in cases like these.

What cases are cases like these? thought William. The doctor preferred to defer judgement.

Judgement came therefore on the hospital ward. The doctors explained the diagnosis calmly. The bumps? Kaposi's sarcoma. A relatively rare disease until a few years ago, but now, with AIDS . . .

For two days William stormed, cursed, wept piteously, accused and then fell silent. Again and again the doctors sat on the edge of the bed. Again and again they described the nature of the disease, the chances, the prognosis. The counsellor came and counselled. Again and again. Slowly William developed a kind of acceptance. It wasn't easy. But then, if he were only to admit to it, the worry had been there for some time. In a sense, it was a kind of relief.

'Have you ever injected drugs?'

'No!'

'Have you ever had homosexual intercourse?'

'How dare you!'

'We don't mind. Nothing shocks us. We're used to it.'

'Piss off!'

'Given blood?'

'Don't be silly. It's my blood. I don't give it away!'

'Required transfusion?'

'I'm never ill.'

'In the past few years, would you say your sex life has been stable and committed?'

'What?'

'One partner? Several?'

'I sleep around, if that's what you mean.'

'I see. Have you ever been intimately involved with a known AIDS carrier?'

'No. Not at the time anyway.'

'What does that mean?'

'It means that there was a journalist in London . . . we knocked about together . . . but she didn't have AIDS, not then.'

'AIDS can remain latent in the body for several years. Did you take precautions?'

'She was on the pill.'

'I see.'

'What's that mean? "I see." Come to the point, won't you?'

'I think you already know what the point is.'

He did. That letter from his friend . . . but he had been having such a good time, he had refused to think about it. Well, he hoped she was dead. Dead and buried. Bitch.

They moved him to another ward, where the counselling was more intense. Life after diagnosis, they told him. He didn't believe it. From what they had said, another illness, even a common cold, could lay him out.

Dying, it has to be said, was becoming an obsession to William.

Death. What was it? Unknown. Not living any more. Nothing. He struggled with the concept. No returns.

Not something you can buy your way out of. But try
as he might, he couldn't get to grips with it. The idea
of life just stopping was unfathomable. Apart from the
purple bumps and the night-sweats he felt fine. Secret-
ly he began to wonder if they'd got it wrong. It's been
known. Or maybe it would just clear up? They told him
the lesions were benign . . . if he ate more fruit, less
instant food, more wholemeal bread . . . Why not? A 'gay
plague', after all. He wasn't really part of it. Sitting on the
outside of the regular group discussions, he developed a
penchant for 'fairy-watching', he called it. Bent, most of
them. Poofters. Some flounced in and held hands, talking
about their lovers. Pathetic. Straight as a die was William,
and proud of it. They probably deserved the disease. He
didn't.

It was Tom who finally surprised William. He seemed
so normal. Quite likeable. William didn't have many
friends, and Tom always took the trouble to talk to him.
Of course he didn't need company, didn't need friends
. . . but all the same he was glad to see Tom. He had a
way of smiling that stirred something in William, like a
kind of comfort.

'If you could just sit with him, Tom, we'd be grateful.
He hasn't adjusted. Half the time we've no idea what's
going on in his mind. He says he's okay but he doesn't
look it.'

'It'll give me something to do,' said Tom, 'I can't
just sit and watch David die. It'll be a challenge.'

'The consultant wants to keep him in. He's afraid
William's just the type to do something rash. It's like
he's blocking it out. He's never suggested discharge.
He just doesn't seem bothered. It's worrying.'

By the third week William had decided that Tom was
definitely okay. A bit quirky, but intelligent. He decided
that he liked Tom when he saw him walk on to the ward
and head straight for him, after a day's absence. Tom
wasn't a patient but he seemed to live in the hospital, so
his non-appearance was upsetting, and his return stirred
a sense of simple gratitude that William had never experi-
enced before.

'Where were you yesterday?'

'With a friend.'

'I thought I . . . ?'

'My lover.' The way Tom said it, so matter of factly, then faced William, as if to challenge him, made William hesitate.

'Is that why you're living here?'

'To be close, yes.'

'Which ward is she on?'

'He.'

William looked away. Bastard. All this time, now he tells me he's as queer as the rest of them. It hurt somewhere.

'Why didn't you tell me before?'

'Because I knew what your reaction would be.'

'I LET YOU DRINK MY SODDING WATER!'

The nurse at the end of the ward stopped what she was doing and looked up.

'Scared you might catch something?'

'Bastard!' cried William, bringing back his fist. Tom caught his arm and held him. William struggled, but Tom's grip was firm.

'You bloody queen. If I'd known . . . '

'You'd what? Shun me like you shun the others? The reason I haven't told you before is because the staff asked me to sit with you, and I could sense your hostility.'

'I DON'T NEED YOUR POXY CHARITY!'

'Call this charity? I'm as desperate as you for someone to talk to.'

'Piss off.'

'For such a city slicker, your vocabulary's a bit limited.'

'What's he got then, your *boyfriend*?'

'My lover? He's got AIDS. I gave it to him. He's dying.'

Tom stated the facts so simply he surprised himself. His eyes smarted. He looked away.

'Shouldn't fuck men. It isn't normal. God's judgement.'

Tom clenched his fists and turned back to William. His patience had snapped. 'What's your excuse then, you little shit? Got a different strain to the rest of us, have you? Specially developed for the average fuckabout man in the street?'

'I'm not a poof.'

'No. What are you?' Tom stood, pushing back his chair so violently it fell over, and walked rapidly away.

He stopped at the door and spoke to the nurse. 'He's hardly worth the effort. I'll not visit again. Dave may be in a coma but at least he's human!'

William watched him leave, a cold, bitter rage blurring his vision. In the space of an hour he had discharged himself. His Porsche sat in the garage unheeded, as he unlocked the front door of Number Thirteen Upstart Quay. His legs felt weak. He went straight to bed and slept.

He woke the following morning with a strange emptiness burning inside him. He phoned an order to the grocery store, then cursed the delivery boy for keeping him waiting when he finally arrived with the food. The food did nothing to ease the emptiness. He drank half a bottle of whisky and slept on the sofa.

When he woke, it was night. He had no idea of the time. In his hurry to leave the ward he had left his watch behind. The alarm clock was flashing. He turned on the radio, forced himself to endure half an hour of the music he had enjoyed so much before, noted the time, then turned it off again.

'I'm not a poof.' he had said to Tom. Now Tom's reply refused to leave him. *What* was *he*?

Property speculator. Previously dealing with stocks and shares. Fuckabout. The lying son of discarded parents. It had never bothered him before. Life's for living, get what you can, while you can. He had made more money in single transactions on the stock exchange than many people earned in a year . . . but of what value was the knowledge to him now? Sharing magnums of champagne with colleagues had then been an almost everyday routine, but now the memory seemed insubstantial, the luxury never fully appreciated. It had always been a kind of game: he was beginning to recognise it as a game he could no longer play.

People had been like instruments – insignificant units to be traded, wholesale, in consolidations, mergers and the like. Companies fail all the time. Stay sharp and you'll manage to find profit from their loss, one way or another. The people whose lives he had ruined were not standing behind his computer: they didn't exist. But even if they had stood before him he would have felt nothing. William was convinced that the economic world was divided unequally in two. There were Winners like William, then there were people like his brother, Posthumous Peter. Wily Williams and Peter Pathetics. The Williams won, were bound to win, would always win. The Peters pattered predictably behind, and lost. They prayed and were preyed upon. They were duped, misled, manipulated and, according to the whims of the Williams of this world, they were dumped. Well more fool them.

William was beginning to doubt his sanity.

Unshaven, in dirty jeans and cardigan, he sat in a corner of the room and watched, uncharacteristically, a film about Christ. When the actor playing Jesus turned finally to the camera, looked straight at him and said: 'I am always with you,' William cried out in pain.

'Sell all your possessions and come with me!' the Man had said. In two days' frantic telephone activity William arranged for the sale of everything but the apartment. He sold the Porsche to a local car dealer who specialised in selling only top quality cars, and whose plush city showroom, with its deep pile carpeting and discreet sales staff, seemed more like the foyer to a grand hotel. A local estate agent, Grabbit & Run, ably assisted by a solicitor whose name was Mudd, agreed to deal with the sale of his accumulated property.

The sense of release felt good to William, like the start of Salvation. He donated some of his money to a nearby church for their roof appeal, sent a substantial amount to his parents, and divided the rest amongst the charities listed in the Yellow Pages.

If his life thus far had been 'soulless' (William knew the word but didn't quite understand), he had been reliably informed through the television screen that he could be saved . . . saved in the sense that, post-expiration, he might earn his ticket to heaven rather than a trip on the down-escalator.

William thought more and more of Peter, his brother. Peter had probably flown straight up to heaven the
moment he hit the concrete. William, it seemed, would
have to buy his way in.

Atonement meant saying you're sorry, didn't it? Well,
he'd said sorry: rather like a naughty boy who wasn't
allowed to leave the table until he had apologised.

Letters of delighted thanks flowed in from the various
charities. He shook with excitement as he read them . . .
surely, when Jesus came to write the Final Report, these
gold stars would influence him in William's favour? And
the church had promised to scratch his name on a few
of the new roof tiles . . . a kind of immortality.

Oddly enough, these good deeds failed to stop the
purple lesions from spreading. Nor did he find that 'inner
peace' for which he craved. He ached inside; felt lost,
empty, powerless. He read and reread the letters until
the words lost their meaning . . .

He decided one morning that giving up his possessions
was not enough. Perhaps he still had to prove himself?

He would go to church.

He arrived to find the doors locked against him. He
couldn't believe it. He had given them money and yet the
doors were locked! He tried again: lifted the heavy brass
handles and pushed. Locked. He leaned back against the
grey stone walls of the porch and wept in frustration. He
thought he had bought his way in. But they hadn't issued
him with a key.

Refused admittance. It began to rain.

For two hours he waited in the damp, cold porch,
hoping someone would come. Nobody came. He lifted
his wrist to check the time and suddenly remembered
where he had left his watch. The thought cheered him.
In the hospital people had spoken to him – even Tom.

Tom. William wondered if Tom's lover was still
alive. Strange how the thought gripped him. Strange,
the realisation that he actually cared about Tom's feelings. Strange, this tightness in his chest . . . perhaps the
cold. He coughed; a dry, brittle cough. He would visit
the hospital, collect his watch and ask about Tom.

The dirty double-decker lumbered to the bus stop.

William entered, dropped a pound coin in the slot, took his ticket and looked for the change machine.

'Move on, mate, there's a queue behind you!' the bus driver shouted.

'But where's my change? It can't cost a pound!'

'No change given – can't you read the signs?'

William walked, slightly embarrassed, to the back of the bus and sat down. The lower deck was crammed full of passengers – those behind William climbed the stairs. He was caught in an inadequate space between a schoolboy picking his nose and a woman with a shopping bag on her lap. Crammed together, not speaking, in a stuffy rumbling machine that crawled from stop to stop. The windows were opaque with steam: outside the rain continued unabated. He had no choice but to look at the other passengers. To left and right, some sniffing, some mumbling . . .

The schoolboy stopped picking his nose and turned his full attention to William. William tried to ignore him, but felt the blood rise to his cheeks in embarrassment as the boy continued to stare. He didn't dare say anything: this was Life, after all, in the raw. Real people . . . probably just itching to beat him up if he complained.

Stop after stop the bus rumbled onwards. Some left, others entered. Frank Watkins sat close to the exit, ripping his ticket into shreds. He seemed anxious and preoccupied, leaving quickly when the bus reached the railway station. Two women were chatting quietly in German. A young man in leathers and black make-up, his hair cut mohican-style, was being teased by a couple of schoolgirls on the seat behind him. A black woman stood, walked to the exit and pressed the bell. An old man in a beige raincoat stood and shuffled towards her. The driver braked suddenly and the old man, arms in the air, began to fall backwards.

It seemed to William to happen in slow motion. The man was falling slowly; listing backwards with an expression on his face of utter helplessness – it was like a dream . . . to left and right, all colours, all ages – punks and old ladies and young shabby men; women with children looking on – all suddenly reaching out, left and right, leaning into the aisle with hands ready to catch him. They caught him. The old man came to rest gently on the floor of the aisle. In seconds half a dozen passengers were helping him to his feet. The black woman brushed down the back of the old man's raincoat.

'Bleddy buses!' she complained. 'Never a thought for the old 'uns!'

The bus stopped; the driver left his cab and came up the aisle.

'What's up? You all right, mate?'

'No bleddy thanks to you!' the woman shouted. 'Stopping like that. You should be ashamed!'

'I couldn't help it! A car come out ... anyway, is he all right? That's the main thing.'

'Seems to be ... Come on, soldier, we'll help you off ... '

And so the old man was escorted to the exit by a posse of concerned passengers, helped down the steps and deposited safely on the pavement.

The passengers rubbed the steam from the windows to wave at the old man, who had been met by his daughter. 'Come on, Dad, I've just mashed. Are you hurt?' The couple walked towards the open garden gate a few yards from the bus stop. William failed to see this. 'He'll be alright,' one of the passengers said, reassured to see the old man's daughter take his arm.

Throughout the bus, dotted with complaints about bad drivers and public transport, the same phrase repeated itself again and again. He was alright: that was the main thing. A brief flurry of activity, short, flushed conversations followed by the same reassurance, then lapsing into silence once again. William – who hadn't reached out – stared uncomfortably at the ceiling, surprised and thoughtful.

At the hospital the clerk at the enquiries desk wasn't helpful.

'No. No property left under your name, mate.'

'But it had my initials on the back ... !'

The clerk tucked the pen behind his ear, sighed and began again.

'Look, mate, it might well have your initials on the

back. It could have your photograph hanging off it –
it makes no odds. I've got a list of all the unclaimed
property and your name ain't on it, and if your name
ain't 'ere we've got nothing for you.'

'Maybe it's on the ward . . . can I just . . . ?'

The clerk stood as if preparing to grab him. 'No you
can't! And anyway, if it was left on the ward I'd 'ave it,
and I 'aven't got it . . . '

His enquiries about Tom proved equally fruitless, as
William had no recollection of his surname, or his lover's
name. He left the hospital, stood outside the doors and
wondered what to do next. He couldn't bear the thought
of going home . . . he coughed again. His chest hurt,
but the pain was nothing compared to the emptiness
that awaited him in Upstart Quay. He felt compelled to
do something.

He decided to visit the Porsche. At least it gave
him a purpose. He walked down the hill and through
the Market Square.

A kind of desolation seemed to be overtaking him:
something dark and aching deep inside. He walked
quickly through the Market Square, not noticing the
group of vagrants until one stopped him.

'Got a light, mate?'

'Piss off!'

He walked on, then stopped. His brother . . . The
vagrant rubbed his ear as though stung, shrugged, then
forgetting the first exchange, walked once more to the
young man.

'Got a light, mate?'

This time William didn't abuse him. He looked instead
at the man's eyes. Dirty, clouded – but kind eyes, surely?
His brother had always seen kindness in other people.
Kindheartedness and honesty had led him to train in
social work, and to the flats where he fell – was pushed
– to his death following just such a request as the one
William had received here, in the square, on this miserable, despairing afternoon.

'Got a light, mate? Few fags? Few bob for a bite to eat?'

William struggled. His brother had died in response,
but William already felt dead – why not pursue the matter?

Why not delve a little in the Real World? What did he have
to lose?

He thought of the people on the bus. 'If I fell, would
you help me up?'

The man staggered a little, looking perplexed. 'Eh?'

'I said ... Oh, never mind. Look – if I give you
money, will you eat with it?'

'I'm starvin' mate! See them over there?' He waved
his arm loosely in the direction of his companions.
'They'd spend it on drink, but me, I don't touch the
stuff!'

William looked again. The man had a bottle of cider
tucked just inside his overcoat.

'I'll buy you a meal. Where do you go?'

'Eh? Oh – aye ... right. C'mon.' The old man took
William by the arm and half-dragged him away, ignoring
the shouts from the others in the square.

Strange to be walking with this man. The vagrant
continued to grip William's arm. His clothes stank of
urine. Just behind his left ear, William noticed, were
specks of dried blood – probably from a fall. He struggled
to contain his disgust. But this was contact, after all. A
real situation. Like the people on the bus – real people.

It wasn't far. Past a large department store, down a
side street that led between a bus station and a disused
railway cutting ... What was that sign on the wall?

He didn't have time to look. The man dragged him on.
Round a corner, over the road and there it was: a small,
steaming, peeling café. Outside the door a drunk lolled
on the pavement, carefully stepped over by the passers-
by. The place seemed to ooze wretchedness to William,
as he followed the man inside.

Steam, overpowering heat and the stench of boiling
bones made him gasp as he entered. He looked through
the haze for his companion: found him seated on a
bar stool, elbows leaning on a narrow counter under
the window, looking at him with a side-smile of eager
expectancy ... Well, he'd come this far ... William
walked to the serving-hatch. Waiting for the assistant to
appear at the hatch, he thought of the direction they'd
come ... conveniently, if his geography was correct,

the car showroom would be only a couple of streets away.

A pinched, agitated face bobbed up through the steam at the serving hatch.

'What'ya want?'

William jumped in surprise.

'Oh!'

'I said what'ya want? Haven't got all day!'

'Oh, right – sorry.' He glanced at the chalked-up menu. 'Two teas, two bacon rolls please.'

The stricken face disappeared in a sea of steam, leaving William to wonder if he'd been dreaming. Then, just as suddenly it reappeared.

'Marge on yer cobs?'

'Agh! What? Sorry?'

'I said, d'you want marge on yer cobs?' An arm, stained and hairy, with a tattooed fish on the back, thrust a bread roll through the hatch, waving it about. William jumped back in alarm, but made the connection.

'Oh I see!' said William. 'No – um – yes, why not?' He smiled at the arm as it withdrew.

Through the steam two hands appeared, pushing two chipped mugs full of brown liquid towards William.

'One pound fifty. Help yerself to sugar. I'll call yer fer the cobs.'

William took the teas and looked for the sugar. It lay in a chipped white bowl on a rickety table to his left – the white granules interspersed with globules of brown. The teaspoons sat in a small dirty glass of water . . . removing one, he broke the film that lay on the water, and gingerly he returned it. He'd go without. His companion could help himself.

They sat side by side on the stools, staring out of the window. The man didn't speak to William. It was raining again. William closed his eyes, then opened them quickly, preferring the squalor around him to the vacuum within.

Not all of them were drunks, William noticed, although at first glance they appeared to be. In the far corner a woman, dressed in a brown raincoat and wellingtons, was chattering incoherently to no one in particular, waving her arms now and then in a burst of anger, then

subsiding to a whisper, then shouting obscenities, then
subsiding . . . No one sat with her. A broad, bearded man
in a flat cap stood, then sat, then stood again . . . unrolled
a paper from his pocket, put it back in his pocket, took
it out again, looked at it, rolled it up and repeated the
sequence. Another woman was sleeping, her head on a
table, resting on a Tesco's carrier bag. A young man in
a dirty paisley shirt – William didn't notice a coat, was
poking ash in the ashtray with a nubb-end. Steam billowed
from the serving-hatch and floated in clouds to the dirty
ceiling. William turned to his companion, who ignored
him. He couldn't stand it. He got up and touched the
man's arm. 'You have my – my cob. I'm going.' He
left.

Rain: insistent, cold, soaking his hair. He splashed
through the puddles – the traffic loud, close, dirty.

At the showroom he stopped and looked in. The
Porsche sat in a position of prominence, in the centre of
the window display. Two thousand pounds more than he
had sold it for. He didn't care. Red – bright red, shining,
chrome glistening . . . He couldn't remember the last time
he'd driven it. So much had happened – he'd had it taken
away, didn't even want to say goodbye – and here it was:
so bright! So alive!

The rain trickled down the back of his neck. He walked
on, through streets he had never noticed before, where
harassed women checked their purses for the money
they'd need to buy groceries, where the shops were
dilapidated, houses were boarded up, men stood in small,
defeated bundles outside Job Centres or in queues outside
dole offices, where the sky itself seemed to press down in
unmitigated misery, trapping those below in a kind of pit
of despair. Places where the sun never seemed to shine.
He walked on, distracted, dislocated, directionless into
the heart of despair, not seeing.

The rain had stopped. It was getting dark.

He came to a wall backing on to the railway station.
He was crying now: the tears refused to stop. He sat
down on the wall in a spot shaded from the glare of the
street lamps, and tried to compose himself. He noticed
the sky. It was dark now, and the clouds were much

smaller, scudding across a bright, round moon. For the first time in his life he concentrated fully on the moon. It was full, and rising high above the rooftops, casting a strange white luminosity upon the wet pavements. She had such a sad face . . .

She was howling. William felt the sound beneath his feet – a deep, resonant thunderous roar . . . But no, it was a train arriving at the station. The sound would drive him mad – but no, it was just a train arriving . . . Then Tom walked past.

'Tom?' William called, hopefully.

Tom stopped and turned. 'Oh, it's you.'

Foolishly grateful to see a familiar face, William stuttered: 'I've been sitting here, and oh, it's good to see you, Tom. How's . . . ?'

Tom didn't let him finish. 'He died, William.'

'Oh . . . I'm sorry. I'm sorry for the things I said.'

'You didn't know any better.'

William didn't want him to leave. 'Tom, I . . . ' then he stopped.

Tom, looking up the road, muttered, 'I have to be going.'

'Do you live round here?'

'No. I help at the Night Shelter.'

'Where's that?'

'It's just there.' Tom pointed to a tall gaunt building a little further up the road.

'What do you do?'

'I make the soup. They like my soup.'

'Who's they?'

'The down and outs. The single homeless. The ex-hospital patients, wandering the streets.'

'Oh. I've seen some.'

'I'm surprised you even noticed them, William. Look, I'm sorry, I have to go.' Tom walked away.

Just like that. This was not a good day for William. Not a good day. He held his arms across his chest and began to rock . . .

But the moon was creeping up on him. She rose above the Night Shelter and little by little, crept along the wall towards him. She caught his foot, then his hand, then one leg, then his face as he turned, hearing a shout from the empty street.

Guilt. Not the guilt of the naughty child, but guilt of the human, of the neighbour. A little of the understanding of the neighbour. He heard a shout. She caught his face. He heard a shout. He looked.

In the distance a train was approaching. It was cold that night, particularly cold. He had lifted his face to the sound.

'Ow! Hell! This bloody thing!'

A little further down the path stood a man leaning against a wall, one foot in the air, pulling at the sole of his shoe. Seemed to be trying to put it back together. Having little success. He returned his foot to the pavement, tried to walk, stumbled and fell once more against the wall.

She had him all, now. Caught in her light. His unshaved face, his designer mackintosh, his curious eyes . . . He called. 'What's up?' He stood, walked to the man.

'What's up?'

'This damn foot. This bloody hole, here. It's sore! Bloody rotten shoes! Look at em, look at em! They don't give me money for new 'uns! Swine!'

'Where are you going?'

'Just down there – the Shelter there.'

'Want a hand?'

William put an arm around the man's waist, supporting him. The old man hobbled forward gratefully, his arm over William's shoulders.

The train was rumbling into the station. The moon caught them both, casting long shadows back along the path. It was cold that night; very cold. But the moon had them.

They walked into her arms.

Escape

'I think you should keep a very close eye on Joan,' Gail said.

Christine squinted through the office window. 'Who's there with her now?'

'Jasmine. But Delia's been specialling her for most of the morning. She was called to Six's half an hour ago.'

'Trouble?'

Gail rubbed her arm tiredly. 'Trouble everywhere, and no staff to cover.'

'Hells bells!' snapped Christine. 'My head's pounding. I didn't hear you leave this morning . . . ?'

'You were dead to the world.' Gail smiled, then caught herself: 'I . . . Do you remember Jack – Celie's husband?'

'I never met him, but you've spoken about him.'

'He's dead.'

'Oh Christ! Oh, I'm so sorry, Gail . . . Last night . . . ?'

'Albert came over to tell me. He sort of attacked me . . . It wasn't that. It was just the shock of it.'

'What happened?'

'I can't tell you now. I need to visit Celie, but no one's answering the phone. Most likely she's with Jack's parents. I'll stay on until Valerie and Julie get back from the student's meeting . . . '

'You shouldn't have let them go . . . '

'I'd no choice! The senior nursing officer's speaking to them, about what happens when the hospital closes.

197

He *insisted* that every teaching ward sends at least two learners.'

'Charming.'

'Yeah, well . . . Ours not to reason why . . . Mary Hollis should be here soon. You'll have your hands full. I'll stay until . . . '

Gail had just passed the ward keys to Christine when the rumble of footsteps and a muffled screaming, growing louder, could be heard from the corridor outside. Jasmine tapped on the office window and pointed towards the noise. Christine shouted to her: 'Stay in the dayroom Jas – we're going!'

The young nurse retreated to her post as Gail opened the office door and the two staff nurses hurried out. Christine was first on the ward corridor and turned to Gail: 'Call the duty doctor!'

First in the procession came a nurse wrapped in a cape, her paper cap hanging by a resolute grip from the side of her head. She almost ran to Christine and handed her the notes.

'Mary Hollis – from Casualty – she's been terrible in the ambulance!'

Behind her followed two ambulancemen, and between them a stretcher bearing a small, shrieking bundle of sheets and flesh; arms waving in the air, legs kicking the sheets away. Jasmine couldn't help but look – the noise was deafening. A woman, returning from the kitchen with a cup of tea, whispered loudly to the student nurse: 'She smells of something – it's horrible!'

'Paraldehyde,' said Jasmine. 'We were warned that she'd been violent in Casualty, but they said she'd be sedated . . . not like this!'

Jasmine checked the dayroom once again. Joan was standing – leaning against the wall beside the dormitory door, but the other patients were talking amongst themselves. Joan's position, and the fact that she was standing, should have set warning bells ringing in Jasmine's mind, but the ward corridor sounded like bedlam . . . Mary let out a piercing scream and Jasmine turned to see one of the ambulancemen doubling up beside the stretcher, grunting with pain. Mary's naked leg was thrashing the air wildly, her foot seeking another point of impact. Christine ran to wrestle with the offending limb while Gail moved the ambulanceman away. When Jasmine returned to her observation of the dayroom Joan had gone. In the distance she heard the unmistakable sound of the dormitory door closing. She blanched, stood, and moved rapidly to the gathered knot of uniforms.

'Staff? Staff – Joan's just gone . . . I heard her . . . shall I go?'

Christine looked at Gail. Gail cursed then whispered: 'I'll go, Christine. Call the central nursing office!'

She dashed into the office, through the office door into the dormitory, sprinted past the beds and out through the fire exit at the far end. Took the stairs three at a time, through another door and out into the grounds.

Gail unbuckled her belt and laid it carefully across the bed, unbuttoned the top button of her pale blue dress and collapsed, exhaustedly, into an armchair. Christine stood at the window, hands deep in pockets, watching a hospital bus warily negotiating the ramps on the perimeter road. They were silent for some minutes, until Christine spoke: 'You couldn't have done anything, you know.'

'That's what they're all saying. It doesn't make it any easier.'

'Where will you go?'

'To the coast – somewhere quiet. I just want to be quiet.'

'Give yourself time, you'll see things differently.'

'I don't know. Maybe . . . I feel as though I've seen too much . . . '

Shh.

The doctor says how are you, Joan? and she says normal, doctor, normal. She doesn't mention the hand, as she knows it appears to be there. I'm very normal, sir. Extraordinarily. More normal than anyone I know.

(The hand went scuttling off on Tuesday, as she tried to write a letter. First came the heavy black lines down the centre of the page, then across and growing frantic then up into the air, yanking pulling wrenching itself free. No blood, but many nerves exposed wriggling thrashing.)

I can't find it, doctor. Shh don't tell. I'm awfully well.
Tick tick tick
Shh now, shh.

' ... Here I am and here I'll stay. Out of reach, with sand and salt water. Beyond pain. They say there's nothing here. Sometimes nothing can mean everything. I shall go to the shore, watch the waves ... '

High windows. Painted storms upon the walls. Ripped wall-paper. Tables, chairs, withered plants. Dirty windows. Dormitories smelling of polish sometimes, sometimes other things.

'Scald the cups before you mash!' Steaming geysers. Heavy afternoons. Rattle of trolleys – food, drugs, food, drugs ...

Small room. Next door muffled voices, a bed shakes. Magazines on the table. 'Have you emptied your bladder? You'd better let me have your watch and earrings, I'll give you them back the moment you wake.' 'I'm just going to give you a little injection and I want you to count backwards ... have a nice sleep and when you wake it'll be over.' Ten nine (I don't ...

She's going, slurred second, gone. Fingers twitch slightly. Mouthpiece ... Ambu bag, two inflations. Quick rub at the temples, ready – ready ...

Wheeled to Recovery, observed while unconscious; begins to wake, spits out mouthpiece. 'Hello Joan? Joan, can you hear me? It's over – you've had it. Would you like a nice cup of tea?' Final room. Tea gets spilt. Patients wander, confused, disorientated. 'Wait a couple more minutes then I'll take you back.' Red eyes, blank faces ...

Dirty windows. Occupational Therapy, Industrial Therapy, more dirty windows. No one sees clearly here. The ward stinks of stale cigarettes. I'm cold.

' ... I dreamt that I held her head in my hands; thumb brushing back the streaks of sweated hair from her face. A round face. Gentle – a gentle face ... I sit on the beach for hours. Sometimes it rains: I don't feel the rain. The waves roll in; I will them to break.

... I dreamt that I saw her and she wouldn't look at me. I spoke to her, and her face was a darkness. The waves swell and roll, swell and roll ... '

They wheeled Mary in on a stretcher. She's so small ... strong as an ox, so they say. They're busy. I have my strength and my shoes. I'm going.

Down the stairs how my heart's beating keep on heart keep on. This door. How long before they notice? KEEP TO THE WALL duck beneath the windows. The trick is to think how they think you can do that. Down DOWN – watch the cars – she's got a cape on – they're out they're after me. Oh legs run for me if ever I needed you I need you now . . .

Bang bang bang over the lawns bang bang bang off the road – keep to the back of the houses – cars cars – oh Jesus get me there get me there don't let them stop me . . .

WAIT. The car's turning. They think the village – so exposed here – bang bang bang – easier downhill – someone's shouting – don't stop – my name – don't stop nearly bang bang nearly.

Wait wait come lorry come fast as you can over the hill come now come see she's running come before she tries to catch me don't let anyone be hurt through me Lord but let me go please let me go . . . Lorry lorry stop shouting nursie time it TIME IT lorry lorry NOW NOW NOW

'I can't reach her. I can't, I can't . . . JOAN, NO, NO . . . '

The sky that day was a vivid blue, and on the horizon layer upon layer of variations; turquoise, pastel – almost pink – blue, dull, misted blue and then the dark, burdened blue of the sea. It was a rare day; beginning with the sunrise blinding her eyes and then later, the vast empty stretches of beach, the light cool breeze, the wide pools of water left by the ebbing tide and vast, firm areas of sand up to the sea's edge.

It was a dream.

Mid-morning, Gail sheltered from the chill of the wind behind a temporarily redundant breakwater and basked, eyes closed, in the heat of the sun. In the distance to her left the sea broke gently, hushed but resonant. To her right, no more than ten yards away, the reeds beyond the dunes whispered their marshy secrets.

So perfect – so few people. Even her mind felt rendered silent by the sonorous beauty of it all, stilled by the sun's relentless heat. Later she walked calmly along the shore.

Further up the coast, she drank tea in an empty

restaurant, trying to switch off the harsh insistence of fruit machines and video games. Few people visited; the shopkeepers had one or two days left before the whole of the east coast closed for the winter. The sense of ending, of closing up, carried a strange irony for her now, and home . . . was just one day away.

The walk back became more and more difficult as the tide crept inward, forcing her further up the beach and finally, after labouring a while through the soft sand, away from the beach altogether and on to the road that passes the marshes. Then, slowly and regretfully, she wandered back towards the village. The sky changed from gold to russet to deeper gold; the setting sun caught as silhouettes the scattered trees in the fields. Away from the sea the breeze had diminished, and the sun's last rays comforted the road beneath her feet. By the time she crossed the bridge over the dyke the horizon had become pastel – misted once again. The faded russet sun dipped its head beyond her vision. She stood at a lamp-post and studied what she could, in the rapidly fading light, of the bus timetable.

She opened her eyes. Rose leaned slightly towards her. 'You'd have stayed?'

'If I could, I'd have stayed.'

'What brought you back?'

'Practical things. I resigned from work that day – in my mind, at least. I had to move out, find somewhere else to live . . . lots of things. And Celie most of all. She must have been so . . . there aren't words, really. I came back to find her.

'I stayed up all that night. I wanted so badly to keep the memory of something nice. I watched the dawn break from a darkened room and through an open window. Below the window the dunes rose, and fell towards the ocean. It was cold. I shivered, wrapped the blanket around me a little more tightly, drew my feet up to keep them warm. It was like the most precious moment of my life – I tried to draw every drop of nourishment from it. My soul seemed to expand in the silence. I felt naked, alone and very still inside . . . '

'What did you see?'

'A confusion of people. The people were dressed in pain. I wanted no part of it any more. Then I thought that, without that confusion, all that there is, is me. And when I'm not, nothing is.'

She closed her eyes again. Rose studied her intently. 'Is it safe to be so alone?'

'Not safe – it's just easier.'

'How do you feel now?'

'Alive,' Gail whispered. Outside, the bulldozers and cranes moved in on the old hospital church. They were breaking God down on Otherville Road.

The Full Price

The following week Gail paced the room. 'I've been lucky. Luckier than most. Usually you take what the State offers, as you're in no condition to refuse. So you don't get offered much. But if you're articulate however, well educated ... If you or your family's important, you're treated with greater respect. I think it's almost a subconscious process: somewhere there's a line that delineates the treatment you receive. Mrs Smith – married with kids, depressed – is treated with drugs, ECT – electric shock treatment. Her progress is monitored on a graduated scale: is she eating? Is she talking? Has she finished her cane tray at occupational therapy yet? Is she socialising? Is she well enough to go home for the weekend?

'Mrs Smith's depression is almost a physical condition: the stages of her recovery are monitored by answers to practical questions. When she smiles, chats, enjoys her weekend at home – when her tray's completed, she's pronounced "better" and discharged. People like Mrs Smith account for a large percentage of the short-stay psychiatric hospital population. And within a year she'll be back. A year after that she'll be back again. Sooner or later she'll be redefined as a "readmission" – no longer acute, bordering on long stay. Does she challenge her treatment? Of course not! Who else can she trust but the psychiatrist? She must *need* ECT every year, that's all. She was taught by her parents as a child that people who sit behind desks always know best. She wouldn't know how to argue. Apart from that, she has a bitch of a time outside hospital anyway. All her neighbours think she's mad because she's been in "the loony bin", so she's no one to talk to – *really* talk to, apart from her doctor, who doesn't talk much anyway. Be grateful for what you're given, she thinks. You're lucky to be given anything. She offers up the cup of her suffering, the nurse passes it on and the psychiatrist/God examines, diagnoses and disposes of it with the stroke of a medicinal pen. And you know, Rose – you *must* know – that when the cup is offered, it cannot easily be retrieved. She trusts the State, rests her head upon the breast of the Health Service, and in return is given piss-poor treatment and a life sentence of hospital admissions and represcriptions. I think Joan knew that. She'd been in hospital before – she knew the routine, she felt the decline, she knew the way her life was heading and she opted out.'

'Joan was Mrs Smith?'

Gail sat down. 'Joan was many people.'

She considered this for a moment, then began again: 'But – *but* – should Mrs Smith be a magistrate or civic dignitary: should she have a degree in economics or a husband who insists on receiving regular reports of his wife's condition, then something quite dramatic happens. She is no longer "the woman with depression", but "the very intelligent woman who appears to be going through a crisis". Suddenly psychiatrists, doctors and nurses alike don their metaphorical bibs and tuckers . . . She's an "interesting case". It isn't enough just to treat her as a "regular". She reads books on the ward! She refuses to attend occupational therapy! The old Mrs Smith would be marked as a "management problem" if she refused *anything*, but in an educated woman it's a sign of spirit. Suddenly everyone starts talking about the psychodynamics of depression: citing Laing or Jung or Freud. Was she abused as a child? Has she been subjected to trauma? The old Mrs Smith *was* abused as a child – was kicked and beaten and molested by her drunken father. She had an illegal abortion at sixteen. The man she intended to marry lost a leg in the war and drowned himself in the local quarry. Her husband and children treat her like shit. Why else should she keep coming back? But no one ever wonders about her. No one ever asks.

'People talk about "going private" but there's really no need. Trust the State, do as you're told and the State fucks you up. Act as though you could run the State, then the State will bend over backwards to help you.'

'Which Mrs Smith are you?' Rose asked.

'Neither. I come from the inside. I'm counted as a part of the State. I mean, look at this . . . ' she waved her hand around the room.

'Do you think you wouldn't have been offered psycho-therapy . . . ?' Rose began.

Gail leaned forward, a zealous light in her eyes: 'Do *you?*'

Rose didn't answer. Anger, she thought. That's good.

Gail continued. It felt safe to talk to Rose – made safe by the therapist's deliberate professionalism. At times Rose seemed to 'give' a little . . . would mention, in passing, that she was taking her dog to the vet that afternoon, or apologise for being late because she'd been 'caught behind a tractor'. Later she would wonder if it wasn't all a part of Rose's skill to draw her clients in.

Sometimes, when Gail looked at the small, middle-aged woman sitting opposite her she became afraid: Rose seemed so ordinary and so vulnerable. She could sense whether Rose was having a good or bad day when they entered the room together: she found herself studying the therapist's face to find the person behind the professional, but then she would catch herself because, in truth, she didn't want to know. Once Rose arrived at a session with a bandaged knee and explained that she had fallen over. The thought of Rose falling over horrified Gail, because if Rose could fall over she could just as easily die.

Why should Rose die? Because she's a human being, a person, and people die.

That week Gail stood on the bed and checked the crack in the ceiling twice every day. By the following session the bandage had gone from Rose's leg. Perhaps she wouldn't die, after all. But Gail didn't mention it.

That would have been tempting fate. Apart from which, she didn't want to admit to Rose – or herself – that she cared about her not dying. She didn't want to admit that she cared. People that she cared about invariably died. The thought touched the place inside her that hurt the most and she recoiled from it, because it held more pain than she could cope with. In time, she comforted herself with the thought that the two of them were never really alone: behind Rose's chair she imagined a veritable army of therapists, who met together each week to discuss their clients' progress. And because they were not alone, not really, Gail felt safer. This therapy business is a lot more sophisticated than I can possibly imagine, she told herself, because the more sophisticated she could make it seem, the less she would be able to understand. The less she understood of therapy, the greater the invisible distance between herself and Rose. There's safety in distance, she told herself. So when Rose, through her bandaged knee, ceased to be superhuman, Gail made her just one of many therapists – just one part of a greater whole ... An instrument of a therapeutic process of which she, Gail, would be the beneficiary. Ultimately. She hoped.

But now she'd done it. This time she'd really done it. Because she was angry – not with Rose, but with everything she knew, and had seen, and in her anger she'd come face to face with the therapist and answered Rose's question with a challenge. She didn't know how it had happened – she'd just been angry ... she didn't even know *what* she had done – all she knew was that she really had gone and done it! She sat on the bus and frowned all the way back to her bedsit. The bus driver, an anxious little man who had no other passengers apart from Gail, assumed that she was frowning at him. The back of his neck burned from her three miles-worth of frowning. He clipped the kerb twice turning corners. He thought she'd never get off. Was it his fault that bus fares had gone up by five pence? Of course it wasn't! By the time she reached her destination the little bus driver thought he'd never recover from all her frowning. When she alighted he turned off the engine and jumped on to the path, shouting after her: 'I didn't do it! It isn't my fault!'

If she heard him, she didn't turn. But he comforted himself with the thought that she probably *had*. She hadn't heard him. She was still frowning when she entered her room. Unfortunately for the little bus driver a feisty old age pensioner – his first new passenger in three bloody miles – had been waiting at the stop when he'd shouted.

'I think it's a scandal!' the old lady muttered.

'You don't even pay!'

'But it's the principle!'

'I didn't do it!' The bus driver was exasperated now.

She wagged a finger at him. 'But I bet you pocket the difference!'

'Silly old bat!' he whispered as she hobbled down the aisle.

'I heard that!' She hobbled back up the aisle and sat directly behind him, where she frowned at him even harder than Gail had done all the way to the depot, and when they reached the depot she hobbled off in search of the inspector, who no doubt would frown at him hardest of all. He didn't deserve this! He climbed off the bus and kicked the front tyre.

He thought he might enter the Navy.

At least they don't frown at sea.

Gail fell asleep before Martha's last client had departed that night, incomprehensibly comforted by the fact that Rose had sustained her anger, and that Rose was *there*. The walls in the squashing room had squashed her a bit today, and the emotion they'd squashed out had not devastated her after all. She felt, if anything, *relieved* that it had begun.

That night she dreamt of a sea of faces: of her mother, or her grandmother, or Rose . . . much larger than life. She woke the next morning feeling like an infant who had spent the night in her mother's arms and realised, quite suddenly, that she could no longer define Rose as any one person – or anything, because Rose had become everyone and everything and she loved her quite helplessly.

She phoned in sick at Pluckett's, bought herself a pack of Polyfilla and set to work on the ceiling.

Projection, she told herself, is all a part of the therapeutic process. It had to happen sooner or later.

That evening, all the cracks in the ceiling had gone.

So she counted the stripes on the sink curtain instead.

She resolved to get the therapy over as quickly – and painlessly – as she could.

She hoped it would go on for ever.

She wished her mother was alive, or that she could be small again.

She wondered whether it might be better just to run away.

She realised what she would be running from.

'Please God,' she whispered into the darkness, 'keep Rose safe. Don't let her die.'

No Snow

'It never snowed when Santa came. And one year, fog
surrounded the little corrugated school when we gathered in the classroom and listened to him landing on the
roof. The classroom looked pretty, bedecked in home-
made pictures of the Virgin Mary and Baby Jesus, big
fat Santas with big red faces, reindeers with horns big
as the branches on a tree, and multicoloured hooves.
This must be the real Santa, I thought, as the one that
turned up at the end of our street a few days before had
been in a festive float pulled by a tractor. We'd grown
suspicious when Santa said the reindeers were resting,
ready for the Big Day, not because the reindeers were
resting – after all they had to rest – but because Santa
sounded very like Mr Merryman from the sweet shop,
who had a stutter. But there were fairy lights all over
the tractor and the float, and Santa Merryman was well
padded and sounded – bar the stutter – very Santa-ish,
so we clamoured at the foot of the float to be next on his
knee. Celie asked for a crown with real diamonds and a
fairy-wand. Celie got a box of crayons. Patrick asked if
Santa could stop his dad drinking. Patrick got a box of
crayons. Billy said it was stupid, asking for things, and
threw a stone at the tractor. Mandy organised the other
children into single file and told them not to shout so
loud. I asked Santa if he could make Mummy better and
bring her home for Christmas. I got a box of crayons. Billy
threw another stone at the tractor and got chased down

the road by the driver. Mandy got well crayoned. Then the Sally Army came and we all sang Silent Night.

'It hadn't snowed then, and it wasn't snowing now, even with Santa on the roof. We stood in rapt amazement as we heard the tinkle of the reindeer's bells. We hoped he wouldn't mind the fog, and we were glad the roof was flat, for the reindeer. Mrs Parrish, our teacher, switched off all the lights and lit the candles. Then there he was, outside the classroom door, as big and red as any of our pictures. We squealed with excitement when he entered. Funnily enough, *he* stuttered too. And the elves had made an *awful lot* of crayons that year.

'It didn't snow at all. In fact the fog stayed thick all over Christmas. It didn't feel right. Not even the lumpy stocking at the end of my bed felt right, but everything was there. I had a water pistol, a box of Smarties, a kaleidoscope, some white chocolate, a sugar mouse and a colouring book – useful for my crayons. Daddy went downstairs to fry up for breakfast – the only day in the year we ate bacon in the morning – and started on the turkey. Granny and Gramps had stayed over. Gramps lost his dentures. Granny said he should be more careful. Grampy made me laugh, pulling funny faces over the banister while Granny made the beds and Daddy cooked the breakfast. I ran excitedly round the house, except for the front room, where I couldn't go until we were all ready, because that's where the presents were. I said it must have been Santa that took Grampy's teeth. Granny called Grampy a silly old man and said if she found them she'd flush them down the toilet. Grampy pulled another face then Dad shouted that he'd put them in a cup on the kitchen window sill, so Grampy came down in his nightshirt, rinsed them under the tap then put them in awkwardly so that one of the teeth stuck out over his lower lip, and chased me round the hall.

'When we were dressed and had eaten breakfast, Daddy opened the front-room door and we all filed in. I tore through the presents – a new nightie, a toy cash register with three bob in the till, a Beano and a Topper annual, a new pair of slippers and an Etch-a-Sketch, chocolates, a box of crayons and (luckily) another colouring book. I

saved Mummy's present until last, and everybody went
quiet when I opened it. A big, soft, cuddly panda. I took
the panda in my arms and held it tight, while Daddy read
out the card to me: "To a very special little girl – his name
is Peter Panda and likes to be cuddled a lot. Be a good girl,
sweetheart, and do what your Daddy tells you. With all
my love, always, Mummy."

'Later, Granny took me upstairs with a kettle full of
boiling water, filled the sink and washed my hands and
face. The heat from the wet flannel felt comforting, and
Granny told me that when we go to see Mummy I must
be a very brave little girl because Mummy has been very
poorly and I must try very hard not to cry. We got my
best frock from out of the wardrobe – my black velvet
party frock, a clean pair of white socks and my best
shiny shoes.

'It was foggy all the way to Anydale, and when we
reached the foot of the hill it was so foggy it looked like a
cloud had fallen and covered the hospital. Mr Harris from
the factory offered Dad a lift as he said it was the least he
could do, given the circumstances. All the way there he
kept sighing and saying what a sad business it was, and
on Christmas Day of all days . . . I clutched a penny in
the palm of my hand to fend off travel-sickness, leaned
against Granny close enough to be comfy and smell her
lavender water, but upright enough not to crease my best
dress. Every time I closed my eyes Mr Harris sighed again
and went on about the sad business and I felt glad that
Granny had put Peter Panda in her handbag safe, so he
couldn't hear Mr Harris going on, because if Peter Panda
could hear Mr Harris going on I'd have to tell him to shut
up in case Peter got upset.

'We walked a long way through white tunnels, out
into a courtyard, past a pool with some goldfish and in
again on the other side. The first door was big and heavy,
with some lettering on that Daddy said was "Mummy's
Ward". Then we turned right and up some stairs that
sounded like metal and felt cold, then right again and
through another door where it felt warmer but smelt of
polish and disinfectant and I didn't like it one little bit.
Then we went down another corridor that squeaked like

rubber and a lady in a blue dress with a white hat on her head came out of the kitchen drying her hands and smiled. Daddy spoke quietly to her, she looked down at me and smiled again, then led us through another door and down a long room with squashy carpet and tables by the windows, then through a glass door into a big, big room full of easy chairs and Mummy in the corner.'

Admissions

Once, as a child, Celie had been sent to bed for eating berries. Now she wondered vaguely whether, like the child, she had again done something wrong. There was a reason for her being in bed. There had to be. Perhaps she didn't want to know.

She had been sick as a child, but this wasn't like a sickness. This was more like punishment. Only the bed felt warm, and the moment she woke she longed to rest once again. And if this was punishment, why the comforting smiles? Why the food prepared for her, and brought to her bedside? Why the quiet murmurs at the foot of her bed, that disturbed her sleep and continued as she pressed her mind back to gentle oblivion? If this was Hell, then why did she wake at times, conscious of small arms around her neck, a small, sweet-smelling head upon her chest and the gentle, shallow breathing of Cindy, her youngest child? Why was Joe, so much the image of his father, always near?

The room had changed. This wasn't her bed. Jack was ... away somewhere ... Faces she recognised came before her as images of infinite sympathy, infinite sadness during those transient breaks in unconsciousness. The doctor. Jack's parents ... and there were flowers too, in a vase close by ... pretty flowers, with names she couldn't remember, but all colours ...

Then she woke fully. Jack's mother helped her to the

toilet. Fragments of what had happened crept towards her . . .

She heard herself screaming. Her cheeks felt wet. She was standing in a corner of the room. The doctor and Jack's father were advancing towards her, she was lashing out, someone was speaking calmly . . . Strong arms took hold – she was on the bed – she felt a needle – oblivion.

When they took her away Celie was mad, and madder still when they admitted her. The soft comfort of sleep had passed, replaced by a terrible rawness; an abrasive torment, an overwhelming agony of grief, guilt, horror and consuming anger. Who could she kill? Someone should be killed. She needed to kill. She chose herself.

With extreme difficulty but infinite care and tenderness, the nursing staff prevented her.

When Gail first climbed the hill to the nurses' home at Anydale, all that she had with her were a case full of clothes and a small nurse's dictionary. When she moved out of the nurses' home to The Terraces, she had accumulated a shelf of textbooks, some popular fiction, a black-and-white portable television, a kettle and a mug. When she returned after the separation, she returned with the same – everything else was sold with the house. It was therefore possible to move to her bedsit with the minimum of fuss – everything fitted into the Mini quite easily. It was done in less than an hour. Her resignation was also simple: she pushed the letter under the senior nursing officer's door when she knew he wasn't in. No fuss. She left her new address – anything else could be dealt with by post.

The mornings were bitterly cold now – quite suddenly, as though Nature had bypassed autumn and opted for winter instead. Christine helped her empty her room and load the Mini, jump-started it with her, gave her a hug and watched her drive away. There was no point in arguing any more. Christine had told her about the hostel job but Gail wasn't listening.

All the villas in the hospital grounds had closed – life was gathering towards the centre of the hospital only – the area most easily heated. The people on the admission wards were being transferred to other hospitals . . . everyone else had been shunted out, one way or another. Christine and a few other nurses spent the last few days working with those patients who were soon to become the new hostel residents . . . little George, who many years before had eaten his budgie; Joseph, who refused to get out of bed in the mornings for fear of not having a bed to return to; Jane, who had never managed to learn how to keep her colostomy clean . . . and a dozen or so others who couldn't, in all conscience, be packed off into the community *without* nursing support . . . The man with the invisible white rabbit on his arm; the man who used to wander the hospital tapping drainpipes all day; the woman who needed a constant supply of what she called 'Black Lagoon Medicine' to stop her from being raped by Beelzebub; the woman with whom Gail had actually communicated one day, as they worked in the linen room together. She was silent now. Only her eyes spoke, but they spoke in a language no one had the patience to understand. These patients were treated to a few days' extra 'rehabilitation' while everyone waited for the hostel paintwork to dry. This is a cabbage. No, it doesn't come ready cooked, we have to cut it up and cook it. But first we have to buy it . . . no, a cabbage doesn't cost five pounds – you must learn to wait for your change. No, there won't be a canteen at the hostel. Or a billiard table. Or a bowling green. Or a cricket pitch. No cinema, no musical appreciation . . . No, I don't think you'll see many of your friends again. We all have to move on. These are the light switches. Lights don't go on and off by themselves . . . always remember to switch them off when you leave the room. No, you won't be able to sit outside on the grass any more. The hostel hasn't any grass. No dormitories. No big tea pots either . . . we'll learn how to make our own tea now!

That night darkness covered the institution like a cloak. The extremities were dead, and cold. What life was left gathered at the centre in a small cluster of warmth. Even the lights in the grounds remained unlit. Johnny stumbled and fell again and again, but Johnny came home, he made it back, and settled down on the frosted ground beneath the squirrels' trees with a sigh of tired satisfaction and fell immediately asleep, content in the knowledge that he could break the bread again tomorrow, and everything would be all right.

Gail's Mini needed road tax. But first it needed an MOT. And before the MOT it needed substantial repair, so she left it outside the bedsit and had it towed away as twenty pounds' worth of scrap. She had made a modest profit on the house sale – enough to pay rent and keep her alive for a few months before she had to look for work. It was enough. The morning after she had moved her possessions to the bedsit she stood in the cold downstairs hallway and ploughed change into the phone. No answer from Celie's flat, as expected. Finally she got through to Jack's parents. The conversation was halting and subdued. Joe and Cindy were staying with their other grandparents. Celie was in hospital. Otherville, yes. Jack's father gave her the name of the ward. His wife wasn't well enough to come to the phone. They hadn't visited yet – he didn't think Celie was up to having visitors, and the way things were with Jack's mother . . . yes, he'd pass on her sympathy. With Gail being a nurse, they might let her visit – would she let them know?

Gail put down the phone and leaned her head on the wall. Then she put the remaining change in her pocket and went outside. She had forgotten her coat, but she didn't seem to feel the cold, although the paths were white with frost. She walked into town, to catch the bus to Otherville. She hoped the walk might clear her mind. She passed a café with peeling paint on the door and steamed windows . . . she looked inside – a couple of people she recognised, but not Johnny. She passed a car showroom with a bright red Porsche in the window . . . a glimmer of recognition passed through her mind and she stood there for a moment, trying to remember. How red it was – such a deep red . . .

Joan stepped out into the road without a backward glance. Horns blared, flesh smacked against metal. As the body was tossed to the kerb Gail heard screaming. The lorry demolished a lamp-post. The driver fell out of his cab clutching his head and everywhere around her was the screech of tyres as other drivers swerved to avoid the carnage. Sirens wailed . . . Pandemonium surrounded her during those endless minutes of disaster but she remained still, conscious but not feeling, cradling Joan's bruised head as the twisted and smashed body was covered in blankets and the pool of blood gathered beneath her. It was only later that she realised the screams had been her own.

Blood red, but brighter. Red like money. She'd known someone with a car like that . . . but it didn't matter – trying to remember things. She thought of Celie and, with dulled but deliberate effort, moved on. The cutting was opposite the bus station. 'YOU WILL LOSE,' the sign said. Gail had to wait for the next bus to Otherville, so she bought a paper and, rather than inhale diesel fumes, walked across the road to the cutting-wall to read the news.

The local evening paper came in two editions – morning and early afternoon. The early afternoon edition expanded the news flash that had just caught the morning edition. So it was there before her on page two: 'MAN FOUND DEAD IN HOSPITAL GROUNDS.'

It was Johnny.

Former Anydale Hospital patient Mr John Jettison, 53, was found dead in the grounds this morning by a security guard, acting for private developers . . . Mr Jettison had been discharged from hospital some time ago as part of the full-scale rehabilitation programme . . . His landlady, Mrs Nora Wadge of 'Goodtakin', Nether Road, said that Mr Jettison 'had a habit of wandering off, but often said he was happier here than at hospital. He had more freedom, you see, they all do.'

Johnny.

A spokesman for the social services said: 'Mr Jettison was not on our list. We cannot be held responsible for the actions of individuals when they are pronounced fit enough to return to the community. Had we been informed . . . but these things will happen, I'm afraid.' A spokesman for the health authority said: 'Once a

person is discharged into the community, his or her
case is transferred to the relevant department of the
social services. Unfortunately it seems that this information was somehow mislaid . . . ' A spokesman for
the hospital said: 'We are in the final stages of closure.
Most of our wards and departments are now closed,
and those that are still open are in the main hospital
building. There is no longer a reason for our staff to
walk the grounds at night. This property effectively
belongs to the developers . . . We simply don't go
that way any more . . . ' Mr Jettison was found at four
o'clock this morning at the back of Villa 14, his former
home. Death assumed to be from hypothermia . . . '

Gail dropped the paper and climbed on to the cutting-
wall. She had placed both hands beneath her on the wall
to push herself, when she was caught from behind by two
Asians who were passing and were quick-witted enough
to see what she was about to do. There was no time to
talk: they grabbed her by the arms and around the waist,
pulling her backwards and wrestling her to the ground,
where they effectively sat on her for five minutes until
the police arrived.

Policemen have strong arms and deep, kind voices. A
siren wailed. A blur of scenery outside the car windows.
They walked a long way through white tunnels, out into
a courtyard, past a pool with dead fish and in again on
the other side. The first door was big and heavy – the
stairs sounded like metal and felt cold. Then the ward
felt warm, but smelt of polish and disinfectant. Another
corridor that squeaked like rubber. A nurse joined the
police and took her hand. Through another door and
down a long room with squashy carpet and tables by
the windows, then through a glass door into a large,
smoke-filled room with easy chairs and heavy tables and
big windows and staring faces and Celie in the corner.

Patients

Something was wrong with Edna Jones.

On the first day she began to swear.

On the next day, Percy returned from work to find one of his best shoes in the oven and the entire contents of their wardrobe piled up in a disorganised heap on the kitchen table. Edna was crying. She couldn't understand why the shoe polish she had used to clean the windows made them dirtier than ever. Percy questioned her about the shoe and the clothes, but if she had a reason for her actions, it was forgotten now.

Percy put her to bed and called the doctor.

Edna was admitted to hospital for assessment.

Percy Jones sat on the settee beside his daughter and son-in-law, who had travelled from their home in Australia to be with him. His daughter gripped tightly his aged hand and questioned him gently. He gave her all of the information that the doctors at Otherville had given him. She tried hard to be strong, but tears gathered at the corners of her eyes as her father struggled with words he had never before encountered, but must now come to terms with as they described the condition of her mother – his wife. Her husband, sitting at the end of the settee, looked away in deference to the old man's grief.

'It was a stroke they said. They called it "dementia" – what they mean is senility, I think. You know your mother is a few years older than me? They say at her age it's difficult to be optimistic about her chances of recovery.

She's like a child – they call it "regressive behaviour". She can remember things that happened years ago, but not things that happened ten minutes ago. And she gets so confused – even about the past. She can remember our wedding – thirty years ago – down to the colour of the dresses the bridesmaids wore . . . then she looks at me and calls me "Sonny". She thinks I'm her brother, but he died fifteen years ago. Then she talks about her mother as though she's a child again. Your Gran has been dead for thirty years. It was when she started swearing that I knew something was wrong . . . she never used to swear. And sometimes she gets violent – can you believe that of your own mother? And . . . '

Percy frowns as he passes the information to his daughter. He tells her the same things time and again. Patiently she listens. It's as though he's trying to understand it himself. She cannot believe that the woman he describes is her mother. Only two months ago she was talking to her mum on the phone and she sounded fine . . . Next year her parents had planned to join them in Australia for a couple of months . . . maybe even to stay permanently, the daughter had hoped. But now . . . this.

Percy takes time in their bedroom, folding Edna's clean underwear and placing it lovingly in a small suitcase. Thermal vests and knickerbockers, stockings . . . All washed by Percy despite the many offers he'd received. She would hate the thought of someone else handling her personal clothes, if she could understand what was happening . . . The clothes were warm, well aired and soft to the touch. Percy washed them thoroughly with half a packet of Dreft, then rinsed them several times before drying them on the old clothes-horse in front of the fire. He found their fresh smell very comforting in the long lonely evenings. Sometimes he could almost imagine her there with him. She'd had that clothes-horse ever since they were married. It had been a wedding present, he seemed to remember . . . How many tons of laundry had she draped over those bars? And still standing, after all these years. It had a solid feel; the wooden bars were smooth with use . . . like the wardrobe upstairs, it had endured. Things don't last the same these days.

From the dressing-table he takes a tin of her favourite talcum powder and nestles it amongst the clean laundry. He bought it for her yesterday. She likes . . . she always liked to smell nice. Large tears that he never lets fall distort his vision; he retrieves the talcum powder and holds it to his breast, rocking a little as he whispers gently: 'This is for you, my pretty lady. My love, this is for you . . . '

His daughter calls him from the foot of the stairs. It's late, she says, they should make a move . . . He finishes packing the case and wearily descends the stairs.

How small he is. He seems to have shrunk, grown old with pain. She notices how meticulously groomed he is, how smart. Does he dress like this every time he visits the hospital? She fights to contain a low moan of pity.

Her husband drives them to the hospital. She sits in the back with her father, who clutches the suitcase to his chest and says nothing. They walk through the car park to the main entrance, and follow the old man as he slowly navigates the long corridors and, turning sharp left, leads them up two flights of stairs to her mother's ward. Her husband has his arm around her: she feels eager to see her mother, but also terribly afraid. Her father pushes open the heavy doors and enters the ward.

Edna Jones is calling to a pigeon through the window.

'Coo coo, coo coo . . . ' whispers Edna. The pigeon sits on a stone ledge outside the window, cocking its head to listen. Then a voice breaks the spell and the pigeon, startled, flies away.

'Edna?'

Edna touches the window, flattening her palm against the pane at the point where, a moment ago, the bird had been. But the glass is cold, and the pretty thing has passed away. She frowns, then tuts quietly. 'It's gone,' she whispers.

'Edna?' The voice again. She turns away from the window. Before her stands a man . . . is it her brother?

'Sonny!' she cries, hugging him.

'No pet, it's Percy . . . '

The old man's heart stirs to feel his wife in his arms and, for a moment, is tempted to keep her there. But his daughter's anxious face forces him to say something. 'Edna love ... Come on, let go ... Sweetheart, look who's come to see you!'

Edna turns from her husband to face her daughter. Percy notices a dark patch on the back of her dress. She's wet again. Edna frowns in concentration over the young woman's face. Her daughter beams with love, her face glistening with tears.

Edna almost smiles, then frowns again. 'Who are you?' she asks politely.

Further down the corridor, the Ward Sister steps quietly in through the half-open side-room door, to check on Gail. 'Has she stirred?'

The nurse sitting on a hard-backed chair beside the bed looks up. 'No. She opens her eyes now and then, but she hasn't moved a muscle all the time I've been here.'

'I'll get you a relief soon. Dr Fawcett thinks Celie should be okay sitting in the dayroom now, so long as there's someone in the room with her. She's very strong willed, that woman. She was talking about her kids to me earlier. I think the doctor's right about her.'

The nurse looked at Gail. She lay on her back, absolutely still. 'What do you think ... ?'

'Did you know I trained under her?'

'Who? Gail?'

'She was the first person who ever managed to teach me the difference between organic and functional psychoses. It was like she conjured up a chart in my mind, with all the different headings and types, and then she brought all the words to life with examples. Then she said, "So long as you keep the chart in your head you'll have a compass. It won't show you where to go, or how to get there – people are much more complicated than that. But when someone asks you, you'll know which way's north and which is west at least!" I've never forgotten it. It got me through one of the exam questions!'

'Did it? Will you tell me?'

'I'll try, but you never know – she might teach you it herself one day.'

'Do you think she'll try again?'

The Sister frowned. 'I don't know. My guess is she's going to keep trying until she succeeds. You saw the fight we had with her. All we can do is keep her sedated, watch her like hawks and hope that the medication will help, or she'll come out of it herself.'

Gail was away somewhere. While the medication kept her far from rational thought, her unconscious mind worked frantically to make sense of a chaos of images and repair what damage it could. She was like a diver, submerged, coming up for a second of air before diving again, knowing that the water was strange and the air too clear to survive.

Three chairs against a black background. Three dark figures – three voices – are seated.

Voice 1 I have washed them down and shrouded them. This was never life. I presume nothing. I accept nothing. Nothing is ever as it seems – I'm human; I perceive more often than I see . . . Nothing is stable – I'm sure of nothing.

Voice 2 You write, but what do you hide behind? You smile, but what does the smile imply? You take the trouble to speak, but what are you *really* saying? Are you strong and sharply outlined, or are you vague? Who do you see in the mirror? Removed from all outward proof of existence, will you still exist?

Voice 3 Where did you go?

Voice 2 We didn't notice you'd gone: we never imagined anything like this . . .

Voice 3 Still, you never know what's going to happen. I could be dead tomorrow – who knows?

Voice 2 You need to make the most of it while you've got it. I never did and look at me. I feel as though I've never really done *enough* – do you know what I mean? I should've done more . . . not that I regret it, but I think if I had my life over again I'd try a little harder – take more risks, you know . . .

Voice 1 (*Quietly*) hammer hammering hammering out hammering breaking through . . .

Voice 2 Some breakthrough!

Voice 1 building up brick upon brick building . . .

Voice 2 When are we not on our own? Tell me when. Give me an instance. I dare you. I defy you.

Voice 3 We welcome visitors. Like my old man used to say, keep the kettle boiling and tea in the pot and you can't go far wrong. It's a poor bloody world, he'd say, if we can't be nice to each other . . .

Voice 1 Poor bloody world. I can't bloody mend you – my roof is all broken my rafters exposed my windows are dirty my door won't close I have birds in my attic and a carpet of hay . . . brick upon brick

Voice 3 'Course thirty years ago you'd be out every morning scrubbing the front step with your hands red and chapped looking up and down the street at the other steps and all the other women would be out scrubbing theirs and you'd shout to each other and laugh and sing sometimes 'course times change and we must change with them but there's a lot to be said for those days all the same . . .

Voice 1 upon brick. No way in. No way out. No step to scrub. No song to sing.

Voice 2 So – brick by brick and curtain by curtain she barricades herself in. This being the only way she can be sure that we are outside and that she . . . exists. For if the hand that hangs the curtain is one of the only pair that function this side of the wall . . . if all doors are locked and intruders prevented . . . If the only heart beating beats within her skeletal cavity . . . then she must therefore exist, and we must be the strangers.

Voice 1 brick upon brick

Voice 3 . . . and the nuclear family being father mother and two point two children Granny in the nursing home well you can't be expected can you? And these walls being paramount you can't hang a thing off them it's the cavities they're all bloody jerry-built you just don't get quality these days . . .

Voice 2 Nuclear. Tidy. Insulated. Like a bomb.

Voice 1 . . . upon brick. It takes time. Behind a farm in Norfolk stands a tree, in the centre of a long-dead

church. The church decays, the tree grows, and blos-
soms yearly. It takes time. And time defiles the body,
not the mind. Time weakens the flesh, not the spirit.
Time hardens the arteries, not the heart, toughens the
skin not the soul, clouds the eyes not the vision. Time
conquers by stealth, but we gain through wisdom. You
are my greatest strength, my hardest sorrow; you are
my means of transport, but not my arrival. You may
be tomorrow . . .

Voice 2 and tomorrow . . .

Voice 1 but only I can walk into you. This dwelling

Voice 2 the seat of existence

Voice 1 a cold

Voice 2 strange

Voice 1 existence

Voice 2 eroding

Voice 1 falling

Voice 2 tumbling

Voice 1 dying

Voice 2 infinite

Voice 1 endless

Voice 2 the seat of the conscious

Voice 1 dwelling of the soul

Voice 2 house of the spirit

Voice 1 carpet of hay

Voice 2 hold on

Voice 3 just hold on

Voice 2 hold on . . .

Voice 1 (Rising) I have washed them down and shrouded
them. I have wrapped them in a sheet and taped a
respectful rose beside their name. I have watched the
metal trolleys roll away. So this is death: this simple
cessation of life . . . but this was never life, never life,
not this . . . The hand is cold, the blood ceases to flow,
but this was never life – this hand, this face, this hair –
never life! Do you understand? Just the dwelling – do
you understand?

Silence.

She had started to move in her sleep. The nurse alerted

the Sister, who went into the clinic to prepare Gail's next injection. The duty psychiatrist had given clear instructions: keep her out for twenty-four hours, until the shock subsides, and then we'll see.

Gail tried to open her eyes. She shuddered as cold flesh pressed against her face. She opened her eyes. It was her hand. The nurse sitting beside her touched her arm: 'Gail?'

She sat up. 'I need the toilet.' Her mouth was dry. She stood: the nurse took her by the arm and helped her out of the room and down the corridor. Gail tried to think clearly. She pushed the nurse away and tried to run – her legs failed her and she fell to the floor. Now two nurses helped her up, walked her back to the room where the Sister waited, an injection tray in her hand.

Gail faced Johnny. 'You shouldn't have done that!' She was angry.

Johnny was digging his grave in the orchard.

Joan put a hand on his shoulder. 'Sometimes we do things,' she said.

The trees were on fire. Jack ran between them. Gail thought it was Jack. A box slid behind curtains. Gail was in the back yard, hanging out the washing. It dripped soot.

'Seen our Albert?'

The sky collapsed upon itself, like a pit without props. She was in darkness. She couldn't breathe. They were holding her down. 'Mum? Mum?' The gas fire was on. A shadow on the settee. The box slid behind the curtains. 'Mum?'

She opened her eyes as the needle pierced her thigh. The Ward Sister gave the injection and stood back.

'I know you . . . ?' Gail said. The Sister smiled. Trees in Winter. 'Let me open the window!'

'Just lie back, Gail.'

Flames. Crisping flesh, falling masonry. The box sliding, whisper quiet. Chimneys smoking . . .

BANG BANG BANG

The Sister put her hand between Gail's head and the wall, guiding it firmly back to the pillow. She struggled, but there were too many nurses.

And then she was gone.

Later, they led her to the toilet, then sat her at a table outside her room with a cigarette and a cup of tea. The nurse beside her helped lift the tea to her lips. The cigarette kept falling through her fingers.

She noticed her arms. They were covered in scratches. 'Who did this?'

'You were fighting, Gail. We had to hold you down.'

'Oh.'

The scratches grew and divided, like sharp sudden frost on a window. They shot up to her shoulders. She clutched her chest.

'Jesus!'

'What is it, Gail?' Another nurse stood beside her.

'I'm breaking!'

Later still they took her into the dayroom, where the television danced in one corner. She covered her eyes. 'Stop it doing that!'.

Celie came across to her. 'Let me sit with her,' she asked the nurse. She took Gail's hands from her face and held them tightly.

'Look at me, Gail!'

'I can't . . . '

'Look at me!'

'There's so many of them, Celie!'

'So many what?'

'People! And they're all talking at once! I tried, but I can't make sense of what they're saying!'

'Maybe you don't need to, Gail. Maybe you shouldn't try. Just stay here, with me. It'll be okay, love, I promise.'

Edna Jones has been given a watering-can. She waters the many feeble plants that litter the ward gallery, asks for more water and, having been resupplied, begins again. The nurses have little time to notice, as each time she returns, a different nurse replenishes the can for her. She shuffles up and down the length of the gallery and talks gently to each plant in turn. No one can hear what she's saying, but she smiles a grandmother's smile as she adds a little extra to the already overflowing pots. If the ward was still, the sound of a dozen little waterfalls would be heard, but the ward is rarely still, and so the steady trickles go unnoticed.

Finally Edna has no one to ask and, being unable to locate the kitchen for herself, places the watering-can upside down on the floor, claps her hands together in a thoughtful manner and shuffles towards the ward exit.

The fire doors are heavy and opening them proves to be something of a struggle for Edna. Nevertheless she is determined, and with effort opens one far enough for her to squeeze through. The door clunks behind her and suddenly she's afraid. It's very dark here, and it isn't like her house. Two flights of stairs: one going down, one going up, and, where she stands, a dim landing of sorts . . . She frowns with confusion and turns to face the fire doors once again, peering through the glass panels into the ward. It's much lighter in there – perhaps she ought to go back and wait until mother comes to fetch her? She pushes at the door but it feels even heavier to open now, and she can't manage. She turns once again to the landing. She wants to cry: mother shouldn't leave her here, it isn't nice. Then she notices another door to her left with a gleaming brass handle. It opens for her and she walks in.

'Edna?' says the surprised nurse who had just opened the door, preparing to leave.

'Is my mother here? Is she here?'

'No, love. It'll be dinner time soon. Shall I walk you back?'

'I can't find the bus stop. Will you show me where it is? Mother will be waiting. She gets angry if I'm late home. Will you show me?'

The nurse smiled gently. 'I tell you what, you come back with me and we'll talk about it over dinner.'

'But where's Mother? Is she in here . . . ?' Edna pushed past the nurse into the room. There were many people here, but she couldn't see Mother. She didn't understand what was happening. Who were these people? She began to cry.

Celie, who had been talking to the consultant and trying not to think about all the other eyes that were trained upon her, rose from her chair to comfort Edna.

'It's alright Edna, don't be scared. Your mum told me she would be coming after dinner. You go with the nurse now, and I'll come and join you in a few minutes.'

Edna left, still crying, and Celie turned to the psychiatrist.

'She asks for her mother every day. It's very sad.'

'It's nice of you to comfort her,' smiled the consultant.

'We all do.'

'Have you heard anything about . . . ' the psychiatrist flicked through the notes on his lap, '. . . Frank? Any news about him?'

Celie, sitting down again, lowered her eyes.

The psychiatrist turned to the social worker on his left. 'Any news?'

'Only that he might be in London. One of the young men said in his statement to the police that Frank had mentioned going to London a couple of nights before the arrests were made.'

'London? Why should he choose London?' Celie was shaking now.

'I think perhaps we ought to leave it there, Mrs Watkins,' said the psychiatrist, nodding to the remaining nurse in attendance.

As the nurse moved towards Celie, Celie clenched her fists tightly and began to scream . . .

'That was a nice pudding!' shouted Edna.

Gail took a tissue from the box beside her and wiped the blob of semolina from Edna's chin. 'It was, wasn't it?'

She sat her down in a chair opposite the kitchen door. 'You stay here, Edna, and I'll make us a nice cup of tea.'

Edna watched gratefully as Gail went into the kitchen, but when the kitchen door closed behind her she began to worry. There was a reason for her sitting here, but she had forgotten what it was. Well, there's no point worrying, she'd better go and find Mother. There was a terrible commotion coming from the far end of the gallery. Someone was screaming . . . Her eyes weren't as good as they used to be . . .

A young man in pyjamas was in his room, lying tightly curled in the foetal position, watching the attending nurse intently.

'JACK! JESUS! JACK! YOU BASTARDS! YOU BASTARDS!' a woman was screaming. People were running up and down the gallery outside his side-room door. The male nurse looked anxious. 'You should go,' the young man said quietly. The nurse didn't answer so he said it again. 'You should go.'

The nurse frowned at him. 'You know I can't leave you, Malcolm.'

'I'll be okay,' said Malcolm. 'All I need is a little peace and quiet.'

'I can't – you know that!'

'I'm not going to do anything,' reassured Malcolm. 'I can't sleep with you here. You could stand just outside if you're worried!'

The door flew open and the Ward Sister whispered urgently to the male nurse. He stood, ready to leave, but his relief failed to appear. He pushed the door open more fully to see what was happening. Celie was screaming and fighting, the Sister and doctors unable to handle her. All the other nurses were busy with other patients. He looked at Malcolm: 'Are you sure you'll be all right?'

'Honestly. You go.'

There was nothing else to do. Someone would be injured. He raced out.

Gail left the kitchen with a mug of tea in each hand, then hesitated. Celie was fighting between where she stood and where Edna sat. Gail hated to see her friend like this. In normal circumstances they wouldn't have been put on the same ward. They probably wouldn't have been in the same hospital. They were from different catchment areas. But these were extraordinary circumstances. There was only one hospital left.

A chance was all Malcolm needed. This was it. He was off the bed and out of the door in seconds, lifting one of the heavy armchairs and hurling it, with all his strength, through the window.

Gail jumped and dropped the mugs when the glass shattered. She spun round in time to see Malcolm preparing to follow the chair out of the window, as it crashed to the ground thirty feet below.

'MALCOLM? NO!'

She launched herself at him and grabbed his arm, but he was stronger and began to pull her with him. Just don't let go, she told herself, as he began desperately to prise her hand away. Gail tried to reach his other arm but he was struggling, fighting, pushing, kicking out, his face white as death, his eyes alive with terror. She could hear the staff running to help, but seconds were all Malcolm needed.

'Let me go, please let me go!'

'No, Malcolm, don't do this!'

His free hand reached for the smashed window frame to give him extra leverage. The shards of glass tore at his palm. Blood poured from the cuts but still he persevered. Then someone else was with them, then another then another . . . Gail let go and Malcolm disappeared beneath a mass of bodies.

That was the last Gail saw of him, but a few days later he sent her a note. It was printed handwriting – each letter clearly an effort – and in green ink. It reached her by an unorthodox route: 'I'm giving this to the chaplain. He says he'll deliver it provided I talk about God and things. He doesn't know what I'm writing. He says you are a nurse. You should know better. He says you saved my life. I'll never forgive you.'

The note fell to the floor. Gail was beating her head on the wall again.

When Edna had her second stroke, she followed Malcolm to the hospital sick ward, where Percy and their daughter visited every day.

Seven days later, she suffered another stroke and died.

. . . Take Edna's condition after her first stroke, stretch it out over year after interminable year. Leave her stranded in the terrible vacuum of dementia. Leave her husband without full reason to grieve, for the body lives on. Let him visit the woman that is still his wife on a ward that stinks of urine, where harassed nurses struggle to cope with an impossible workload. Not for a few weeks, but for years Percy must live with this. Five years – maybe ten . . . She might even outlive him.

If he outlives her, if she dies after several years of

questionable life, for whom can he grieve? The woman he loved is lost behind years of ugly reality. The memories he cherished are stained by the grim truth of her incontinence, her emptiness and that of her neighbours. Death of mind awaiting death is all he knows. Will he live long enough to remember the woman she was? Will he ever remember her fully, or just this shell?

A quick death is kinder. It leaves memories intact.

A small blood clot on the brain can render a top-ranking civil servant incoherent and doubly incontinent. A Government minister cannot legislate against the death of his brain cells. Doctors dribble, pacifists become violent and grandmothers swear. A society made classless on a hospital ward. One day we shall all be humbled.

Only pray that the day never comes.

They heard of Edna's death on the ward within hours, and mourned for the loss of her. Even dementia cannot steal a good soul.

Would that all souls were good.

The Witch and the Poor Boy

Frank Watkins had spent a month living rough on the streets of London and was looking, if not quite derelict, then a little the worse for wear. He had survived by robbing the dossers of their Giros; catching them between the Post Office and the off-licence before they had the opportunity to spend it all on drink. At least, that was what Frank told himself – if he prevented them from drinking he was doing them a service, in a way. He had bought a Stanley knife for protection at the first opportunity, and it had served him well. It wasn't safe on the streets.

Frank was careful to rob only the old drunks, for the younger ones were sober more often than not, and capable of defending themselves. Some didn't drink at all. Some were just plain crazy, thought Frank, discharged from the old asylums into the nearest gutter, and incapable of looking after themselves. These were the ones to avoid, by virtue of their unpredictability. But the drunks were easy prey. All they needed was one drink to top up the booze already in their systems, then they'd be smashed out of their brains and hardly able to fight back.

The bruises and scars on Frank's face attested to the fact that he didn't always make the right choice. They all fought back: that wasn't the problem. It was only when their drunken fists failed to miss their targets: that was when the problems arose. Still, he had youth, strength, quick wits and a Stanley knife on his side, so the superficial cuts and bruises he received were nothing compared to the mess he made of them in return.

Nevertheless, times were hard, and more than once Frank thought of his home with longing. To have a roof over his head would be nice: cardboard boxes weren't always easy to find. Furthermore, he had developed a little habit that cost a lot to sustain.

Frank shivered and rubbed his arm. One of the many puncture-marks that resided there had become inflamed and sore. He didn't need a doctor. All that he needed was in London, in a syringe, just waiting to be injected. But to get it he needed money. Heroin doesn't come free.

When a poor boy is lost, he must needs come home. So Frank had returned to his roots, to his old stamping-ground . . . but not quite.

When a prodigal son returns, it is usually to his parents. If he returns by the front door asking forgiveness, he will be forgiven.

But Frank is not visiting, there is no one to ask forgiveness of, and the house he has just entered by smashing a back window belongs to a certain Agnes Wormole.

He is not careful. He sees no need to be careful here. Who, after all, is likely to come to her aid? Who'd want to protect her? He shakes and perspires and sniffs occasionally, but not from fear. Getting the money has become a matter of urgency.

Mrs Wormole had been on the Rat Alley gang's 'to do' list – she was loaded, they were certain. They had even watched her house one night. She'd be easy. Easy-peasy. Now this belief shone like a beacon before Frank, dragging him back from London to risk arrest in the hope of finding enough to finance his addiction. He could handle her. He'd find out where she kept the money, take it, then fuck off back to London and out of harm's way.

But she heard him. She heard the glass break, even though he'd muffled it. Over the years Mrs Wormole had developed an acute sense of hearing. A deaf gossip is a poor gossip, after all.

While he crashed around the front parlour, opening drawers and rifling through their contents, Agnes took

from beneath her pillow the scissors she had kept sharpened for many years against just such an eventuality.
While he shone his torch around the room, cursing quietly, she was also cursing, but her words were silent, rapid
and incomprehensible as she and the scissors descended
the stairs.

Frank crouched down at the fireplace to examine something. He had been in houses before where the fire was
never used, and often they kept the money there, hidden
behind a decorative screen. On the floor beside him were
two heavy silver-bottomed antique candlesticks that he'd
found on the mantelpiece. He shone the torch along the
edges of the screen, pulled it towards him and with his
free hand groped the sooty darkness. There appeared to
be nothing there, but just to be sure he let the screen fall
to the floor and, still crouching, shone his torch into the
hearth. Nothing in or beneath the grate . . . He crouched
a little lower and shone the beam up the chimney. Usually
there was a ledge they kept the money on . . .

Red hot, piercing . . . he yelled out in agony and fell
sideways to the floor, lifting his hand to protect himself.
It came again: the stab and then the terrible wrench as
she pulled the scissors free. In a blur of terrified pain he
saw a face, distorted with rage, leering down at him. She
said nothing, but lifted the scissors once more and fell
upon him.

Jesus. Jesus. He would die. Was it her? Her breath
was foul to him as she hissed with effort, pushing the
scissors further and further into his belly. Jesus God he
would die. Already he was losing it, she felt so strong.
He gasped and gurgled, his hand flailing the air for her
throat, face, something, anything. He would die, oh Jesus
God the pain . . . His hand fell weakly to his side. The
blackness was closing in. Still she was pushing into him
until it seemed her hand followed the scissors into his
belly, turning them upwards towards his heart. Blood was
pouring from him, from his back, front, nose, mouth. He
couldn't breathe for the pain . . . then his hand fell upon
one of the candlesticks and with superhuman effort he
brought it up to strike her once, then again, then again
. . . She fell forward, malice undiminished, and with her

final breath forced the blades a . . . little . . . further . . . home.

Three days passed before the milkman paused to consider why the milk was still on her doorstep. He knocked on the old woman's door. Receiving no response, he bent down and lifted the letterbox. He squinted, sniffed, then sniffed again. The sweet stench of rotting flesh assailed his nostrils. He stood quickly, retched, then retched again.

Three untouched pints on the doorstep. Three days had passed. Already the milk was sour.

'Community Care'

The hostel had once been a doctor's house. It stood tall and wide, but strangely alone, at the centre of a residential neighbourhood. Yes, right at the heart of the community stood a living monument to the principles of community care. But principles are one thing. Practice is another.

The old doctor had half-converted two adjoining houses into one, so that at one time one front door was to his home, the other to his surgery. Now there was only one front door.

To reach the hostel Christine took the ring road that ran parallel with Beckwood Estate, passed Harvey's Emporium – once a thriving music-hall, now used as a cheap warehouse for Budget Buy, a local supermarket chain. She turned left at the old Baptist church, now boarded up, that sported a huge poster of a glittering hi-fi system and a legend – referring to the trading company's credit facilities, that said, 'They made it so easy!'

She crossed the railway line and turned right at the following junction. She parked in the car park of the old Swan and Thistle – now also boarded up – and walked the last ten yards to the hostel's front steps. The building was an architectural interruption in an otherwise perfect latticework of red brick terraces that spread outwards towards the railway line and downhill as far as the gasworks. At the foot of the hill a gasometer rose and fell, altering the horizon daily. Behind Christine, over the road, they had almost completed another DIY superstore, for a company which boasted 'Everything for Your Home!'

On the corner of the street directly opposite the Hostel, a tiny off-licence persevered in the face of almost indomitable odds to remain open. The windows and door were hidden behind steel mesh. The owner, now in his sixties, had inherited the shop from his father and struggled, even now, to maintain the 'personal service' that had once meant so much. Despite having been burgled eight times in the past two years, vandalised twice, physically assaulted once and once threatened with a knife, old Stan still retained a good stock of warm Mars Bars, indigestion tablets, Brillo pads and milk. Living proof of the Great British Spirit and the last reminder of the fine old days ... Days when the Baptist church had a strong local congregation; when the whole district, it seemed, flocked to the Emporium on a Saturday night. When *everyone* had a job if they wanted one. When, every weekday morning, factory sirens sounded from every direction, giving Stan the cue to turn his shop sign to 'Open'.

On Sundays the factory men, keen to get the most from their weekend's leisure, would call at Stan's for a packet of Woodbines before marching off with their mates in their stout work boots to the canal by the gasworks, where they'd fish with home-made rods and lines, smoke, hawk, spit the factory dust from their lungs in the cool morning mist and talk quietly amongst themselves. Then back to Stan's for the Sunday paper and straight to the Swan and Thistle for a few pints to help them over the bevvying of the night before and to set them up for Sunday dinner. The womenfolk would call into Stan's after the morning service for baking powder, cornflour, lard or eggs. Then on Sunday evenings Stan would close early, climb into his best suit and head for church, where he'd join the factory men, all starched and red eyed from their afternoon nap, in raising their voices to the Lord. Short and squat as he was, Stan could belt out the hymns with the best o' them. Then to the Swan and Thistle, where someone would buy Stan a pint for looking after his little lad when he fell over in the street outside his

shop the other day and Stan would nod and smile and join
in the laughter and get quietly, jovially drunk. Later he'd
stagger past the doctor's house singing, 'We plough the
fields and scat-ter . . . ' at the top of his voice, unlock
the side door to the shop and, often forgetting to lock the
door after him, heave himself up the stairs to bed. There
he'd lay, drowsy and content, listening to the laughter of
his neighbours leaving the pub, and then he'd drift off to
sleep thanking the Lord for giving him such a damn fine
life and damn – hic – fine friends . . .

Since the riots, all that had gone. Now Stan needed
his alarm clock to remind him when to open the shop
because, however hard he strained to hear, not one factory siren called out across the city. Many of the old
community had left. Now the people were younger and
their eyes were full of either hatred or fear, and no one
gave a fuck about the silly old sod in the corner shop.
When the Baptist church was forced to close, they held a
jumble sale on the premises to try to reopen it. The jumble
sale was raided by a gang of youths – one with a shotgun –
who cleared all the trestle tables of clothes, and then took
the trestle tables. There had been no question of calling
the police: the three parishioners present were threatened
with dire consequences should they be foolish enough to
'give trouble'. Within weeks those three parishioners – and
their families – had left the area. So that was the end of the
Baptist church. The Swan and Thistle was simply terrified
out of existence. Of the old days only Stan was left: kept
in business only through the custom of the people in the
hostel over the road.

Behind the hostel the council cleared a couple of
blocks of tenements, rehoused the people in a new concrete tower block on the Beckwood Estate – miles from
their roots – and then built an 'adventure playground' with
a playing field, that would hopefully encourage the local
youth to vent their anger on footballs instead of people's
heads. And now, while eight-year-olds sniffed glue in the
wooden 'play tunnel', the local youths gathered in knots
in the far corner of the playing field, plotted against
the police and dealt in drugs. A fourteen-year-old had
recently died from hepatitis after 'shooting up' with a

dirty needle near the goal posts and a five-year-old girl was in a coma after sniffing glue in a crisp packet by the swings.

'I'm dead, where do I go?'

A little man in large round spectacles, hopping agitatedly from foot to foot, held Christine's jacket with trembling fingers as she reached the hostel steps. Christine smiled and put an arm around the little man's shoulders: 'What do you say we go in and make a nice cup of tea, George?'

'Chrissie I'm dead. Dead Chrissie dead.' Then he let loose her jacket, hurried up the steps and, after holding open the door for Christine to follow, ran awkwardly into the hall shouting, to no one in particular, 'Chrissie's here. I'm dead, dead, Chrissie's here!'

He looked poised to knock on the office door, but instead turned on his heel and half-ran, half-stumbled, up the stairs to his room.

Christine frowned as she followed him in. George hadn't been the same since a little girl on a tricycle had thrown a stone at him and caught him on his temple. The injury had been superficial but for weeks George had refused to leave his room. Now he was so agitated that he seemed to dance all the time.

They'd tried to find him somewhere else to live but the beleaguered health authority couldn't help him and some bloody fool at the social services had written to say that, although this had obviously been a 'painful and regrettable' experience for George it was all, in a sense, part of the 'rehabilitation process'. 'As a member of the community,' the letter continued, 'he must learn how to interact, not run away at the first sign of trouble!'

Christine wondered if she and the letter-writer shared the same community. Someone had daubed 'MADHOUSE' on the hostel walls again. Someone else had defecated on the steps. The kids came out at night in gangs to peer through the windows and torment the residents. They were living on a knife-edge and now, to cap it all, the council was rumoured to be about to withdraw funding. She and her colleagues seemed about to be given the task of rehousing George and sixteen other – just as vulnerable – people. But rehousing them where?

Someone had recently described the Health Service as a 'sinking ship'. As far as Christine was concerned the ship was already under, but still sinking to almost unbelievable depths. What would come next? Would they rehouse George and his companions in health authority cardboard boxes in the Arboretum, and employ Christine and her colleagues to do the soup-run? She turned the handle of the office door and shook her head thoughtfully. She had a terrible sense of the future. Soon she would have to get away – when this was over. She'd emigrate, perhaps – to a place where people *really* care about each other. Was there such a place? Or did it all cost?

George dropped the lock on his room door and sat down on his bed. Herbert had stopped talking again, so George had altered his diet to seed and little pieces of apple. His head still hurt from the missile, but when he looked in the mirror he couldn't see the mark. He could only see himself. Frankly, he thought, that wasn't very much.

He took a Granny Smith from his bedside locker and settled down with the hostel's kitchen breadknife to cut it up. Around him, there was little proof that he existed. A few old apple-cores, some bird seed scattered on the carpet, but nothing else. Nothing to remember himself by. One of the other residents had torn up his old copy of *The Librarian's Friend* and his briefcase had been stolen long ago.

He shouldn't have the breadknife. But it was nice and sharp. He sliced easily through the apple and then let the blade rest on the inside of his wrist. He pressed the knife as deep as it seemed prepared to go and then released the pressure. His veins seemed bigger, and bluer, than before. He pushed his spectacles back into position – they had almost fallen off the end of his nose with the exertion – and then peered curiously at the blue serrated indentation that the knife had made on his skin. He couldn't have done that in hospital. No sharp knives in hospital. He stared at the breadknife. The blade caught the sunlight. He thought he heard a voice and held his breath, then whispered, hopefully, 'Herbert?'

His window exploded.

'Hey, fuck-face!'

'Four eyes!'

'Leather head!'

'Hey, *ya cunt*, why don't ya just *die*?!'

George stood up, shook the glass from his trousers and walked to the window. In the playing field – a long way down – a couple of youths were staring up at him. One had sores around his nose and mouth. The other was staggering.

'Fuck-face!' shouted the one with sores.

'Shit head!' shouted the staggering one. They were convulsed with laughter.

George looked at the window pane. It was really rather tidy. Just a few bits of glass stubbornly sticking to the frame. He knocked them clean with his elbow.

Someone was banging on his door: 'George, are you all right?' and they were shouting: ' . . . then he fucked yer mother too then he blew yer fuckin' brains out and put you in a ZOO!!!'

He'd asked for a high room. 'To see things!' he'd said. He'd seen lots of police cars and ambulances since he'd been there. On the playing field. And heard sirens in the distance . . .

'George? Let me in . . . '

. . . and those weeks that he'd stayed in his room he'd lived like a bird in a cage. However high he was, there were always people looking in on him. The kids in the field outside, or the staff inside. The wardrobe was too small for him to climb in and the bed too close to the floor for him to hide underneath. A bird in a cage. Perhaps it was punishment for never setting Herbert free. Birds don't – shouldn't – talk. Birds fly.

'Herbert?' he whispered again.

'LOONY TUNE LOONY TUNE LOONY FUCKING LOONY TUNE . . .'

Busy busy busy. He brushed the glass from the windowsill with his hand and climbed on to the bed.

'Who's on duty?' someone was shouting outside his door.

'Then get the keys off him – quick!' Someone was trying his door handle. Bending slightly, he climbed out of the window and crouched on the sill. The boys on the field had been joined by an older youth in a black leather jacket who, staring up at George, smiled and began to clap: a slow, rhythmic handclap of the sort you hear at a performance, when the audience are impatient for the show to begin. The two other boys, helpless with mirth, tried to compose themselves and join in.

George felt the breeze on his face.

And then all three of them were standing there: clap, clap, clap. They were no longer laughing. They were excited. Their eyes were hungry for the main event.

He didn't need his glasses now. He removed them and let them fall, shattering on the concrete yard three storeys below. His door was being unlocked but he closed his eyes in a moment's ecstasy, hearing only the sound of distant thunder, or a drum-roll . . . he raised his hands in the air, leaned forward . . . how easy it was to fly, after all . . . A sudden rush of air.

The door flew open and Christine fell into the room. The window was empty. Outside, the three youths cheered.

Nora Wadge, Johnny's landlady, had been grateful for the publicity her former lodger had, through dying, provided. She built an extension in her back yard and, with a few 'modest' alterations to the main building, now had room for another six guests. Ever willing, she – through her contacts in the social services – had helped the hostel staff to rehouse their residents after the tragedy of George Beagle's death. Furthermore, she had gained a lover and close business partner in the form of the bloated Harry Retch: a fellow entrepreneur with a bed & breakfast of his own three doors down from hers. Now Harry had a gut the size of a dustbin that hung obscenely over the waist of his trousers, and a vest that looked as though it had cleaned sewer walls, but Nora knew she could sort him out. Clean shirt, roomy jacket and you wouldn't know him as the same man.

What a future they planned! All that stood between them was a couple of empty houses and an old woman whose memory was back in the reign of Victoria.

It wouldn't be long. Things were flush for the B & B industry these days: a shrewd accountant and a bit of business acumen was all that was needed for her and Harry to buy their way along the street towards each other until they met romantically, shrewdly, gloriously and lucratively smack dab in the middle! So, whenever she had a visit from a social worker she'd put an arm round one of her intimidated lodgers and cluck about how mental illness was 'such a sad business' . . . but in private, with Harry, she had to laugh – as it certainly hadn't done her any harm!

George's death had certainly been unfortunate, but it had also been opportune for the council, who'd been looking for a way to shut the hostel down.

So now the hostel was empty. Cleared. The furniture had been stacked in the large living-room. And the staff were sitting on the office floor, sharing a bottle of wine. Only the office window was left to be boarded up, then they could hand the keys over and go.

It was a large bay window. A three-board job. But the council workmen were being unusually efficient. It didn't take long.

As the first board was hammered into place a male member of the team began to weep.

As the second board went up Christine said: 'Everyone raise your glasses!'

As the final board closed them in they raised their glasses in a toast.

'But to what?' one of them asked. No one could think of anything.

'Just drink the wine,' Christine said.

They drank silently, then someone whispered: 'I didn't think they could make it as dark as this!'

Stan watched the closure through his shop window. Then he watched the staff begin to leave. His heart felt heavy. He went to the door, hit the Yale lock with his thumb, pushed the bolts home – top and bottom – and then, with one final, weary glance up the street, turned the sign to 'Closed'.

In the distance the gasometer was emptying again. A monolithic steel structure, immense and grey and lacking a soul, dominating the landscape but a blind servant to intractable laws: gas, and no gas. Supply and demand. Physical laws: the breath of the people, rising, falling, up and down, supply and demand, here today, gone tomorrow . . . It was emptying fast.

There would be no horizon soon.

Recovery

The nurse had some free time. Gail sat in the dayroom and watched her. First, the nurse spent ten minutes trying to make a silent woman talk. The nurse was nineteen, the woman fifty-five. In the end, tired of trying, she leaned across to her: 'You won't talk to me. So how do you expect to get better, if you won't help yourself?'

Then she moved on.

Another woman was writing. She sat down beside her and leaned across: 'What are you writing?' she asked. The woman turned away. The nurse stood. 'You shouldn't keep things to yourself!' she said, clearly offended.

Little by little, Gail watched her circumnavigate the room. She felt like a segment of a dartboard. She watched to see where the dart would land next.

The nurse sat a while with an old man who had recently lost his wife. For a moment, Gail hoped she might see something better, as the nurse reached across to take the old man's hand. But then the nurse noticed a colleague waving a sandwich at her from the dining-room and pointing at the tea tray on the table, ready for the staff's morning break, so she patted the old man's hand, said: 'Chin up dear, life goes on!' before waltzing off for her break. When she returned she came with another nurse, discussing the frock she'd wear for a party that night. They sat down together and flicked through a couple of magazines, chatting quietly. Then the other

nurse was called away and the dart was aimed again.
This time at Celie.

Celie sat, stoically resigned, as the nurse prodded
and poked about. But when the nurse asked: 'Do you
think you'll marry again?' Celie left the room. The nurse
raised her hands as if to say: 'You've got to ask!' and then
slumped down beside Gail.

'So, what have you got to tell me, then?'

'Come with me,' said Gail, leading her out of the
dayroom and into the empty doctor's office.

The nurse, disconcerted, left the door open wide, just
in case – well, you never know – better safe than sorry, eh?
Safety first. Look after yourself. No one will do it for you!
Oh, she was full of them, those neat little phrases; she was
full of it! But Gail must have something really important to
say, so she sat by the door, crossed her legs and tried not
to think about the party. Someone outside turned the radio
up for her: 'Don't worry, be happy!' the song went. Her
favourite. She tapped her foot in rhythm. A good song –
and so true, so very profound. Her mum said that these
people needed a good kick up the bum to snap them out
of it and – well – she was inclined to believe it herself.
Nothing on this ward that a bit of hard work wouldn't
cure. She'd just come from a geriatric ward: she knew
all about hard work. Oh yes.

Between that ward and this she'd had a couple of
weeks' training on the types of illnesses she was likely to
find on an admission ward – and how to nurse them. She
had been told to expect trouble, but she'd not encountered trouble yet. Nope. Mostly it was taking them down
to occupational therapy or for blood samples, X-rays –
stuff like that. Otherwise it was a bit of a doddle. You
have to watch people in case they run off but otherwise
– well – you could just talk them round. Keep the pecker
up! her mum used to say. How true that was. How very,
very true. 'Don't worry, be happy . . . ' She wondered if
Bill would be at the party tonight . . . anyway – task in
hand! Gail was at the window with her back to her. Her
shoulders were all tense. But they'd said at Report that
she was responding better and not suicidal any more: not
likely to go through the window – bloody good job too, as

the nurse wasn't sure what to do in those circumstances.
She expected you just lunge after them and grab them by
the collar or something . . . just grab them and hang on.
Bet it wasn't a pretty sight, some patient splattered all
over the courtyard. Her mate Sheila had seen a 'jumper'
already. It didn't seem fair. She always missed out on the
action . . .

Gail hadn't said anything yet. She'd better start her
off, get her going . . .

Her best, most sympathetic smile: 'So, what do you
want to tell me, Gail?'

Gail turned from the window and faced her. She
really turned.

'What the hell do you think you're doing? What's
your name?'

Ooer. Was this trouble? 'Karen,' she responded.

'You're a self-important little shit, Karen. Did you know
that?'

Some people need to get things off their chest. She could
take it. Karen was a nurse; strong shouldered. She took it.

'Why?' she asked, with infinite – sacrificial – patience.

'You really don't know, do you? And if I told you,
you still wouldn't be any the wiser. What do you call
what you were doing out there? Counselling? Dear God.
If that's what you think it is, give up now. Don't go any
further. Have you considered another career?'

'I've only just started this . . . '

'Yes, Karen, you have only just started. So who do you
think you are, picking people off like you were doing in
the dayroom? Have you got any idea of the damage you
can cause?'

'I was only talking. We've got to talk. It's our job.'

'Not like that it isn't. You had absolutely no respect
for anyone in that room. No concern for their feelings.
What were you doing? Fishing? Is that how you fish?
Throw concrete into a river and hope it hits one on the
head?'

'What?'

'What do you know about life? What the fuck do
you know about life? And you think that your uniform gives you wisdom? I've never in my life seen a

worse example of abuse than I did watching you just now.'

'I wasn't . . . '

'You weren't thinking, that's for sure. Do you put your brain in gear when you come on duty? And you had no respect for anyone. Are you playing games with us? Does it make you feel good, when no one answers you back? Does the uniform give you a sense of power? Is it a nice way to pass the time, playing "nursie" to people who'd rather be left alone?'

'Sister said I was to try forming relationships . . . '

'Then I pity your boyfriend, Karen. What did you do – did you say, "We're going out together me and you, no argument"? Hasn't it occurred to you that people have a right to privacy? Can't you get it into your thick skull that people only come into hospital at the very worst moments in their lives. Just because they're vulnerable doesn't mean you can go barging in there with your great flat feet, treading on feelings, doing what the hell you like!'

The Sister arrived, concerned at the noise. Gail was shaking with anger. Karen had paled slightly. So the Sister leaned against the door jamb and Gail addressed her instead, conscious that her feelings were getting slightly out of control. She reached into her pocket and lit a cigarette, taking a deep drag before continuing. 'It's irresponsible of you to let her loose on us. Who's likely to complain? Get her to fold linen or something, but don't give us to her like toys she can examine and drop when she gets bored. We're not monkeys in a cage . . . '

'I know that,' the Sister said, trying to calm things down.

'Then why . . . why let her loose? For Christ's sake, she hasn't a clue! She asked Celie if she'd get married again! And she said to Godfrey: "Chin up, life goes on!"'

Gail paced the distance of the window, leaned her hand on the sill to steady herself. 'Don't let her assume that her uniform implies wisdom. Don't half-teach her about counselling and give her an excuse to blunder her way through people's minds between making the beds and the morning break. To offer words without

genuine empathy is to ask someone you don't know
to go naked before you while you remain fully clothed.
Does that make any sense, Karen? Are you listening?'

Karen nodded, by now as white as a sheet.

'And how does the naked person feel, paraded before
some smug little shit who wouldn't *dream* of undressing
in public? Is that therapeutic? No – it smacks of imposition – of bullying – it's like mental rape. And imposition
is right at the heart of the disease in the psychiatric
service. Doing something for someone implies giving –
it implies a gesture of value. But doing something to
someone makes that person a victim of your actions.
And psychiatry is exceptionally good at making victims
out of ill people. Closing down the old hospitals is just
a continuation of that process. Did anyone respect the
wishes of the old people, in hospital for thirty years or
more, who wanted to stay in hospital? Like Hell! No right
to vote, or complain, or ultimately to choose. Victims.'

Karen was struck dumb, not by her words but by
Gail's agitation. She was wondering if she might be about
to see some action, after all. But then Sister tapped her on
the shoulder and made her leave the room, shutting the
door behind her. It looked like half the ward had heard
the noise. Everyone was staring at her. She needed a fag.

The Sister sat on the chair and looked up at Gail.
'Any suggestions how we change for the better?' she
asked.

The question had the required effect. Gail calmed
a little.

'Do you think I'm mad?' she asked Sister.

'No. I think you've been ill but no, you're not mad.'

Gail smiled. 'No lectures about madness not existing?'

Sister laughed gently. 'No.'

'Was it just me, or is she bad?'

'You know I couldn't . . . '

'She's bad. She's dreadful. She's the worst. And you
know what makes it even more terrible? She'll dismiss
everything that I've said to her because "I'm a patient".'

'I'll talk to her . . . '

'I doubt that things will ever change for the better.
How can they, with attitudes like that?'

'Give her a chance . . . '

'Why? Why should I? We're not animals. She can't "use" us for training. When she does that amount of damage in such a short time . . . We're too good at tolerating crap from people like her, because we don't feel able to complain. And you know what sickens me the most about her? She will always, always, keep her own opinions. You can see it budding already. That arrogance. She will always be right. She'll never lack confidence. But I hope I never see her again. Look, Sister – it's time we – you – nurses – decided on who or what we are. Because in our confusion we're leaving a legacy of damage that will persist even if we close every hospital in the country!'

Karen, a little later, was assigned the task of writing some of the notes. She checked through the Kardex. Phrases like 'psychotic', 'unmanageable', 'erratic' and 'management problem' fairly leaped off the page at her. She thought about what Gail had said . . . well, all right, she might be a nurse but she's a patient now. A patient. Her words don't count.

A good nurse keeps good records, but she'd had a hard day and she needed a long bath before the party. So when she reached Gail's entry in the Kardex she tried to think of a word that might say it all without her having to write it all down. She checked through the other notes again. Some nurses wrote a lot of notes. Some seemed to say everything with just one word. She stuck the pen between her teeth and chewed on it . . .

'You might be advised,' the Sister later said, 'to think about what Gail was saying to you, and why.'

But Gail was a patient. You don't think about what they have to say, not really. 'Course you do if you're counselling, you have to listen hard then, for your notes later, but Karen hadn't been counselling Gail. She'd counselled a few of the others that afternoon, but Gail just blew up when she went to speak to her. Just blew up. If she, Karen, was qualified, she'd have given Gail an injection then . . . into the side room, no messing! Shouldn't let her go on like that. She didn't make sense . . . well, she wouldn't, would she? That's why she's in here! Anyway, what would say it all? I know!

She marked the date in the margin and scratched her pen over the paper's surface. Then she initialled it. Oh, but it said it all in just one word, didn't it? She puffed with pride and looked at the entry again. 'Verbal', she'd written.

They were paddling.
    'I hope no one sees us!' said Celie.
    'Why?'
    'Well, we're a bit old to paddle.'
    'I think we deserve a paddle, frankly.'
    'But if they saw us . . . '
    'What can they do to us? We're already mad!'
Celie laughed. 'I bet there's frogs in here . . . '
Gail frowned.
Celie looked at her: 'Do you remember . . . '
    'No!'
    'You have to let it go, Gail. You have to.'
    'Don't Celie, please . . . '
Willow trees grazed the water's surface. Beyond the willows' tent ran a wall. Grouped behind the wall battalions of yellow metal sat patiently: dumpers, bucket loaders, tipper lorries, skip lorries, cement mixers, trailers, and a crane with a ball that hung menacingly over the edge. Ready to climb the hill. Ready to rape the bowling green with heavy skid marks, take a swing at the hospital church, hammer away the patients' canteen, crash through walls and vandalise the last remaining sanctuary of the lost. But for now they were silent. Somewhere, in a room that creaked with democracy, a minister sat with a contract in front of him. He looked at the suits that surrounded his desk, wiped the spittle from the corner of his mouth, sighed once and signed on the bottom line.

Gail sat in silence. Rose waited. Finally, her client began to speak.
    'There was never anything I could do. Not in reality. Too much was burnt, too much destroyed, and I couldn't stop it, any of it.'
    'Where are you, Gail?'
    Gail tried to breathe evenly. 'Paddling.'

'With whom?'

'Celie.'

'When?'

'In hospital . . . No.'

'No?'

'I don't want to talk about it. It hurts, Rose. I think I want to die.'

'Just say the words.'

'I don't know the words. Oh God, it hurts!'

'Tell me what you see?'

'I don't know. A bridge. A dam. Rocks.'

'Trust me, Gail . . . '

'Cool water tickling my toes. Celie laughing . . . '

'Go on, it's okay . . . '

'We were standing in a stream, gathering odd rocks and bits of wood to make a dam. We were fifteen or so. "There's water still getting through," said Celie, wading to the dam.

'"That's because we haven't finished yet." I found another rock.

'"I spoke to Mam last night. She says I could stay on at school if I wanted. She says there's no reason why we shouldn't have a brainbox in the family. She says I might like it better when I get into the sixth form, and a bit extra education wouldn't hurt, she says. If I stayed on, Gail, would you stay on? We wouldn't have to wear uniforms and Patty up the road says it's like moving to another school when you stay on. You get treated with respect. But I won't stay on if you don't, Gail."

'"I bet there's frogs in here." I'd found a patch of liverwort just beneath the bank.

'Celie laughed. "Do you remember when Billy collected them snails and put them in his mam's purse?"

'I smiled and looked around for a stick to poke the liverwort with. Ten to one there'd be rocks below, and if there were frogs, I'd rather not feel with my fingers. The stream felt deliciously cool. I wanted to stay in that stream for ever. Tears filled my eyes. I couldn't have said anything, because the things that I wanted to say went beyond words. I remembered the two of us on our first day at school, holding hands as we ran across the playing field.'

'Gail?' Rose leaned forward. Gail was standing at the window now, leaning with her hands against the glass. 'All Malcolm needed was a chair. He could have done it. I could do it. I think I want to, Rose. I want to go. It hurts too much. Perhaps some people aren't meant to live.'

Rose came and stood beside her. 'What people?'

'But it can't be right, can it? All this pain? Oh and Rose, what they're doing to people I love. What they're doing. No one asks. No one stops to ask. It all just *happens*, Rose, and I can't do a thing about it. I never could. And I'm not sure that life is worth . . . this.'

'Tell me, Gail. You were in the stream. What happened?'

'NO!'

'What happened, love?'

'A memory.'

'Tell me.'

'The doctor had told Dad that it wasn't a temporary thing with Mum after all, not like the last time, when I'd been little. They hadn't thought it might be more than that at first, but she went blind suddenly and they did some tests and found she'd got something wrong with her brain. She started fitting and they moved her to another ward, where all the old people went. Dad wouldn't let me see her. He said it would be better to pray for her at home . . .'

'Gail?' Celie was calling her.

'I still can't believe that they burnt my mum. That she was in the box that disappeared behind the curtain. I'd seen things burn at bonfires. The crematorium had a chimney. The chimney smoked. They put Mum's ashes in an urn on a ledge in a courtyard with flowers everywhere and lots of other urns. I don't know what happened to the urn. I cried because Dad cried, but I didn't feel anything, because I didn't believe they could really burn people, and especially not my mum.'

Celie paddled up behind her. She put a hand on her shoulder.

'Gail?'

'Billy's mum. Do you know what she did with those snails?'

Celie said nothing.

'She chucked them on the garden and threw salt over them.' Gail couldn't look up. Celie hugged her.

'You could stay with us if you wanted, for a while. You're like my sister. You're my very best friend. Don't cry, Gail, don't cry.'

'Deirdre said that Dad blamed me for Mum's death. I caused her to die just by being born. I shouldn't have lived. I shouldn't . . . '

'They burnt kilns, and bonfires. Salt burnt snails. They shouldn't burn bodies. They shouldn't have burnt my mum.'

The memory was so vivid and so long suppressed that it hit Gail with the force of an explosion. She began to rock back and forth, and with the scream that surged to the surface from the deepest place she felt it all, again: Her dad in the garden: 'So fragile, makes you think when you step on it . . . '

Johnny in the paper: 'Found dead in the grounds of Anydale . . . '

Joan jumping into the lorry's path: 'Joan! No! No!'

Her mother, holding her close: 'My baby . . . '

Malcolm: 'Please let me go!'

And Jack, settling down with Celie by the gas-fire: 'There's not much hope for anyone, Gail. You just have to fight your corner, and not let them knock you down . . . '

Albert, in the dark night: 'I've been *inside* you – remember?'

So Gail screamed that day until the scream became silent, aware of nothing but feeling everything, ignorant of the voices in the room as Rose ushered worried staff away and shut the door after them. The cool stream played around her feet, and there was Celie, and developers' trucks, and death, and pain, and guilt, and anger, and uniforms, and suits, and loss, and death . . . The casing shattered, the bomb exploded and she was falling, falling, with the earth falling away, until she felt strong arms around her, holding and supporting her, and a sudden sense of warmth reached the darkness, and she held on to Rose for her life.

Alf's Heart

Nellie felt old. Since spending all that money on the slot machines she felt older than before. Old and wasted. Her face felt grey, and there were shadows developing under her eyes that refused to wash away.

Alf felt like he belonged in the knacker's yard. He put his head in his hands and leaned on the kitchen table.

The kettle began to whistle, so she lifted it and poured a little, to warm the pot. It was no use saying anything, at times like this. Just brew the tea and slice the ham. A nice bit of ham it was, too. Off the bone – not a lot, but enough to fill a plate. Enough for the two of them. Just enough. When he was younger he'd've chewed at the bone as well, and made her laugh. But his dentures were dodgy now.

Teapot filled and stirred, she replaced the lid and sat down at the table to butter his bread. The plate of ham sat in the middle of the table. In a striped mixing basin beside it was some lettuce and a few small tomatoes. Half a jar of pickle and a small bottle of salad cream stood to attention beside the teapot. Alf sighed, stood and went upstairs to change.

Recently he'd taken to walking the city for jobs. He walked over the hill and caught the bus outside the Philistine Arms. Despite Nellie's protests, he said the exercise was good for him. And anyway he'd had enough of being told by pimply youths in the Job Centres that he was too old ... Fifty-eight wasn't old at all. What did they know? So he walked the old roads, round the old factories, went in and introduced himself. Not that there were many of the old ones left. Most of the buildings still upright were used as warehouses now, and in the place of the others were blocks of garages that they called 'Industrial Units'. He wore his best suit and his feet ragged and no one had any time for him, not when there were so many young lads around. Experience and a damn good work record no longer counted for anything. When he was a lad, his dad sent him round the factories looking for jobs and it had paid off because it showed you were eager and not likely to swing the lead. But not now.

Nellie wondered when would be best to mention the bath.

'Have you seen the ham?' she asked him.

'Just give me a minute ... ' he shouted as he climbed the protesting stairs one by one, pausing halfway for breath. He could see her through the open kitchen door, buttering his bread in the same flowered apron she had always worn; frayed at the edges now, the pattern faded. Buttering his bread. He felt a rush of frustrated anger. Silly old woman. Girdled and dowdy. Look at her there in her brown check dress, tartan carpet slippers, varicose veins and ...

He leaned over the banister and shouted to her: 'Have you had your hair done today?'

She came out of the kitchen, wiping her hands anxiously down her apron front: 'I was trying to tell you ... '

'What?' he snapped.

'The bath ... '

'The *what*?'

'Our old tin bath – I sold it.'

'You did what?'

'I sold it to the lass next door. In Gail's house. I sold it. She wanted the coal scuttle ... '

'They've got a coal scuttle ... '

'No. I think Albert took it for his mum. I saw him nipping down the back lane with it last week when I was dusting upstairs ... '

'Don't go on, woman. What does she want the bath for? Carrying coal? They can't be that daft?'

'No, they're having gas central heating . . . '

'They've got an upstairs bathroom already! What do they want our bath for?'

'She wants to hang it on the wall.'

'You're having me on!'

'I'm not. They've got this funny black metal furniture. She says the bath on the wall complements it.'

'Our bath?'

'She says it makes the house more traditional. She says she wants it to be like a proper miner's house.'

'With a bath on the wall?' He sat on the stairs and laughed in astonishment.

'Did you tell her that I've never been a miner?'

'She said it didn't matter. She said it was antique.'

'Oh, go on!' Then he stopped laughing.

'They can't have it!'

'But I've sold . . . '

'How much?'

'Forty pounds. I got some nice ham . . . ' She pointed at the kitchen.

'How much is left?'

'Thirty – I had my hair done . . . '

'Right!'

He stomped up the stairs. She returned to the kitchen in tears. She could hear him in the bedroom; traced his footsteps from bed to wardrobe as he changed, the pause as he stooped over the bed, laying out his suit for the morning. Checking for creases. Then the steps again, to the wardrobe, the clatter of hangers, the door shutting, the key turning . . .

He came downstairs with a pair of well-worn, brightly polished boots with steel toe caps, laces knotted together and slung over his shoulder. She hurried after him as he opened the door: 'Alf, don't . . . '

'They'll take these. Let 'em hang a pair of working boots on their bloody wall. They're no use to me now anyway . . . Where's the rest?'

He held out his hand. She reached into the pocket of her apron and handed him three ten-pound notes.

He looked at them, then at her. 'Pieces of silver!' he said. When he shut the door behind him she sobbed.

Later, with the old tin bath returned to its rightful position under the stairs; the ham, lettuce and tomatoes untouched on the kitchen table, they passed the evening in silence. He polished his shoes, then read the paper. She poked and replenished the fire from time to time and tried to read a romantic novel about a nurse and bricklayer. Later, she remembered to cover the ham and salad with plates and put them on the side. Perhaps they'd eat it tomorrow. And when they went to bed he turned to one wall while she turned to the other. As the final, glancing blow he'd even separated their denture pots on the bathroom windowsill.

The following day dawned brightly: she opened the kitchen windows to let out the steam and inhaled. It had rained in the night, but lightly. Already the pavements were dry. Only a few scattered raindrops on the window panes and the smell of fresh, washed earth remained as reminders.

He'd gone, but he'd made himself a couple of ham sandwiches for snap.

She'd not for one moment imagined he'd have cared so much about the bath. Moving here was like coming to a palace. They didn't need to go outside to use the lavatory any more. They didn't need to keep the bath either. And they'd left the old boiler behind. But he'd taken the ham, so she felt a little less hurt by him. All that job-hunting must have been getting him down. She was boiling his handkerchiefs: she felt more kindly disposed. Only words, after all.

In the square, the pigeons grew bolder. Alf dipped his fingers into the crumpled paper bag, drew out two small pieces of bread and dropped them to the ground. The pigeons surged and fought, flew up to stand beside him on the low stone wall, pecked inquisitively at anything remotely resembling food: gum, droppings, paint . . . He reached again into the bag; finding it empty, he shook what crumbs remained on to the wall beside him and smiled as the birds on the wrong side hopped over his thighs and dropped boldly into the feathered mêlée.

Soon the crumbs had gone and the pigeons flew away.
He pulled his cap a little further over his eyes and leaned
back, grateful for the warmth of the sun to soothe his old
bones.

Old bones. He wondered if she'd kept the bone? And
she'd got him the ham specially. He'd always liked a
nice bit of ham ... He felt ashamed. He felt affection
and pain mingling and pulling. He still loved her, after
all these years. She'd been crying more of late. He wished
he could buy her a new dress, or take her out somewhere
... She was going through the change – and those new
neighbours! He smiled. The lad was trying to light a pipe
when he went in – not having much success either – Alf
could tell he didn't know how. And the girl was cooking
something foreign. They'd already installed a gas fire in
the front room. The lad looked slightly ashamed when
he saw Alf looking at it. 'Coal's so expensive!' he said,
embarrassed.

'Nowt to do with me, lad. I've just come for me bath!'

And his Nell had been right. It was hung on the wall.
Rope plant holders and great spidery plants everywhere,
plain grey walls with a sliver of black paper trimming
over the skirting board. Black tubular furniture – leather
seats, looked like. And the old bath on the wall! He sat
in the sunshine and laughed. What *is* the world coming
to? They'd taken his boots like a shot – pound to a penny they'd be up on the wall in the bath's place by now.
Well, it was no great loss, and his Nell had managed a
trip to the hairdresser's – no harm done. Except for the
way he'd treated her. He remembered his wife on their
wedding night – her hair had been long then, and blonde
– and in the morning's sunlight as she lay beneath him,
her face all warm and her hair tousled and spread like
so much gold across the pillow ... So she'd gone grey
– what of it? He'd probably sent her grey – and the baby
they'd lost. Where age had roughened her features other
features had developed. The laughter lines. They'd had a
good few laughs in their time, although not so many this
last few years ... And her forehead was marked with
years of hardship and wisdom. Still beautiful to me, he
thought. She deserved more.

Nellie pulled the bath into the hallway and knelt beside
it. She looked around the rim. Then it hit her like a
thunderbolt. The day Alf blushed when she found him
in the back kitchen of their old house on the Beckwood
Estate. He'd been soaking in the bath – she never knew
how he managed to soak in it. She sat in it, but only
long enough to have a good scrub down. When she
wanted a nice long soak she'd use the slipper baths
at Beckwood Baths – she hated lugging the damn thing
outside to empty it afterwards! He'd been cleaning his
toenails with a penknife, but she could have sworn he'd
been scratching something on the rim . . .

She never thought to look. She was always too busy
keeping house. She'd scoured it a thousand times, but
she'd never really looked at it. Now she looked. The
marks were faint but still legible. It wasn't long after
she'd discovered she was pregnant – before her miscarriage. For a few weeks they were *so* happy. She
switched on the hall light and knelt down beside the
bath again. Now she could see it! He'd blushed that day,
and she pretended not to notice because men don't like
to be seen blushing. And he emptied and cleaned it out
as she was busy with the vegetables for dinner. Oh Lord!
See what he'd written: 'Alf/Nell, 1951' and beside it a tiny
heart!

Alf wandered round the city centre. He hadn't the
heart to look for jobs today. There wasn't any point.
Apart from which his heart was back home, with his
wife. He tried three florists, but it was silly as he hadn't
any money. He stared through shop windows, looking
for ideas, but his Giro wasn't due for a few days yet. He
had to get her something. All this job-hunting had made
him feel old, but inside he was as young as any of those
lads in the square . . .

Nellie bustled round the shops. She'd make him a fine
dinner – shepherd's pie had always been his favourite.
In his younger days – think of it! Not every girl's ideal
man but to her he'd always been handsome. When they
were courting he took her dancing twice a week: the
waltz, quickstep, the cha cha cha! And all the friends
they'd had – those good friends . . . Most had moved

away now, with the jobs. The old estate had become rough and unfriendly. Alf had stuck it out to the bitter end at the factory; he'd always believed that they wouldn't close it down – it mattered too much to the community. He thought they'd see sense. But the old values changed and no one cared what happened to the community . . . One day the factory gates opened as usual, then the next they were closed for good. And that was the end of it. She bought the onions and hurried home.

The smell of mince, onions, cheese and potato flooded the kitchen and drifted into the hallway. His slippers lay beside the fire. She'd changed her dress, tidied her hair . . . she felt nervous and excited, waiting for him.

The front door opened. She went to greet him. In his hand was a single red rose. He blushed and stammered: 'It's . . . '

'Oh Alfie!'

'I couldn't get . . . '

'I saw what you put in the bath. My life, I'd never seen it before . . . '

'I shouldn't have made such a fuss . . . '

'If I'd known I'd never have dreamed . . . '

He gave her the rose. 'To say I'm sorry. And – well, you know . . . '

She hugged him.

'I took it from the rosebed in the square.' He smiled affectionately, foolishly. 'Should have seen the looks I got . . . "What's that old fool doing . . . "'

'You're *not* old!' she murmured.

' . . . climbing over the wall? One black youth even offered to pick it for me. Drew quite a crowd. But I didn't care, I didn't care. My heart's been bursting all day, for you.'

. . . And later that evening, after the dinner she'd cooked for him, and the rose had been placed, prominently, in a crystal-clean milk bottle on the mantelpiece . . . After he'd stoked the fire, they sat together on the settee, watching the flames dance and roar. She laid her head on his shoulder. He put his arm around her: loving, protective.

Upstairs, the gap between the denture pots had closed again.

Downstairs, two pairs of tartan slippers on weary feet were toasting. And two hands, wrinkled and callused with a lifetime's industry. Gripping.

Digging In

My, but it was raw tonight. Albert stepped off the bus, dug his hands into his pockets and dashed across the road. A five-minute trot was all that stood between him and a pint of ale in the snug warmth of the Thresher's Arms.

He'd grown tired of Sheila. His mother and Sheila got on together a little *too* well. He was a young man – he could have any pub – come to that, any woman – he chose! He reached another crossing and was forced to halt: the traffic was heavier here. He kicked an empty beer can in impatience and spat on the pavement.

Then he saw her.

Tall, a little on the heavy side with broad hips and a big bosom. Black skirt suit and white blouse; hair cut like Princess Di's, rouged cheeks and eyes plastered with navy-blue eye shadow, she walked carefully past him on black court shoes with three-inch heels.

Suddenly pubs seemed less interesting to Albert. He watched her. She couldn't walk fast because her skirt was too narrow around the knees. Her shiny black handbag looked full enough to have a brick in it, and she held it defensively as though expecting to be mugged. You can't blame her round here, he thought. She was wearing the scent he had once bought Gail from a discount drug store: cheap but potently feminine. She must have had a bath in it, for the full strength of the perfume ballooned out some four feet behind her like a parachute, overwhelming

Albert with a giddy desire to be up some back street with her in his arms.

He removed his cap, smoothed back his hair and followed her.

At the entrance to the working men's club he caught up with her and offered to pay her admission. She looked up at him from behind her false eyelashes and smiled.

'Let's go to the bar,' he said.

'Me friends are over there, sittin'.'

'Tell them you've got company.'

'Not backward in comin' forward, are yer?'

'You won't regret it,' he grinned at her, his words heavy with innuendo. She blushed beneath her tinted foundation.

'Eileen? Eileen! We're over 'ere!' her friends shouted. They were sitting between the farthest trestle table and the wall, a pile of bingo cards beside the ashtray. They'd saved her a place. The half-pint of lager and lime awaited her arrival.

'I can't!' she waved and shouted to them, laughing at their gestures when they saw she was with someone. Albert leaned against the bar as he ordered, so Eileen was free to point at his back and mime to her friends, 'I've got one!'

They raised their glasses to her with hoots and wolf-whistles, then left her to it.

He bought her a large gin and orange which she drank while the first 'turn' died the death on stage, desperately trying to keep the jokes coming despite being almost completely ignored.

He chatted her up during the bingo, ensuring that her glass was never empty.

By the time the star turn had begun to sing 'My Way', her legs were buckling. He whispered something to her but she was singing, so he took her arm and led her out.

It didn't feel cold in the small wooden park shelter, even though the night was bitter. She was too drunk to notice anything but the feel of his mouth on her breasts and his fingers steadily climbing her thighs. It wasn't passionate. He was a little rough, but she didn't mind.

And when he tore her skirt in his efforts to get it down she couldn't have cared less. She gasped with pleasure as he pulled apart her legs and entered her. Somewhere in the back of her mind it registered that he wasn't wearing a condom, but as each energetic thrust brought her legs higher round his back the thought of being unprotected made her more excited still. He was having her, but she was having him as well, as much as she could because she wanted it. She wanted it. He could make her pregnant, but she gripped him tighter still. She was having him.

When it was over he collapsed beside her on the wooden seat, lit two cigarettes and handed her one. She picked her skirt up from the floor and stepped into it.

Albert looked across at her. 'I'm sorry I tore it, love.'

'It's okay. It'll fix.' She tidied her hair as best she could, buttoned up her blouse and sat down again.

The cold was beginning to bite; she felt more sober.

'You married?' she asked.

'Separated. Why?'

'Just asking.'

'Are you?'

'It's been offered, but I like a good time too much.'

Albert inhaled deeply on his cigarette before speaking, smoke rising from his mouth and nostrils. 'Was that a good time?'

'You shouldn't have to ask. You heard me.'

'Mm. You allus that noisy?'

'The men I've been with say it turns 'em on. Can't 'elp it.'

'Known a lot of men, have you?'

'One or two.'

'Don't you ever want to settle down? Don't you want a family?'

''Course I do. All me sisters are married. I'm aunty to eight kids. I love babbies.'

Albert smiled, stood and threw what remained of his cigarette into the shrubbery outside the shelter.

'C'mon, then, Miss Good Time, I'll walk you home.'

The Healing

They sat together in the candling booth. Pluckett's under-manager, Arthur Stone, patiently guided Gail through the various procedures. He wore a short-sleeved shirt. Gail tried to blot out the intimacy of their dark-curtained surroundings and concentrate instead on the job in hand. He smelt nice though – of clean perspiration and subdued aftershave. He spoke quietly, in warm, measured tones: 'Look for anything that shouldn't be there. Any cracks, or traces of blood . . . anything less than perfect, put in the tray to your left. If an egg looks bad, drop it in the melange bucket on your right. And this clipboard is for marking the melange . . . '

'I remember,' said Gail, pleased that so little had changed. The eggs floated past her on the conveyor belt, illuminated by the light beneath the belt – the 'candle' that enabled the 'candler' in the booth to note and remove any imperfect eggs as they flowed unceasingly between the chickens in a hidden part of the factory, and the boxes at the other end.

'Don't forget that you record any eggs dropped by the girls outside. They'll shout to you – always remember to mark them down. Other than that it's a breeze . . . There's one . . . ' His hand reached out to the top row of eggs, removed the damaged egg and leaned behind Gail to pop it gently into the large cardboard tray. It was a quick, almost unconscious action which gave Gail a moment to notice the soft down of blond hair on his extended forearm, and when he reached behind her something stirred between them: they both knew it.

She coughed nervously. 'I think I'll be okay.'

'Good, good.' He didn't look at her, but backed slowly – almost reverentially – from the booth; leaving her to reassemble the sudden chaos of sensation that his movement had aroused, and concentrate instead on eggs.

When a job had been vacant a few months before, Gail made a point of visiting Nellie Wain. Nellie took some convincing – she'd been a housewife for thirty years, she said. But Gail said what's that, if not a full time job? Go on Nellie – you'd enjoy it . . . And Gail grinned and pleaded and tugged at Nellie's arm until Nellie laughed and gave in. At the interview, Pluckett asked about her job experience and she told him, quite bluntly, that she'd had thirty years' hard labour looking after her husband and, compared to that, a production line was easy! Pluckett liked her, and gave her the job. Alf still went to the library every day, but he shopped, and vacuumed occasionally now, and took up cookery evening classes and he wasn't in the least bit humiliated because times were changing and his home was happier now than it had ever been!

Nellie flourished. In fact, she proved so good at the work that Pluckett was tempted to train her as a supervisor, but for the time being Nellie was happy doing just what she did. She discovered herself capable of big belly laughs – deep and infectious, that lifted the working atmosphere on the production line so much that the other women saved their jokes especially for her, because when Nellie laughed it was like a party and time just *flew*!

Nellie watched the young man leave the candling booth and saw the expression on his face. Well well . . .

Arthur was a quiet, shy man with fair, handsome features and calm hazel eyes. At thirty-two, he had never married, although he had considered it on more than one occasion. His parents had divorced when he was seventeen: he shied away from repeating their mistakes. He was earnest in his commitment to the women he loved, but his relationships always stumbled as they moved towards the altar. He didn't want to stay single all his life; he needed a companion, but to him marriage was like setting a relationship in cement, from which it could never expand and grow. Sometimes he felt like the loneliest person on the face of the earth, although his many friends helped to fill the detached house he had inherited through his parents' bitter divorce.

Arthur had taken more than a passing interest in Gail from the moment she began work at Pluckett's, but felt restrained, somehow, by her detachment. She was not cold: she smiled when spoken to and she worked well with the other women, but something seemed to set her apart from the others – something she held back. It wasn't his nature to pry, and factory work precluded all but the most mundane conversation. So he watched her with a shy nervousness that reminded him of his adolescence. For her part, she seemed hardly aware of him. It was impossible to meet in the canteen during breaks, as the other women teased him unmercifully about his private life anyway. And in the evenings she left with the others in the company bus while he collected up and recorded the punch-cards. All he could do was all he was doing: taking advantage of any situation that put the two of them together and hoping that, if he persisted, she might eventually notice him as a human being and not just her immediate boss.

It worked, finally, that day in the candling booth. It was required of him to sit with her. It was his job. But in such close proximity it was impossible for her not to notice him, and she had noticed him. He hardly dared wonder what she thought. Too many nights spent thinking of her had made him inordinately sensitive: he could only hope that, whatever touched her consciousness that day in the booth, it would not be unkind towards him. He hoped not. In fact, whatever passed between them in those few minutes suggested the opposite, but he was afraid to believe what he instinctively felt. Loving someone as much as he found himself loving her, *without knowing*, made him feel naked and exposed, as foolish as a child, and as vulnerable. That night he watched television absently, alone in his house, the phone off the hook, knowing that he had to seize the moment before it fell away from her memory completely.

How to do it was the problem.

The next day Dame Fortune intervened in the form of Nellie. Gail had never told Nellie what had happened to her – she visited her once, a month or so before telling her about the vacancy at Pluckett's, but that left a huge gap in her life between then and when she'd sold the house next door. Nellie could only guess at what could have happened: she remembered the look on her dad's face when he came home from the war . . . She wondered how bad Gail's war had been. But Gail wasn't telling and Nellie wasn't asking. The other women had noticed Gail's detachment as well. In another woman they might have interpreted this as stand-offishness, but in Gail it was different because it was clear she *tried* to be friendly. The factory girls knew when an egg was bad, just by looking at it. Gail wasn't a bad egg; she was suffering and, if she'd only let them in, they'd help her just as they helped each other. If only she'd open the damn door.

Nellie had discovered the door handle. She wasn't about to let go. Gail and Arthur would make a nice couple. So she whispered something to Ada five minutes before the morning break, Ada passed it down the line and, when the breaktime bell rang, at least five of them were meeting at The Merry Maid in town at eight o'clock. Five would do. Now they just needed the young couple. Ada asked Arthur and Nellie asked Gail. When Arthur hummed Ada mentioned that Gail would be there, and when Gail hesitated Nellie mentioned Arthur. The pair of them agreed so easily that Nellie and Ada still had time for a cup of tea before break ended.

That night Gail and Arthur were subtly manoeuvred into position by the girls. Florrie, who accidentally sat between the two of them, was hastily despatched to the bar with a ten-pound note. By the time she returned with the drinks the concertina bum-shuffle, started by Nellie, had removed the gap and squashed Gail and Arthur securely behind one of the tables. That should do it! thought Nellie. It did.

Later, when Arthur invited everyone back to his house

for coffee everyone magnanimously declined, but when they were in the car park saying goodnight, Gail found herself bundled into the passenger seat of Arthur's car by several strong female arms. Gail was a little drunk from the gin they'd slipped into her lager and unwilling to protest when Nellie planted a kiss on her cheek and whispered, 'You have a good time now.' Arthur, ever the gentleman, played along when they ushered him into the driver's seat and shut the door. He pulled out of the car park and on to the dark street with Ada and the others running after the car laughing, while Nellie stood and watched them go with the kind of tears in her eyes that people usually reserve for weddings.

He pulled up outside a garage and turned to her. She seemed relaxed. 'I'll take you straight home if you like,' he said.

She looked at him. Not past him, or through him, or beyond him, but fixed her eyes directly upon his. His heart stirred. 'No,' she replied.

He introduced her to the house.

'It seems too large for you,' she said.

'It was my parents'. Mum kept it on when they separated. The divorce wasn't settled until I was eighteen. She met Jim. He had his own place. She never got round to selling this, and now I'm trying to buy it from her. It didn't cost that much when they married. She seems content to sell it to me.'

'Nice,' said Gail.

'Yeah. Mostly. It's cheaper than trying to buy my own place, but sometimes I feel like a pea in a drum, when I'm on my own.'

'You should see where I live.'

'I'd like to sometime.'

Her eyes widened a little, as though she'd been sleeping inside them and had woken to a distant sound. His heart constricted. He took her hand and gently led her upstairs.

Flight

All roads lead to this.

'I heard from Christine last week,' Gail said to Rose at their final meeting. 'She moved to Scotland with a co-worker when the hostel closed. They set up a sort of therapeutic community in the Highlands. They own three sheep, two goats, a chicken and a pig. The community's ten strong now – she says it's unlikely to expand, as being small makes them almost self-sufficient and less dependent on the Authorities. No one wants to leave. She sounds very happy. She says they're saving for another pig as Albert . . . '

'Albert?'

'Albert the pig. She thought I'd like his name . . . '

Rose laughed.

'Albert's lonely . . . You know they held a remembrance service for Anydale, when it closed? She saved one of the service booklets for me, but with all that followed she forgot. She found it again a couple of weeks ago so she sent it on, together with an open invitation to stay with them . . . '

'Will you go?'

'I might.' Gail smiled. 'I saw Mandy Potter on television the other night. She's an advertising executive now. She's part of the Government's campaign team selling shares in water to the public. She's probably just the sort of person they need.'

'What about Celie?' Rose asked.

'She took the kids back to her mum and dad's. She says she's no intention of moving away again. She's got a paid job with the Citizens' Advice . . . I keep meaning to visit her. She sounds very dynamic on the phone. Very political . . . '

'Aren't you political?'

'Not like Celie. She's very forthright. She helps people practically *and* emotionally. With me it's just words. I always get the rest wrong.'

'Don't words matter?'

Gail smiled and stood to leave. '*Something* matters, Rose.' Then suddenly she knelt down beside the therapist's chair and took the older woman's hand. Rose had eyes like pools of deepest brown.

'Who *are* you?' Gail asked.

Rose returned the younger woman's grip, smiled gently but said nothing. Her eyes gave the answer. In them Gail saw a reflection of herself. She frowned: 'But I'm not your only client. Where are *you*?'

Rose laughed. 'I'm safe,' she said.

The frown lifted from Gail's forehead. 'I'm glad. Keep safe, Rose.'

Gail chewed on a barley stalk. The sky over Anydale was purest blue; small cotton-clouds drifted like ice in a clean ocean. A low plane from the nearby airfield droned overhead, ascended vertically, looped the loop then flew away. She smiled when she thought of the Anydale Spotter. She reached behind her head, let loose her hair, shook it with an uncharacteristic flourish and stood.

She walked down the hill with her arms outstretched and the breeze on her face. She could still hear the plane in the distance.

She sat on the kerb, caught the next bus back to the city and when it pulled up at the bus station she crossed over the road to the cutting-wall.

The sign had changed. Like her thoughts, the message had altered. It seemed kinder now, and bolder – even optimistic. The change was recent: the paint was thickly new – unlike the older, fading letters.

As she stared at the change, a thousand random

images passed behind her eyes, a thousand uncollect-
ed thoughts, a thousand faces, a thousand voices and
through them all she heard one voice clearly speaking and
she knew it was her own: 'You shout and beat your head
upon the window pane. The one with arthritic hands, the
one I kneel before . . . the one who says, "I won't cry."
Your heart bursts before my eyes. You chatter endlessly:
we have to feed you. You die in our absence. You die
daily. You warm your hands against the one lit bar of an
electric fire. You curl into a ball and try to sleep. You
drown in the silence. You pace the room and rattle the
door-handle; you lay your head against the sill and try
to breathe the night. You are tubes and wet sheets; you
scream as we turn you. You wait for the dawn and the
dawn never comes. You fold his clothes and stack them
neatly on the dresser; you dust his memory. You pray for
an answer and I don't have one. I don't have any.

'I see your eyes before they close. I have held your
many hands so often I feel them still: some work-worn,
some soft, some thin – so thin – so pale. I see you in the
street, reflected in shop windows. I see you with your
prayer book. I hear you mourn the death of your child;
I see you rise, naked and starving, from your mother's
arms – wasted arms, lifeless eyes. You are mugged in the
street, abused, victimised, left for dead.

'So what is there? I don't believe in anything. You are
struggling to live . . . and yet, beneath the pain and ever-
endurance, you are the sweetest song – my night of dense
forest, my early morning. You dance in the cornfield: in
every stalk that grows, ripens, dies . . . We *all* dance for
a day, however cold the season. Some nights as I raise
my face to the wind I see you rise from the cities and
the graves . . . I see you in your thousands, tumbling
from the stars, all the stars – some living force . . .

'There are links and there are chains: we circle endlessly. I may not see you again, but I never lose your
hand. I may not ease your pain, but I never lose your
hand. And I'm not sure of life – it hurts so much sometimes. I can't mend the breaks in you, I can't heal what
aches in you . . . I don't believe in anything, but I'll still
hold your hand.'

Gail peered over the chasm's edge. It was too far to let people fall. And no use simply praying that it would cease to exist. She thought of Malcolm – letting go of him had never crossed her mind. If words were all she had, she'd use them. There were no angels here – no devils. No beating wings, no infernal horns. Just people. Good bad mad sad people.

It was time to take the strain again. A warm strength flooded her. She smiled.

Arnold the insurance man could see her smiling. He saw no reason for anyone to smile. What was she smiling at? Someone had painted a sign on the opposite wall of the cutting . . . A big sign, with one of the words crossed out and another added. That much he could see. She was nodding now, very subtly, nodding and smiling at the sign. He saw no reason to smile. It annoyed him very much.

Arnold was not sleeping well. He had been having restless nights ever since he had given a lift to that man who set himself alight. Not sleeping well had affected his health. He resented it. He resented his involvement in that man's suicide. He hadn't asked to be involved.

He had built his career on offering people security against accident, fire, flood, loss of limb or eye, and ultimately loss of life. Security was his business. He respected life – particularly when insured by his firm. To be associated through no fault of his own with a man who committed suicide had damaged his credibility, had knocked him off the promotional ladder, had relieved him of his company car and relegated him to his original position with the firm.

Arnold had become once again a knocker and tapper of doors. The shame of it! To be brought so low through the actions of another!

He still wore his suit and carried his briefcase, but gone were the days of high-flying responsibility, gone the respect of his peers, gone the business trips, all expenses paid . . . Arnold was once again pedestrian, collecting weekly premiums from low-income families. He saw no reason to smile.

Arnold crossed the road and walked along the path

until he could see her face. She was daydreaming. He
squinted at the sign, but couldn't read it. No doubt he
could if standing where she stood.

Arnold the insurance man was on his rounds. These
low-income types were the very devil to pay up for their
premiums, so Arnold caught them on Sundays, when
they were bound to be home. They annoyed him very
much, these poor people.

She looked poor, but her eyes betrayed a certain
zeal – a certain passionate intensity that refused to be
humbled. This disturbed Arnold, for Arnold had been
humbled. Arnold's only satisfaction was visiting clients
who were, by nature of their poverty, much humbler than
himself.

It wasn't just her smile, but her appearance. She wore
red, perhaps as a statement: red top, grey jeans and red
sandals. She looked like a torch. People pretending to be
torches annoyed him very much.

Arnold the insurance man was down, but he was far
from out. He had invested shrewdly in stocks and shares
prior to his demotion, and his investments were paying
well. In a little while, Arnold planned to go into business
for himself. He was tired of insurance and planned to be
a capitalist. He already had his potential customers – the
people he visited. To a man, or woman, they needed
money desperately and he, Arnold, would supply it.
Lump sums, no questions asked . . . underground loans
with substantial rates of interest repayable *ad infinitum*.
He could think of several young men prepared to collect
on his behalf for a reasonable wage – no questions asked,
DHSS not informed . . . Young men prepared to break the
occasional limb if required . . . Ah, but the future looked
good! Still, he saw no reason for her to smile.

Arnold the potential capitalist followed the young
woman's eyes, but still could not read the sign. He looked
down into the cutting, to where a giant advertisement
hoarding concealed the old railway tunnel. He'd heard
the rats down there could kill a man . . . Arnold closed his
eyes and imagined the stench inside the tunnel, the damp
oozing from the sooty walls, the heavy shuffling through
the darkness and, for the first time in over a year, Arnold

smiled. It was a thin, pinched, mealy little smile and it
lifted the whiskers growing on his cheeks. He rubbed
his chin thoughtfully; his claw-like hand stained with
the blood of a broken biro. He would make his fortune
underground.

Once again he looked across at her. Still smiling:
what right had she to smile? She looked too proud, too
bright, too perfect . . . She was invading his territory. It
angered him.

Arnold crossed the road and crept stealthily towards
where she stood, leaning slightly over the cutting-wall,
her back to him. He put down his briefcase and looked
around. It was Sunday and the city was drowsy, som-
nambulant, barely alive. See how the breeze lifts her hair!
See how she stands like a beacon, lighting up the grimy
pavement! As once another man had stood, at the foot
of the very throne of this nation! How dare he! How dare
she! Well, I won't let her!

Arnold the tunnel-dweller viewed his quarry from
behind, established the point at which to strike and,
with one final glance around, sprinted across the road
and channelled all his energy and momentum into one
violent shove just below her shoulders. She cried out in
surprise as she flipped head-first over the wall, her hands
flailing the air for something to grasp.

But the descent was inevitable and irreversible. The
sides of the cutting declined steeply. Neither handhold
nor foothold existed. She fell.

Arnold straightened his jacket and tie and looked up
at the sun. How bright it seemed today, how enticing!
He felt a thrill of accomplishment. No one had seen. The
people were sleeping.

Now he could read the sign that had pleased her
so clearly. The word that had been crossed out was
'LOSE'. The sign now read: 'YOU WILL WIN!'

Had she imagined it was meant for her? How mis-
guided these poor people are! They're not sharp, they
lack aggression, they trust too much . . .

My, Grandfather Mammon, what a powerful business you are!
All the better to manipulate you, my dears . . .

Ah well, let them sleep. These people of Albion,

these great trusting masses, so vulnerable, so infinitely malleable . . .

Arnold picked up his briefcase, and looked once more at the sign.

'YOU WILL WIN!' it said.

'Yes,' thought Arnold smugly, as he turned to walk away.

'Yes, we probably will . . . '

The small yellow remembrance booklet followed her down and came to rest, opened on the most-read page, caught in the bars of a rusted, broken-backed shopping trolley. And while the light lasted; before shadows filled the cutting and the night's creatures left the dripping tunnel to rustle through the city's debris . . . to find whatever lived, or tried to grow, or was warm with their sharp, incisive teeth . . . Before darkness fell upon the city as a whole, the jaundiced booklet gave its final message to the approaching night. It read: 'O God our Father, we have sinned against You in thought, word and deed: we have not loved You with all our heart; we have not loved our neighbour as ourselves . . . '

The darkness came, and what was left fell into shadow. At the foot of the page, in bolder type, two words were still discernible: 'SERVICE ENDS.'

. . . And then the rats came to feed.